NOWHERE
NEAR
GOODBYE

a novel

BARBARA CONREY

Nowhere Near Goodbye
Red Adept Publishing, LLC
104 Bugenfield Court
Garner, NC 27529
http://RedAdeptPublishing.com/

---

1.   http://StreetlightGraphics.com

The first time I imagined this book was when a friend lost her granddaughter to glioblastoma. I wanted to create a procedure that would remove this brain tumor in its entirety and allow the patient to live a long and happy life. Of course, this book is a work of fiction; there is no procedure like the one I created for this book.

All these years later, this disease still rears its ugly head and destroys all who wander into its path.

I dedicate this book to my friend Leah Ferguson, who can do no more than stand by and watch as her mother fights this battle with courage and dignity.

Prologue
Kate: 1982

My headaches went from "not a big deal" to the size of Montana. Then my eyesight took a hit, then my stomach and my equilibrium—and equilibrium, for those who needed it explained, was a word meaning *balance*. I was unable to stand on my own two feet without tripping over them.

Mrs. Clark's advanced-level reading class was where I first noticed I couldn't see the assignments written on the blackboard. No matter how many times I squeezed my eyes shut, hoping that when I opened them—again, again, again!—I would be able to read the words and numbers written there, all I saw was a blur that didn't mean crap to me.

I tried to remember the last time I easily read the board, but I couldn't. And so I did what kids did when they were scared but too stupid to admit it: I hid my symptoms as long as I could.

Eventually, fear won out, though, and I told my mom I thought I needed glasses. Actually, that wasn't true. *I* didn't tell her; I made Emma tell her. Because that was the kind of friend Emma was. She would do anything I asked her to, no matter what.

My mom made an appointment with the ophthalmologist—no simple optometrist for me—to see if I was right. To see if Emma was right and that I needed glasses. That visit didn't go so well. It didn't go so well in that the ophthalmologist, Dr. Wells, examined my eyes for what seemed, even to me, to be a long time. And the longer he looked, the nicer he got, and he was not a nice man, so that must have been an effort for him.

"Why don't you scoot on out to the waiting room and have Miss Carol send your parents on back?" he finally said, patting me on the head like I was some little kid.

I couldn't get out of there fast enough.

Miss Carol—whom I will forever remember for her fondness for skintight faux leather pants—also patted me on the head before calling Mom and Dad into the office.

Which left me alone in the waiting room.

Sometimes, I didn't do so well alone. I would find myself doing mindless stuff that could be interpreted as destructive. Sometimes, I wasn't even aware of what I was doing until the damage stared me in the face.

On that particular day, what caught my attention was a loose black thread from one of the little dots sewn onto my chair seat in the waiting room. Pulling those threads out was like peeling dead skin from my sunburned body. I knew I shouldn't, but I couldn't help myself.

I'd been taught to respect other people's property, but I picked those dots gone, every last one. I'd just managed to kick the evidence of my destructive ways into the corner when my parents came to get me.

Turned out I didn't need glasses.

I DIDN'T TELL ANYONE. Except Emma.

"I'm dying" was what I told her when she walked into my room. Those were my exact words, because there was no point in beating around the bush. No one had told me I was dying, but a showstopping statement was easier than admitting I was scared shitless.

Emma listened to what I'd just dropped on her and was, like, "Oh my God!" Emma didn't believe in God, yet that was how easily he'd slipped from her lips.

Unable to move forward, unable to turn around and run like hell, Emma tried to process what I'd just told her. "Are you sure?"

"Yes, I'm sure." Like I would make that up.

She backed up until she leaned against Harrison Ford and Carrie Fisher—the poster of them from *The Empire Strikes Back*. It was taped to my closet door. Once Emma's back hit that poster, she slid down its length until she sat with her knees up around her elbows.

I tried to explain what I knew, which wasn't much. I tried to tell her how I knew I was dying, the trick my mom had taught me even though she'd warned me not to tell anyone.

Mom said if I wanted something badly enough, I needed to imagine how I would feel once I got it. And if I could do that, I'd know it would happen. I told Emma how I imagined seventh grade and growing breasts—having my sweaters fill out with something that didn't look like I'd pasted a couple of Hershey's Kisses to my chest—and I saw nothing. Not even me.

My mom was right. Emma looked at me like whatever brain cells I'd been born with had left town in a hurry. She jumped up from the floor and threw herself down on my bed, once again invoking God's name. Then she said nothing. I thought maybe she'd forgotten what we were talking about. She did that sometimes. One minute, she was present and accounted for, and the next, she was off in her own little world, thinking about something that had nothing to do with me.

Then she let me have it. "You think that works? Tell me you don't. Tell me you do not think that if you can't see yourself in the future, it means you have no future. Just because *maybe*, maybe once or twice, you saw something that actually happened, some 'thing' that made you think you were God's best friend, you now think just because you can't see yourself with breasts, it means you're dead. You are *not* God's best friend, and you do not know what's going to happen in the future."

Normally, Emma accepted what I said without question, but that time, she not only didn't believe me but also retaliated in anger.

"So does that mean you don't want to look at what I found in my dad's medical books?" Sure, I was testing her. I wondered whether she believed me.

Emma's eyebrows practically hit the roof. "Have you lost your mind?" She scooted over and pushed my copy of *Ramona Quimby, Age 8* onto the floor, making plenty of room on my bed for me and my dad's medical books.

I wasn't allowed in Dad's home office when he wasn't there. But not being allowed to do something had never stopped me from doing it. Warning Emma not to spill a drop of the Coke we shared, especially not on my dad's stuff, I told her what I'd learned so far. "It's called GBM—short for glioblastoma. It usually happens to old men, men my dad's age, I guess."

"So why's it happening to you?"

"I don't know. Maybe I got lucky?"

We looked through those medical books like we were thumbing through the pages of *Playboy*; we knew we shouldn't, but we couldn't help ourselves.

What we learned was that it wasn't going to be pretty.

What I had was a shitload of cancer and not just the wee bit my dad pretended it was. It turned out my diagnosis was glioblastoma multiforme. That was a mouthful. We learned that because along with my dad's medical books and his notes, we found my case file. That was another reason doctors shouldn't treat members of their own families—it was too easy for them to find the stuff that shouldn't be found.

By the time my symptoms became a nuisance—around the time I couldn't see the damn blackboard at school—my tumor had already burrowed in, made a home for itself, and hung a few pictures. Maybe put up some curtains. It had no plans to vacate.

Some brain tumors could be surgically coerced—just a fancy word for *bullied*—into packing up and getting out, but my tumor seemed content right where it was. Like an octopus with a bazillion tentacles, each tentacle had wrapped itself around a different part of my brain. That was the kind of tumor I had. The kind that wouldn't be happy till I was dead, even if my dad refused to say it.

"Look at this!" Holding up one of the research papers like she'd just found the answer to world peace, Emma read it to me. "This is a clinical trial, whatever that is, and some people survived. Look at it. These are people who lived!"

I looked, and Emma was right, except she had missed the note my dad had added. "These are *miracles*. See my dad's notes? He calls them miracles. They don't know why these people survived."

But that didn't stop Emma from grabbing on like God might just pencil me back in. "If those people got a miracle, maybe you will too. Don't you see?"

I ripped the paper out of her hand. "Where do you think miracles come from?" That stopped her cold. "They come from God, Emma." When that sank in, I let her have the rest of it. "Why do you think God would send a miracle my way? Because the world can't live without a kid who never follows the rules?"

No one knew better than Emma that I wasn't all that good. Or nice. Far as I could see, there wasn't much reason for God to reconsider my fate.

Chapter 1

Emma: Present Day

Peeing on a white plastic stick was not something I did every day. Even though Tim knew as well as I did that the only babies in our future were the ones we might adopt someday, he convinced me it couldn't hurt to at least rule out pregnancy as the cause of my crappy lethargy of the last couple of weeks that had me heading to the couch the moment I dragged myself home from the hospital each night.

I agreed to take the pregnancy test, but I wasn't sure why. I hadn't thought about what hope would be raised by taking the test. I hadn't thought about the smile that had started in Tim's eyes and moved down to his mouth as each day passed with no sign of my monthly cycle.

"What does it say?" I sucked in my breath and waited for my husband to give me the results of a test I never expected to take, much less pass. *Breathe in.* I looked around the bathroom for something to focus on. *Slow, slow. Okay. Now, breathe out. Nice and slow.* If I didn't concentrate, I would end up breathing into a paper bag.

While I waited for Tim to tell me the test results, my eyes darted from my wedding ring—still in the porcelain dish where it waited for me to slip it back on my finger—to the pewter bowl filled with sea glass, a gentle reminder of the first time that Tim and I had walked together on the beach in Saint Thomas.

Finally, I settled on staring at my reflection in the full-length mirror directly across from where I perched on the lip of our old claw-foot tub. I never could decide if I liked the placement of that mirror. No, that wasn't true. I liked it just fine until I stepped out of the tub and the first thing I saw was me.

I barely hit five feet and weighed ninety pounds only when I was dripping wet. My straight brown shoulder-length hair hadn't changed since I was a kid except for the blond highlights I'd finally worked up the courage to try. Tim described my eyes as the color of chocolate and expressive as hell. But he was a writer, so it wasn't surprising he would come up with a better description than the reality: just plain brown.

"Hey, how are you doing?" Tim grabbed my hand and squeezed gently, interrupting my thoughts and encouraging me to hold on.

"If I'm pregnant, I hope the baby looks like you," I told him, catching sight of his raven-black hair and eyes the exact color of the emerald on my finger. Hopeful words, but what I thought was: *if I'm pregnant, I don't know how I'll ever finish my research.*

How could I be pregnant? I was infertile, empty. That was what I'd been told. And yet... and yet I couldn't look at Tim or the applicator and not picture a houseful of kids and a dinner table laden with big bowls of food. And little children clamoring for attention. I imagined noise and laughter and silliness in my grown-up world and all the fun that came with a big family.

It could happen. If I were pregnant, I could be pregnant again. And again.

I suddenly wanted to spread the wealth so one child didn't need to carry the burden of perfection alone. Perfection was a burden, and that was what only children did: aim for perfection.

When I thought of big families—and right then, that was all I thought of—I thought of not being the *only*, of not feeling around in my pocket for the key to the kitchen door at the end of the school day. I thought of not stepping into silence.

My mouth was raw from chewing on my cheek, but that didn't stop me from asking again, "What does it say now?" I believed in protecting myself from disappointment. So I wanted to get it over with, and yet there I was, opening myself up to all kinds of hurt with thoughts of Christmas mornings and presents piled so high under the tree that the ornaments on the bottom branches disappeared in the pile of carefully wrapped packages.

Because I wanted the test to be positive. I hoped it wasn't just some cruel joke and all I had was the flu.

"Emma?"

What if I've gotten my hopes up and there's nothing inside of me? What if I'm just as barren as I was last month?

Tim's mouth was moving when I looked at him, but I didn't understand his words. The scene was like those old-time silent movies where it was impossible to watch the actor's lips and read the script at the bottom of the screen at the same time. I told myself to concentrate, but it didn't help. Whatever he said disappeared into a jumble of sounds that meant nothing.

"Emma!"

Giving up on words, Tim gathered me up from where I sat on the side of the tub and pulled me into his arms. Then I knew it was just some cruel hoax. The test said, "Don't be stupid," even though, against all odds, I'd prayed for it to say "baby."

There's no place to hide from yourself when you're waiting for the pain to find you. But that was what I wanted to do: hide. I'd let myself hope when that was the very last thing I should have done.

I tucked my head into Tim's shoulder. *Don't let him see how much this hurts.* Then I burst into tears. And I never cried.

Lifting my chin gently so that I was forced to look into his eyes, Tim smiled and whispered, "Don't cry, baby. Don't cry. You're pregnant! *We're* pregnant!"

Pregnant. *Pregnant!*

I swore to God, and I didn't even believe in God, that I heard in that instant the whisper of an infant's cry. Instead of the creaks and groans of the two-hundred-year-old house we called home, instead of the ticking of two grandfather clocks, instead of the drip of the powder room faucet that Tim had never been able to fix, I heard the cry of my child.

Pregnant? Is that what he said?

Tim, being a believer in both God and happily ever after, pulled me even closer. Pregnant. I was pregnant. *We* were pregnant.

"We're having a baby," he whispered, cupping my face in his hands. "We're having a baby!" His joy was transparent. He was blissfully unaware that as soon as I'd heard the positive results, I struggled between what I wanted and what my work demanded.

I laughed and tried to put work out of my mind, at least for the time being. *Let me have this moment.* That was all I asked.

Tim moved his body slowly and swept me with him in a dance that took us between the tub and the old armoire that held fresh towels. The space clearly wasn't meant for dancing, but that didn't stop us from bumping into the sink and the tub, rattling the bottles of lotion and shampoo on the shelf as we made our way from one end of the room to the other.

"What are you thinking?"

I can't tell you what I'm thinking. That was what I was thinking.

Chapter 2

"What are those things you stick in electrical outlets to plug them up?"

"Safety outlet covers?"

Tim nodded. "We need to get about a hundred."

We'd finally wound down from celebrating the results of the pregnancy test, and while I lay on my side of the bed with my mind floundering between my research commitments and my promise to Kate, I placed my hands on my belly and imagined the little life growing inside me.

Tim reached over and traced his finger over my jawline and across my lips. "You look like the cat who swallowed the canary. What's going on in that head of yours?"

I couldn't help the happiness that tugged at my lips. "When we were kids, all the other girls our age pushed baby dolls around the block in tyke-sized carriages, and all Kate wanted was to pretend we were Amish. I guess that's what comes from living in Intercourse, Pennsylvania. Only she always got to be the boy so she could wear overalls and play baseball while I always had to be the girl with an apron wrapped around my waist—I think we were five at the time—and all I'd wanted was to play with those dolls. And now here I am, pregnant. I'm going to play with dolls!"

I didn't tell him the rest of it. While he'd been busy calculating the number of outlet covers we would need once the baby started crawling, I was trying to lull myself into believing I could have a baby and find a cure for GBM.

"And anyway, I don't think we need to worry about safety outlet covers just yet."

His grin melted my heart. "Maybe not. But we don't want to leave things for the last minute." He moved from safety outlets to fencing in the backyard. I knew how excited he was about the baby, and I didn't want to do anything to mar his happiness, so I kept my worries to myself.

"Do you want to call your family? Tell them the news?"

I turned on my side so we faced each other. "Seriously? Do you think they'll be excited?"

Tim tried his best not to laugh, but his eyes betrayed him. "Maybe not. Maybe we'll just wait."

My family was the only family we had other than Tim's sister, Amy. Tim's parents had been killed in a car accident a few years back, but we both knew there would be scant enthusiasm from my family. If a new addition to the family didn't have four legs and a tail, they would be hard-pressed to offer congratulations. "We'll call Amy in a few weeks."

I turned the light off by my side of the bed and closed my eyes. Tim was still mumbling about fence designs, and I hoped the sound of his voice would put me to sleep, but I couldn't get Kate out of my mind. I'd never admitted to her how I'd envied those little girls from our childhood who changed diapers that mostly stayed dry unless they'd been lucky enough to have one of those dolls that peed and cried on demand. Just as well. She would never have let me forget it.

While those girls learned to never—not even once—leave an infant unattended on the changing table, I was busy scaring the bejesus out of myself by attempting to prove I was every bit as brave as Kate. I never was, but I never stopped trying.

We'd thought our lives were blessed, right up until we were eleven and Kate was diagnosed with a brain tumor. The few years we'd had, between kindergarten and playdates and sixth grade and her death, had been the happiest years of my life.

I would have bet we'd never be friends. Of course, I'd have bet Kate would live to see the age of twelve too. But I was wrong on both counts.

Kate and her family had filled a hole in my life I hadn't even known was there. My family's life revolved around puppies. Beagles, mostly. They rescued beagles, nursed them back to health, then sent them on their way to forever homes. While I walked into an empty house at the end of the school day, Kate's mom waited for her with milk and cookies on the table, eager to hear all about her day.

I'd thought my family was normal. Kate's family thought differently.

"My parents were talking about you last night."

I'd stopped walking, sure I'd heard her wrong. We were in the park in Kate's neighborhood, traipsing along walking paths we knew better than our own backyards, and I waited for her to tell me what they'd said.

"Well, actually, they were talking about your family."

Kate had hedged when I'd asked what was said.

"I'm not supposed to tell. Dad didn't think I was listening because the television was on, but I was, and when he realized I'd heard every word, he told me family discussions stay in the family. And what I'd heard was a family discussion."

"Why did you bring it up if you weren't going to tell me?" I'd demanded, not even sure why I was so angry.

Kate never was able to keep a secret. And sure enough, five minutes later, she'd told me. "He said your parents spend too much time worrying about dogs that need saving and not enough time with you. And my mom said they were too busy to see your loneliness."

Right about then, I started going to Kate's house after school. Kate thought I was missing a prime opportunity to experience freedom. She thought she would love—"at least once for the love of God" was exactly how she'd put it—to ponder her day before regurgitating it.

Then she'd looked at me and said, "Ponder. It means..."

I knew what it meant.

Chapter 3

"What do you mean, complications?"

Tim and I sat in chairs across the desk from my OB-GYN, Jamie Jamison, when I asked my question. Jamie was my friend, and I'd known him since medical school, but still, I couldn't look at him while I waited for his answer. Instead, I stared over his left shoulder at the bird's-eye-maple credenza he'd carted into his office when he accepted a job with the hospital. My view, which included his medical books and the antique baby scale I'd given him as a gift when he'd finally narrowed down his specialty to obstetrics, offered no answer, but it was easier than looking into his eyes and seeing his unasked questions.

Jamie's office was on the same floor as mine at the hospital but in the opposite wing, which made it convenient for me and only a ten-minute drive for Tim. Since our appointment was at eleven, we planned an early lunch before I was due back in my office to meet with a new patient.

Jamie referred to my chart. "I don't want you to get your hopes up, either of you." He looked up then, maybe more at Tim than me. Maybe he thought Tim would support him in whatever he was trying to say. "I don't want you making plans."

"Plans?" Even that one word was slippery in my mouth. What I wanted most was falling through my fingers.

"Emma, you know what I'm talking about. You know the extent of the injuries you sustained when you were a child as well as I do. Don't make me be the bad guy here."

14

Jamie's words took me back to Dr. Goldman's office the day he'd explained the long-term effects of a car accident that had sent my body through the back end of a station wagon parked on the street. He'd treated me like an adult and not just some kid whose parents took up the remaining chairs by his desk. "I'm sorry," he'd said. "It will be difficult, if not impossible, for you to conceive."

The abdominal pain that had brought us to his office in the first place was caused by pelvic adhesions from the surgeries that had saved my life after the accident. At the time, Dr. Goldman's words hadn't mattered, and by the time they did, I had pretty much accepted that if I wanted to be a mother, it wouldn't be through childbirth. When Tim and I decided to marry, he understood that if we wanted children, we would adopt.

I looked up when I realized no one was talking. Jamie leaned against his desk with one ankle crossed over the other, his ruse for appearing casual when he was anything but, and I waited for words I knew I didn't want to hear.

"The chance of miscarriage is high with pelvic adhesions. I know you know that. You don't need to dwell on it, but you do need to keep it in mind. This pregnancy, if it continues, will alter your current way of life considerably. And could be very hard on your body."

I nodded. Jamie was well aware of my schedule at the hospital; he knew what my research meant to me. I would need to be vigilant. I shut my eyes. *I need to stay off my feet, rest often, take even more time away from the hospital. Can I step away from my research?* My chest tightened as the thoughts consumed me.

Tim was probably not even aware of how tightly he held my hand. I would have asked him to loosen his grip, but I needed that pain to help me block out worrying about cancer protocols and four-teen-hour days at the hospital.

Silence again filled the room as we both grappled with Jamie's words. I wanted to cancel our lunch plans, cancel my afternoon patients, go home, and pull the covers over my head.

Tim stood and pulled me up along with him. Jamie stood, too, and reached out his hand to Tim before he pulled me in for a hug. "Try not to worry. I'll schedule an ultrasound, and we'll take it one day at a time."

"WHAT ARE YOU DOING in here?" Tim whispered as if he knew without my saying a word that he needed to tread lightly.

I'd been thinking about dreams when Tim wandered in and found me sitting on the floor in the second-largest bedroom in our house: the bedroom closest to ours. The one I'd privately earmarked as the nursery the day I saw that positive pregnancy test.

That test result was a dream come true. Just like buying our house five years ago had been a dream come true. My dream. As a kid, I had loved the house, even though I'd never seen the inside. I wondered what made something stick in a kid's head. I was familiar with houses like the one I'd grown up in, a farmhouse built more for its ability to keep everyone warm in the winter and cool in the summer. And I was familiar with the houses in Kate's neighborhood, bastardized colonials my dad said were designed more on a whim than on any house plan he was familiar with, but there wasn't another house around like the Caldwell Estate. It was a piece of history. And I'd wanted it.

The house sat on a big plot of land all by itself between where I'd lived and Eden, so every time Kate and I walked past it, we had to stop and stare.

I'd been sure I would grow up and live in that house, but Kate hadn't understood why I would want to. "Who would want to live in a house that makes you think of butlers and downstairs maids? I bet they even put a red velvet rope across the doorways of rooms they don't want people tracking mud through. Just like they do in museums."

Kate had picked up a small stone and skipped it across the stream that ran by the property. "Besides, living here would be way too complicated. I bet they even dress for dinner."

That had stopped me cold. "What do you think they wear?"

That had fascinated me: dressing for dinner. But as soon as Kate turned toward me, I knew I'd been tricked. "What do you think? Prom gowns and tuxedos."

We had both bent double with laughter at the thought of sitting down to a bowl of beef stew while wearing a corsage and some fancy dress. Then we'd continued on to my house to see the latest rescue puppies.

That dream of owning the Caldwell house came true. Why couldn't a new one? The bedroom nearest ours was empty, but I had so quickly envisioned its occupant. That was how fast I went from never thinking about babies to thinking only about babies.

"Hey, where are you? You look like you're a million miles away." After scooting down so he sat next to me, Tim laced his fingers through mine, and we sat silently, each of us lost in our thoughts. We were both quiet people, forgetting sometimes that our thoughts were also silent.

I wanted to fill the room with hope and possibilities and love. I wanted to fill the room with a future. But I was afraid to say any of that. Instead, I said other things. "We can adopt."

Tim's fingers fell from mine. "What?"

I sat up straighter. "We can adopt." Since I'd brought it up, I fought for the courage to keep going. "Maybe Jamie's right. Maybe we need to rethink this. Maybe..." I sighed, knowing it was important to say the words out loud, even though they were a lie. "Maybe this isn't the baby for us." I forced myself to look at him, knowing that I needed to strengthen my words so we would both believe them.

"Why are you saying this? I thought you wanted this baby?"

If only it were that simple. "Remember? We talked about adoption before I agreed to marry you, and you were fine with it. We're only thirty-five. We planned on waiting until I'd completed my research so we'd both have more time. We planned on you publishing another book or two. There's still time. We don't have to have a baby yet."

I ran out of words, and when I looked at Tim, I was afraid I'd disappointed him, even though everything I'd said was meant to save him from heartbreak. What I didn't say was that if we didn't have that baby, I could keep my promise to Kate.

"I think I'd like to paint the ceiling sky blue and then add puffy white clouds. Maybe do a mural on one wall. What do you think?"

"What?" It was as if Tim had heard nothing of what Jamie had told us, of what I'd just said. "What about what Jamie said? That we shouldn't get our hopes up? That this pregnancy is going to change everything good in our lives that we take for granted?" My voice splintered on those words, but I had to say them. I had to stop the wanting before it destroyed us both. I had to stop... this. The hope.

Tim squeezed my hand and wrapped his arms around me. "There will be a baby. Look. I made a list. Grab your shoes. We're going to the paint store and buy everything we need to turn this room into the most beautiful nursery for our most beautiful baby."

"But..."

"No buts. Grab your shoes. Now! Go. Go. Go!"

"Wait!" As quickly as he'd pushed me up, he pulled me back until I was kneeling in front of him. "Before you go, I need to do something." He leaned over and placed his lips on my flat belly and kissed me where our baby, no bigger than the size of a pea, hid inside of me.

"There. Her first kiss."

I was stunned. "Her? This baby's a girl?"

"Yep, this baby's a girl. And she will be perfect."

Chapter 4

Sooner or later, I would get used to stripping from the waist down, slipping on a tissue-thin hospital gown, and covering the lower half of my body with a sheet starched within an inch of its life. But not that day.

Once I was settled, Tim reached over and took my hand. "Comfortable?"

I wiggled my eyebrows. "Just peachy."

Before Tim could do more than snicker, the technician walked into the room.

"Good morning! I'm Cheryl. I'll be taking care of you today." Cheryl straightened the sheet that covered me and firmly grasped the hand Tim wasn't holding. She gave it a good squeeze. "Comfy?"

Tim and I looked at each other and grinned like fools. We locked eyes while Cheryl went about the business of looking at our baby and explaining what she saw.

"Okay, ready to see what's going on?" Cheryl stood poised at the end of the examining table and waited until I nodded; Tim squeezed my hand.

I thought about how sure he was that our baby was a girl. I hoped he wouldn't be disappointed if he was wrong. I didn't even think about what I wanted. I wanted healthy. I wanted someone to tell me nothing would change when a baby entered our lives. I wanted to finish my research. I wanted—

"Mom? Dad? Take a look at the monitor. There's your baby. What do you think?"

Tim moved closer to the monitor as if he could reach out and trace the image with his finger.

Cheryl gave us time to look our fill. "Everything looks good. You look to be in your eighth week, just as you thought." The room was quiet as we all stared at the image of our baby. Then Cheryl held up her hand as if directing traffic. "Listen."

I held my breath. As if that would help me hear better.

"That's your baby's heart beating."

I pushed myself up on my elbows. "It sounds like—" I couldn't think what it sounded like. I'd heard the same sound during my obstetrical rotation in medical school, but I'd never been able to describe it. "It sounds like—"

Tim beat me to it. "Her heart sounds like the ocean."

Cheryl laughed; the sound was feathery and light, seemingly out of place on a tall, big-boned woman. "It does. But we don't know yet whether that heartbeat is male or female. It's a little early. Maybe by your next ultrasound. But right now, I'd say your baby's heartbeat sounds happy."

That was exactly what I wanted: happy. And healthy.

TIM WAS RIGHT. THE next ultrasound proved that our baby was a girl.

We saw Jamie every two weeks, and as each visit passed and we heard our little girl's heart continue to beat strongly, Jamie began to feel what he called "cautiously optimistic."

We spent hours poring over books of baby names and saying them out loud. Then we'd snuggle up on the couch with our arms wrapped around each other and try them out—"try them on for size" was how Tim put it.

"Listen to this." Tim raised his voice until it was high and fluttery. "My name's Danielle. What's yours?" He cocked his head. "You know, when a new kid moves in next door?"

I squirmed around a little so I could face him. "First, there is no next door. The closest neighbor is in Eden. Second, I don't like Danielle. Someone's sure to shorten it to Danny, and then people will think she's a boy."

"Okay. What about Samantha?"

I shook my head. "Sam. They'll call her Sam." I lay back and rested my head against his chest.

While Tim dreamed up new names, I finally worked up the courage to tell him the name I wanted. "I'd like to name her Kate." I wasn't superstitious. Well, maybe I was, just a little.

Will naming our daughter Kate remind me of my Kate? Will I look at our Kate and remember my first day of kindergarten when my Kate wore jeans and a T-shirt and I'd been stuck in a pink ruffled dress and white cotton socks? Will I look at our Kate and remember how my Kate had rolled her eyes when she'd seen that damn dress? And I'd loved her even more?

But Tim's body stiffened at the mention of Kate's name, even though he knew how much I'd loved her.

"What's wrong?"

"I'm not sure that's the right name."

"Why?" I sat up and turned toward him. It wasn't just his answer that surprised me; he sounded like he was walking on eggshells. Tim knew Kate's story. He knew how much I'd loved going to her house at the end of the school day. How Mrs. Bennett had always been home waiting for us with a glass of milk and a home-baked goody that we'd gobbled up with the frenzy of kids who had eaten lunch at eleven and needed to hold our growling bellies in check until the end of the school day.

Tim pulled me down so I was once again snuggled tight against him. Gently, he explained. "I think naming our daughter Kate would be too much of a reminder of how sad you were when Kate got sick. When she died."

I'd had my heart set on the name Kate. But maybe Tim was right. Maybe naming our baby Kate would remind me of more than just her cancer.

"You could be right." I hated admitting it. But maybe I needed to remember all of Kate and not just that she died.

Tim lifted his head and peered into my face. "Well, that was easy. I didn't expect you to give in so quickly. How come?"

It surprised even me how quickly I'd given in. "I put Kate on a pedestal. Not just after she died but before. Even before she was diagnosed with cancer. The fact is, she wasn't always nice. Maybe if we name our baby Kate, I'll remember more than her cancer. Maybe I'll remember that she made me feel bad. Not all the time but sometimes, when she was being especially vindictive."

"Vindictive? Kate?"

I laughed. "Well, not really vindictive." I fiddled with the button on my sweater. Put it in the buttonhole and took it out. Put it in. Took it out.

"She just got to me sometimes. And I usually never saw it coming. Once, we were walking back to Eden from my house, and she mocked the T-shirt I wore. Told me it was a shirt a six-year-old would wear. It was a silly thing to get upset about, but I was eleven, just starting to realize that clothes mattered if you were a girl, and I was having a hard time keeping up with the other girls."

I started to dig at the callus on my thumb, and Tim placed his hand over mine, his way of encouraging me not to let the stress of my memory get to me. I laughed and kept talking. "This was soon after she'd told me she was dying, and I don't know—I'd thought she'd change after she knew she had cancer. But she never did. She'd said that if I was waiting around for her to become a good person just because she was sick, I'd be waiting a long time."

It didn't sound like much, but Kate said stuff like that all the time. "I don't know. I was a sensitive kid. But maybe you're right. Maybe we shouldn't name our baby Kate."

Tim nodded, settled back, and pulled me with him so we were once again nestled together. "How about Amy?"

"After your sister?"

Amy had delivered her first baby at Johns Hopkins. That was how Tim and I met—in the hospital cafeteria during my residency. Tim had been grabbing a cup of coffee after visiting his sister and new nephew, and I'd just walked off a twenty-four-hour shift, and all I could think about was food and sleep. We had bumped into each other. Literally. And one thing had led to another. A bumping of shoulders led to a few lunches, and a few lunches led to a couple of dinners, and a couple of dinners led to lots of wine. And lots of wine led to where it almost always led: breakfast.

I liked the name Amy just fine. I even understood why Tim wanted to name our baby after his sister: she was the reason we met. Kate wasn't the right name, but all I could see was confusion with two Amys in the family.

"How about Alison?"

We played with that for a bit. Tim did his falsetto voice again. "Hi, my name is Alison?" He ended his sentence on an upbeat so it sounded like a question, and we laughed even more.

We looked at each other, and at almost the same time, we said, "Ali. Her name is Ali. Not Alison, just Ali. After no one."

We congratulated ourselves on having made a momentous decision. Then I let my hopes get the best of me. "Do you think...?"

"Do I think what?" Tim undid my ponytail so that my hair fell past my shoulders. He stroked my hair like he always did when he felt satisfied with the both of us, and as always, he gave me plenty of time to spit out what was going on in my head.

But I changed my mind; I shouldn't press my luck. "Oh, nothing. I'm being silly."

I struggled to get up, but Tim pulled me back. "Oh no you don't. You're not silly. What were you going to say?"

I inhaled deeply then let my breath out slowly. "Do you think we'll have more babies?"

Tim chuckled. "Do you want more babies?"

I didn't have to think about that. "Yes," I whispered, not wanting to wake the gods who took away good luck. "I want to fill every bedroom in this house with babies."

And just for that moment, I wiped Kate and cancer and research out of my mind.

Chapter 5

We kept our pregnancy a secret. Not even our families knew. Not at first. Not even Miss Maggie, and Miss Maggie, in addition to being a friend of the family, had always been the keeper of my secrets.

A pregnancy could be hidden for only so long, however, and I knew that other than our families, Ned needed to know. We'd passed the first eight weeks, and I would soon need to buy maternity clothes, a task I was almost embarrassingly eager for.

Tim sat with me at the kitchen table the morning I planned to make my big announcement. It wasn't even light outside, but he always got up when I did so we could have a few minutes together before we started our day.

"Odds are, Ned'll show more excitement than your parents did."

I thought back to last night's call. Dad had been in the barn with the dogs, and I'd thought for sure that by having Mom on the phone without Dad yelling in the background about needing one thing or another, she'd hear my news and be happy for me.

"A baby? That's nice, dear."

I'd felt the beginnings of a conversation in those few words, and my hopes had risen, but then she ended the call with "Gotta run. Dad needs me." I'd blinked, looked at the phone in my hand, and tapped End Call. No matter how much I wanted to, I never got used to their apathy.

Tim tipped his mug to mine. "We'll figure it out. All of it. The baby. Your research. Your family. My book. Who knows? Ned might even have some suggestions."

I nodded. I'd held off telling Ned as long as I could.

I ALWAYS FELT THE NEED to rap lightly on Ned's door before I walked into his office, even though he told us frequently that if the door was open, we were free to interrupt him. In that way, he was different from most of the department heads at the hospital, where it was generally expected that an email request preceded a meeting.

While I waited for Ned to look up from his desk, I reviewed once again what I wanted to say. I was prepared for him to be surprised. As a good family friend and my mentor, he'd been aware that my chances of becoming pregnant were slim. But I expected that once I told him the news, he would show more enthusiasm than my family, and he'd help me figure out a way to free up my schedule but continue my research. Ned had always been there for me, and he would be again. I looked forward to the slow smile that would light up his face when I told him our news.

"Can I close the door?"

Ned's eyes brightened. "Are you here to tell me you're leaving?" He could easily joke because he knew I would never leave. I had to force myself out the door each night and could barely wait to get back in the morning.

I closed the door, stepped in, and tugged at my skirt before I took the chair in front of his desk. Papers and charts were strewn from one end of his desk to the other, and as my eyes swept over the mess, I caught a glimpse of the results of the latest clinical trial. I hoped maybe he would discuss them with me once I'd told him my news.

My heart felt full. Ned was not only my boss; he was also Kate's father. More of a father to me than my own. He was the easiest man in the world to talk to, so I just jumped in, suddenly wondering what I'd been so nervous about.

"I have some news." Those words reminded me of when I'd announced I was getting married. He hadn't been happy then—not at first. I was too young, and there was too much research to do. He'd had his reasons. But I'd proved him wrong. My marital status hadn't stopped my research; I rarely walked through my front door at night until after eight. It worked for us. Tim spent all day writing in his home office. He barely came up for air until early evening, then he needed time to decompress. By the time I got home, he was ready to be part of the real world instead of the one he'd created in his mind, and I was always eager to tell him what was going on at the hospital.

"Oh?" Ned took off his glasses and laid them on the only clear spot on his desk. "Well, don't keep me in suspense. What's up?" His eyes never left mine, and his smile covered every inch of his face. If he was also remembering the last time I'd gone in there announcing news, nothing on his face reflected it.

I wet my lips. The slightest bit of apprehension tugged at me even though I'd mentally told myself I was being foolish. "Tim and I—" I wet my lips again for good luck. "Tim and I... we're pregnant."

There. I'd said it. The cat was out of the bag. Or out of the room or wherever the hell the cat was supposed to be.

Ned continued to look straight at me, and I waited for his congratulations. But he stayed silent.

"Did you hear what I said? I'm pregnant."

Ned was silent, and my earlier apprehension reared its ugly head. "Ned? Did you hear what I said?" My voice rose, and I hated myself for it because I didn't want to make a scene, but his silence unnerved me.

Ned picked his glasses up from his desk and returned them to his face. "I heard you." That was all he said, but still, I sat there. I waited for more. Our silence grew uncomfortable, and I moved to stand.

"You don't have time for a family right now." Ned's jaws were clenched so tightly I was afraid he would crack a tooth. "Babies take time. You don't have time to care for a baby."

He said what I'd been thinking ever since I learned I was pregnant. He was voicing my greatest fear, but the severity of his reaction surprised me. Maybe he'd misunderstood. Maybe he thought I'd said we were thinking about having a baby.

Then he dismissed my announcement altogether. "Have you looked at this phase two clinical trial from Duke? They've got some fascinating data here. We need to make a trip down there, talk to some of their people."

I didn't want to hear about Duke's findings, not just then. I wanted him to acknowledge my pregnancy and tell me it wouldn't affect my search for a technique to stop the glioblastoma tumor from recurring.

I pushed back my chair and stood. "I'm pregnant! Can't you say something about that?"

The scowl on his face reflected that of a stranger, not at all the man of my childhood who had always had a smile and a word of encouragement for me. "I just did. I said you don't have time for a baby right now."

His words filled my head, and there was nothing I could say in response. *Ned is right. I don't have time for a baby right now. What was I thinking?*

Chapter 6

The baby growing inside me didn't exist for Ned. If anything, his attitude grew harsher whenever he discussed what he insisted on calling my "little predicament."

And after days of him acting as if I didn't exist, I'd been summoned to his office. When I reached out to rap on his open door, Ned looked up from his phone and waved me inside. "I have a friend in Chapel Hill who's willing to perform the procedure, and once that's taken care of, we can combine the trip with a stop at Duke. Did I tell you? They're evaluating the possibility of using DCA as a treatment for slowing the growth of certain tumors in adults. They should have those results right about the time we arrive."

My mind raced through possibilities of what procedure he was talking about, but I was sickeningly sure that I knew.

"Don't just stand there. Come in and close the door. And stop rubbing your stomach like you think I'll rip that baby right out of you." Ned reached for the calendar on his desk before I could even react to his comment. He flipped through pages until he apparently found what he was looking for. "How about a week from now? That'll give you plenty of time to tell Tim about the trip to Duke."

I closed the door, took a few steps into his office, and forced my hand away from my stomach. "Plenty of time?"

"Yes. Plenty of time to get rid of your problem."

"Problem?"

"Will you stop repeating everything I say? Yes, your problem. Our problem. You need to focus on your work, and I've arranged a solution." He looked almost proud of himself while I stared back at him in horror.

"Are you talking about an abortion?" My knees felt weak; just saying the word left a foul taste in my mouth. I took two steps backward and leaned against Ned's office door.

"Yes. Abortion. It's not a dirty word."

My hand moved upward to my stomach again as if to ward off his words. He'd mentioned abortion as if he were talking about returning a shirt because he no longer cared for that particular shade of blue. "Ned!" His name splintered in my mouth. "You don't just undo a baby."

"Don't be ridiculous." He leaned back in his chair, clearly unfazed by the cruelty he'd just unleashed. "It's done all the time. You wouldn't even need to tell Tim. Just explain that sometimes nature takes its course. Gets rid of mistakes. Tell him your doctor said you could try again in a year or two. That will give you the time to complete your research."

When Ned stood and moved around his desk toward me, I sidestepped his reach. He seemed to misunderstand my reaction and tried to assure me of his good intentions, when really, the thought of him touching me repulsed me to my very core.

"Don't worry. I'll take care of everything."

I flinched at the casualness of his words. "I can't do that. I can't get rid of this baby." It wasn't that I didn't agree with a woman choosing to have an abortion. I did. As long as it was her doing the choosing. Ned had no right to make that choice for me.

Ned was no longer the man I once knew. He was not the man who'd held out his hand and talked me down from that old apple tree when Kate died and I'd refused to go to her memorial service. He was not the man who said we would figure it out together when I'd asked what my life would be like without Kate. *I don't know who this man is.*

"No? All right, then."

I lifted my head. "What's that supposed to mean?" Was he going to drop the subject and help me work around what he clearly considered an inconvenience?

Ned moved behind his desk and sat. When he spoke again, his voice was cold and flat. "Hand all of your files over to David, will you? That way, he can get up to speed before we leave for Duke."

"We?" Even to my own ears, my voice sounded pathetic.

"David and I. I'll be taking David with me. You'll be busy enough with your patients, and..." He paused to look me up and down while I stood frozen by the door. "And your health. Close the door on the way out, will you?"

Once again, I was filled with grief when I left Ned's office. Our personal relationship would never be the same.

Ned and David had traveled to Duke and brought back case studies of patients whose survival rate had been extended from eleven months to, in some cases, almost fifteen months. It was the most encouraging news we'd seen in years, but I didn't see the results so much as hear about them; Ned had David present the findings at the next staff meeting.

I sat in the last chair at the back of the room and watched while David, whose over-the-collar blond hair had been styled within an inch of its life, moved forward with findings that should have been mine.

WHILE LITTLE GIRLS dreamed of marriage and babies, I watched Kate lose the ability to walk and talk. I watched as she lost the ability to swallow food or control the simplest of bodily functions. While little girls dreamed of marriage and babies, I watched Kate die. And after she died, I attached myself to her father because he hurt like I did, because he found in me the same thing I found in him—hope. But now, that same man breezed past me as if I were toxic.

Weeks went by, but I kept quiet at home about Ned and the hospital and what it was like to find myself on the outside looking in when I'd always been Ned's golden girl. Instead, I forced myself to focus on Tim's enthusiasm, hoping it would be contagious. I wanted to feel the same joy he felt, and when I couldn't, when I was too tired or too stressed, I forced a smile into my words and willed the tight band of pressure around the base of my skull to disappear.

More nights than not, I would no sooner lower myself onto the couch to relax than Tim would have in hand either a how-to baby book or a piece of baby furniture that he'd bought for the nursery. And the more I managed to keep my voice calm and pleasant, the more my migraine escalated, and I would gently push away the book or the rainbow unicorn lamp or the musical unicorn mobile that he'd found for the baby crib.

Tim saw that I suffered. He just didn't know why. He would slide my legs over so he could join me on the couch, rearranging my legs on his lap, then his fingers took over where mine had futilely attempted to squeeze out the tension that, day by day, continued to escalate.

"Maybe you need to take an early leave," he murmured one night while I relaxed into the relief his fingers provided.

I stiffened. I wanted to pretend I hadn't heard him, but instead, I opened one eye and looked at him with what I hoped he would mistake for humor. "Have you lost your mind?"

I refused to give in to Ned's bullying. He would never be satisfied with David. It was only a matter of time before he saw that for himself.

Chapter 7

The first time I felt Ali kick, I was at the grocery store, reaching for a box of Dunkaroos. I was so startled I dropped the box and had to lean on my cart to stay upright, then I laughed when I realized that what I'd felt was what I'd been waiting to feel. I hadn't understood it would feel like that.

I pulled out my phone and punched in Tim's number. At that very moment, our baby was alive.

"What did it feel like?"

I tried to remember so I would remember the next time. "Weird. It felt weird. I thought it would feel different, harder, but instead, it felt more like bubbles in my belly. Or maybe that I'd passed gas." I laughed again. I couldn't think of any other way to describe it.

My relief from that first kick was monumental but short-lived. Within hours, my worry built again, not much different than a teakettle filled with water that turned to steam when the gas was turned on and heated the water. And in no time at all, the whistle blew. As soon as I felt the next kick, I relaxed. My baby was alive, but from one kick to the next, I worried I would lose her. That was my fear. That was one of my fears. The bigger one hid behind it: Would I be able to handle a baby, my patients, and my research?

I found myself waiting for that bubbly feeling or maybe the feel of a leg or an arm. A knee. A foot. Those little kicks, the ones some women found so annoying, gave me hope. That and the steady thump, thump, thump of her little heart.

EACH MONTH, I GREW rounder, and I cherished every pound I gained. It meant my baby was growing. While I celebrated the growth of my belly and endured nausea that forced me to carry soda crackers wherever I went, I continued to worry about my career. Even without my research, I wondered how I would ever keep up the schedule I'd followed for the last few years.

I never told Tim how quickly I'd fallen from grace at the hospital. I never mentioned that Ned had given David my research findings. I never mentioned walking into a room of my peers while knowing I'd lost my place as Ned's favorite.

While I worried, Tim continued to fill the nursery with every state-of-the-art piece of baby furniture money could buy. Most nights when I came home from the hospital, he had something new to show me, and I worried it was too soon, too much. But Tim wouldn't hear a word of what I said.

He painted the nursery with a blue sky and fluffy white clouds, and because we knew we were having a girl, he added pink and yellow flowers to the garden mural he'd painted on one wall. The other three walls were the palest apple-blossom pink. He finished the room with window seats under the dormer windows, then he built shelves under the window seats.

After the crib was delivered and assembled, Tim couldn't wait to show me. He led me up the stairs with my eyes closed, directed me into the nursery, then uncovered my eyes. "Ta-da!" Like a magician, he proudly showed off his achievement.

One look at the crib, and the changing table with drawers underneath on the left, and an armoire on the right, and nightstands with little lamps that twinkled like stardust in the dark, and I burst into tears.

Tim blinked. "What's the matter? Don't you like it?" He pulled me into his arms and tried to hold me, but I bent over from the nausea that rose in my throat. Tim seemed shocked by my reaction but no more so than me.

I'd let Tim have carte blanche in choosing baby furniture. The few times I had a free night or weekend, I was so exhausted that the last thing I wanted was to go shopping. So it wasn't that. It wasn't that Tim was taking over. It was my fear of how our baby would take over my life.

All those months, I'd walked by that room, and other than twinges of worry, I had managed to keep fear at bay. But that night, my fear roared, and I wanted to change my mind. I wanted to send the baby back where it came from.

Tim pulled me down, so we both sat in the rocking chair he'd picked for those middle-of-the-night visits and feedings where we could hold Ali close and rock her to sleep. He rocked me until the muscles in my chest relaxed and I could breathe evenly.

Our dream was coming true, and I was falling apart.

Suddenly, I knew that Ned had been right. I'd been in the middle of a series of groundbreaking clinical trials, and I'd let him take my findings and give them to David while I'd dealt with the inconveniences that accompanied a pregnancy. The timing was wrong; I agreed with him on that. But timing had nothing to do with miracles. And Ali was my miracle. Except I felt like I was losing everything.

I couldn't tell Tim any of what I was thinking. I refused to mar his happiness, his joy.

And then I did, anyway.

WE WERE WEEKS AWAY from Ali's due date, and I couldn't keep quiet any longer.

"This was a mistake."

"What was a mistake?" Tim placed the dinner plates on the table. "Sit. Eat. You're eating for two, you know."

"Tim. Stop. You need to listen to me."

"I will. Just sit. You shouldn't be on your feet so much." He held out my chair, and I walked over to the table and sat. Tim took his regular chair across from me. "Now, what's so important you need to tell me?"

Words tumbled out of me like Slinkys making a mad dash for the bottom of the steps, and while I talked, the bloodred juices of the prime rib on my plate nudged at my stomach. "I can't have this baby. I can't." And because I needed to make sure that he understood, I lied. I looked right into his eyes and spoke words I wasn't sure I meant, words that would hurt him. "I don't *want* this baby."

Tim's face looked like I'd slaughtered a baby lamb on the kitchen table.

"Why?" Just one word, yet it sliced into my soul.

Whatever I said next would affect the rest of my marriage, yet I hadn't prepared any words. I doubted there were words that would let me rid myself of that baby but not lose my husband. So I said nothing. I sat there. I stared into my hands as if the answer were hidden beneath my fingers, waiting for me to uncover it.

At first Tim did nothing, and our kitchen was filled only with old-house noises that we barely noticed after having lived there for so long. When he stood, it was so fast he knocked his chair backward. I flinched when he picked up the dishes still filled with our untouched dinner and threw them into the sink, the sound of breakage emphasizing the words that spewed from his mouth. "The baby's almost ready to be born, and *now* you decide you don't want her? What do you propose we do? Drop her off at the fire station on the way home from the hospital?"

I was so startled by the anger in his voice that I flinched again, only that time, my chair edged away from the table so that I was seated facing Tim rather than the place where my dinner plate had just been.

Tim's eyes grew wide when he saw my fear, and he was clearly devastated to see that I was afraid of not just his words but also of him. He walked over to where I sat and knelt before me. He placed his head in my lap. Then he lulled me with memories, with words soft as silk.

"Remember when we first moved into this house and it was just so ugly, with the brocade wallpaper and the water stains on the ceilings? Remember how we talked about filling all these bedrooms with kids when we found out we were pregnant with Ali? Remember? I thought that's what you wanted. You kept saying six, and I kept saying four. Four would be plenty. And now, and now you don't even want one?"

His voice broke, and he hid his face in my lap as if he should be the one ashamed.

There was so much I wanted to say. It wasn't that I didn't want kids. It wasn't that I didn't want that baby that I'd just begun to envision with coal-black hair and emerald-green eyes. But I couldn't. I had to put Kate first. I had to. I couldn't give up.

I wondered whether that dinner we never ate might be the first step to the end of my marriage.

I didn't know if it was Kate's cancer, or her death, that set me on the course I followed. What I knew was that I wanted—no, I *needed*, like the air I breathed and the food I ate—to stop the thing that grew inside a person's head and destroyed not just that person but also everyone who loved her. And sure, when I was a kid, I couldn't have put into words what I thought I could do that no one else had been able to, but I had to try.

Chapter 8

When Tim was called to New York for an emergency meeting with his publisher, we both heaved a sigh of relief.

"I'll only be gone overnight." He stood in the front entryway, shifting from one foot to the other, his duffel flung over his shoulder. I wanted to reach out and straighten the collar of his shirt. Instead, I kept my hands at my sides.

"It's fine. The baby's not due for three weeks. You'll be back tomorrow night. Go." It was my job to get him to go. I understood that.

He leaned toward me, one hand on the doorknob, and I drew in my breath. But then he shook his head slightly, pulled open the door, and was gone, taking with him all the horrid words we had screamed at each other over the last few weeks.

I closed my eyes; I was relieved. He wouldn't be there to judge whatever emotion played across my face. I wouldn't have to look into his eyes and see how fast he shuttered his pain while he waited for me to turn back into the woman he thought I was.

Later that same night, I'd stood from where I'd been ensconced in the wingback chair in the family room, ready for bed, when the dribble of warm water trickled down my legs. I immediately felt dizzy and sat down, then I popped back up, not wanting to get the chair cushion wet. I knew what it was, but the shock of it made me look at the puddle on the floor in disbelief before I yanked off my sweater and threw it on top of the spreading mess.

My mind had refused to touch on the final stage of my pregnancy, and whenever Jamie had mentioned it, or Tim, I had blocked them out. As if I could prevent it from happening.

I thought about next steps. It was late. Tim would be in his hotel room because he had an early-morning meeting. But he'd be crushed if I didn't call him.

We agreed he would take the first plane home and meet me at the hospital. If everything went as planned, he'd get there before the baby.

My contractions were coming faster. Obviously, the backache I'd had all day—not really bad but never going completely away—was more than just payback for spending too much time on my feet. Soon, I felt both a tightening and rolling sensation that told me I had to move.

It never dawned on me to call my mother. I needed to go through labor on my own, in penance, maybe, to all the women who prayed for that moment yet never had the chance.

The drive to the hospital was short, but I was panting by the time I pulled into the hospital parking lot and headed toward the ER entrance. I stopped the car to make sense of what I saw. Every space was filled. Even the not-spaces were filled. *What the hell? Did a plane crash?* Then I started to cry. The tightening and relaxing of my belly came faster, and the spasms grew stronger. All I could think about was how much I wanted them to stop. I'd changed my mind from that long-ago moment when Tim and I had danced through the bathroom in celebration of our pregnancy. *Why can't I just change my mind?*

I threaded my way through the regular parking lot until I finally found a spot. My cell phone rang just then, before I'd even pulled the key from the ignition. I'd meant to turn the phone off, but I caught sight of the screen—it was Tim. His words came fast, and I struggled to understand him. "I can't get a flight." I heard him take a deep breath, and when he exhaled, his next words were less garbled. "There's a freak storm here, and all the flights are canceled, but don't worry. I'm renting a car, and I'll be there as soon as I can."

Nodding as if he could see me, I hit the end call button. Before I could turn the phone off, it rang again, but I ignored the ringtone and shut the damn thing down. Tears and snot ran down my face when I hauled myself out of the car. *Stop feeling sorry for yourself.* I stood still, tried to get my bearings, wiped at my face with the sleeve of my jacket, and headed through the parking lot toward the hospital. *For God's sake, just pull yourself together.*

I rested against random cars when the contractions hit, but eventually, the automatic doors to the ER sucked me in, and I was quickly swallowed up by nurses who recognized me. There was no triage; I was immediately whisked through those magic doors that held the key to help. That was the benefit of being admitted to the hospital where I worked.

I was taken to my room, where Jamie was waiting. He was the only person I'd called. "So... it's time, huh? You're a little early, but she's big enough. Everything'll be fine."

"That's easy for you to say," I muttered, thinking that if I'd been born a man, all my problems would be over.

Jamie laughed. As close as we'd once been, I'd never mentioned my change of heart about the baby, and I wasn't going to tell him then. Besides, to Jamie, pregnancy was a miracle, and he wouldn't be offering me sympathy.

The contractions kept coming closer and faster. Several hours later, I was wheeled into the OR, and the anesthesiologist administered the epidural. I silently hoped for relief, but it was minimal. My contractions were centered in my back, and instead of experiencing a release from pain each time a contraction stopped, I experienced the constant throb of a toothache times a thousand.

I was determined to ride it out without complaint. I didn't believe in a higher being, but I believed in sin. I believed in lakes of fire and brimstone. Mostly, I believed in everlasting punishment. And I believed I was experiencing mine.

I sucked ice chips and tried to remember why conscious breathing was critical. I was exhausted, but it wasn't the physical and mental exhaustion I was used to, that of back-to-back surgeries with no time to rest between them. It was an exhaustion I'd never experienced before—filled with pain and fear and the knowledge that I would never be up to the task of loving my child.

"Okay, Emma? It's time to push. When I say push, you push. Got it?"

"Got it."

"Push. Hard!"

I pushed. Sure my insides were being ripped out, I pushed again. And again.

And finally, "Okay. One more time. Push like you mean it."

I pushed like I meant it and silently cursed Jamie to hell and back. I felt a slithering wetness escape my body, allowing me a momentary relief. For maybe three seconds, the room went still—with just a hint of expectation that forced me to lean forward.

Then I heard her cry.

Nobody had warned me that the sound of my baby crying would make me want to rip out my heart so it would stop hurting. Then I wished Tim had made it to the hospital and that I wasn't alone.

MATERNITY WARD NURSES needed to readily assess when a new mother needed assistance. They needed to guide and comfort women who were clearly overwhelmed. And they needed to do it without criticism. At least not overtly. My nurse hovered; she waited for a signal from me before she placed in my arms what felt like the weight of a carburetor wrapped in a pink blanket.

Once more, I wished I'd paid more attention during my obstetrical rotation or at least had friends with babies. Or at least had friends.

I forced myself to look at my baby while she nestled against my heart. Then my nurse seemed to decide it was safe to leave us alone. I held her close and tried to empty my mind of all thought. I held her close so I could grow accustomed to the weight of her.

I didn't want to look to see if she had Tim's dark hair and green eyes or if her ears were shaped like mine or if she had my widow's peak that I'd hated as a kid. But I did. And she was perfect.

And I fell in love with my baby, and I was just so sure of my ability to keep her safe.

Chapter 9

A small patch of sunlight stretched from the window and would soon reach across the blanket and poke at Tim's eyes where he lay sound asleep, slumped in the chair next to my hospital bed. A small smile played on his lips even while he slept, and I reached out and traced one finger lightly across his mouth. It was the first time I'd touched him in months.

He opened his eyes. "Hey."

"Hey yourself. What time did you get here?" We spoke softly even though there was no one but us in the room.

Tim yawned and stretched his arms out over his head. "Not soon enough. You had the baby without me."

"I did. Some things just can't be helped."

"I'm sorry I wasn't here." Tim drew his hands over his face as if he could wipe away the stubble that covered his cheeks along with his exhaustion. "I should never have gone to New York."

How quickly I'd wanted him gone. "Who knew she'd come so early? We did okay."

Tim nodded; he never took his eyes off me.

"Stop looking at me." I felt naked when he looked at me.

He reached for my hand then turned it over and ran his finger lightly across my open palm. "You did more than okay."

"Oh, I'm not so sure." I laughed. But then I winced, closed my eyes, and drew in a breath.

Tim's chair scraped against the floor, and when I opened my eyes, he had moved from sitting beside the bed to standing. Eyes wide, he leaned in. "What? What's wrong?"

I laughed, that time not so enthusiastically. "Nothing. Sit down." Moving my hand gingerly across my middle, I reassured him. "Maybe it's just too soon to laugh."

"Was it hard?"

I felt myself still at Tim's question. I could only think about the good parts. The parts I wanted to remember. "Well, I wouldn't do it again tomorrow."

That made us both smile. "Have you seen her?"

Tim nodded. "Right after I was sure you were all right. The nurse said they'd bring her in as soon as you were awake. They wanted to make sure you got some sleep. She's—Emma, she's beautiful."

"She is. She looks just like you."

Then the dam between us broke, and we both started talking at once. I had so much forgiveness to beg. "I'm—"

"No. No, it's me—" Tim reached for my hand again. He brought it to his lips and kissed it as if he were sealing a promise. "We'll figure this out."

And I was sure that we would.

Chapter 10

I woke to the ringing of the telephone.

I'd dozed after nursing Ali, unable to keep my eyes open while I waited for Tim to return with the car seat and clothes for the baby and me. I never even woke when the nurse brought in a breakfast tray. But the phone was ringing, and I lifted the receiver to my ear.

Before I could say a word, I heard my parents singing "Congratulations" in my ear.

"Thank you." I yawned. Then I carefully stretched my sore muscles.

"A little girl! Tim called to let us know. You must both be so happy." Their voices sounded excited, and I smiled.

"I'm being discharged today. So if you want to see her..."

There was a pause. If I were a writer, I'd have called it a pregnant pause. "Oh no. We can't come today. We have a meeting with some important contributors today. There's no rescheduling people who want to give you money."

"That's okay. You can stop by the house..."

"We will. Just wanted to call you quickly. Tell you how happy we are. We've got to run now. If there's anything we can do..."

"Her name's—" But they'd already hung up.

I shook my head. It was a typical family call—for my family, anyway—and I'd been a fool to get excited, but I refused to let it bother me. Not that day.

My eyes felt heavy, and even with the interruption, I was slipping back into sleep when the sound of footsteps startled me awake. It wasn't the soft padding sound of rubber-soled shoes but instead the slap of leather against tile, which sounded angry and threatening.

My eyes flew open, and Ned was pacing between my bed and the bassinet where Ali slept. He looked wrinkled, as if he'd slept in his suit. His normally well-trimmed hair looked in need of a trip to the barber, and he hadn't bothered to shave. I would have bet he hadn't shaved in days.

"Ned?" I blinked, unsure whether I was dreaming, but when I opened my eyes again, he was still there.

"What are you doing here?" I'd barely seen him over the past few months other than for staff meetings and consultations. He'd stopped coming to the house for dinner about the same time he'd suggested I rid myself of the baby.

He'd slipped out of our lives without Tim even noticing; first, because he'd been busy planning for the baby, and then later, when I'd told him the pregnancy was a mistake. If Ned even entered his mind, it might have just been to wonder how much he'd influenced my change of heart about motherhood.

Why is he here? Now? I peeked into Ali's bassinet to assure myself she was sleeping peacefully. "Is something wrong?" For Ned to come by, something had to be terribly wrong. "Ned?"

He never looked up from his pacing. Never answered me. And the closer he came to my bed, I noticed that he smelled—

"Have you been drinking?" *That can't be right. Ned rarely drinks.*

I asked again, "Ned! Have you been drinking?" I tried to keep my voice low; the last thing we needed was a nurse popping her head into the room, demanding quiet and finding the chief of Oncology drunk.

He stopped pacing when he again reached the bassinet where Ali slept, blissfully unaware of Ned's presence or the rage he'd brought into the room. He stared at her little body bundled snugly in a pink-and-white striped blanket and with a little pink cap on her head.

My palms itched. "Ned?"

When he finally turned toward me, my only thought was that I wanted him to move away from the bassinet.

"What about your promise to Kate?" His words were slurred, and he weaved slightly. He leaned toward the bassinet and slowly reached out one hand, but instead of grabbing hold, he steadied himself against the wall. I exhaled.

"How are you going to keep up your research if you have to stay home and take care of... of *this*?"

I'd been calm, or I'd thought I was, but I felt my face grow hot. "This? *This*? *This* is my daughter. She has a name." *Why is he bringing this up now?* For months, he had barely spoken to me. David was his new prodigy. David was being groomed to move forward with Ned's research when he retired. Ever since I'd told Ned I was pregnant, everything had been about David.

I couldn't help myself. I felt my jaw set and my eyes harden. "You hardly need me to keep that promise. You've got David."

I worried as Ned continued to stand near Ali that the noxious fumes emanating off him would wake her. I couldn't remember when babies first developed a sense of smell, but I was pretty sure it was early. Right then, I regretted my lack of interest in obstetrics.

"Could you move away from the bassinet? I don't want you to wake the baby."

Ned looked around as if he had no idea where he was standing or what was next to him.

"Ned?" I pulled myself up from the bed and moved to stand protectively by Ali's bassinet. "I think you need to leave."

Ned smiled, but his smile reached nowhere near his eyes. "I'm not ready to leave. David isn't you. He doesn't have your determination. He doesn't have your skill. I need you."

Ned's words were everything I'd wanted to hear over the last few months. But it was too late. I had Ali. "Ned, I—"

"My child is dead." He spoke so softly I wasn't sure what he'd said. Then he spoke again, and I heard every word. "My child is dead." He straightened his shoulders and pushed out his chest. "You promised her you'd never stop searching for a cure."

I shook my head, not believing he meant what he'd said. "I was a *child* when I made that promise. You can't hold me accountable for what I said then, but yes, I meant it. And I *will* keep my promise. But right now, I have to stop. At least for a few months. I have Ali. I can't give her up. I've wanted her my whole life. What do you expect me to do?"

Ned looked at me with what might have been pity. "I think you know the answer to that." When he stepped toward me, I stepped back; I couldn't bear for him to touch me. "You can have other children. Do you really want to focus on one child when you could save hundreds? Thousands?"

Then he walked out. The Ned I knew had been a loving father and not just to Kate. He'd been more of a father to me than my own, but the Ned who walked out of my hospital room was a man I didn't know.

I was still standing by the bassinet when Tim walked into the room with a fistful of discharge papers and a quizzical look on his face. "Was that Ned I just saw in the hallway? He looked like he'd been drinking."

"Mm, I don't think he's feeling well, but I doubt he's been drinking."

I didn't know why I felt the need to protect Ned. It was just something I did.

Chapter 11

Two weeks later, I stood at the top of the basement steps with Ali in my arms, knowing that her blanket would offer little protection if I let her slip and thump down each steep, rough-hewn step.

I imagined it from the safety of the doorway: eyes flung open in shock, her little face bright, bright red, arms flailing as she rolled from step to step. I closed my eyes, wanting to erase that image from my brain, but I couldn't. When I envisioned her little lungs filling with that stuttering high-pitched wail babies made when pleading in the only way they knew, I thought I'd lost my mind.

What would it be like to let her fall?

I stared down into what was no more than a root cellar lit only by the bare bulb hanging at the bottom of the steps. I knew in that way one just knew things that I wouldn't even have to toss her: just open my arms and she'd be gone.

When I looked at the infant in my arms, she slept soundly, more certain of her safety than I was.

Feeling as if I'd been slapped in a room full of strangers ready to judge me, I stumbled back from that open doorway. My arms trembled from the weight of her small body, but I pulled her even closer to my heart, afraid that I might lose hold of her.

The musty smell inching up from the basement almost sickened me but not nearly as much as the darkness of my single fleeting thought. Only Ali's innocence, her tiny fingers splayed in serenity, her baby birdie mouth puckering in and out—making those little sucking sounds babies made when they thought all was right with their world—allowed me to hold on to some scrap of sanity.

What was I thinking?

I didn't know. I'd stopped thinking, maybe. And feeling. Who pictured their two-week-old infant bouncing from step to step until there was no breath left within her little body? Ali was our miracle. She was what I'd wanted first. What I'd wanted always. What I thought I'd never have, and once I had her, I thought of ridding myself of her because my life revolved around patient files and life expectancies and clinical trials.

And because Ned told me I should?

How will I ever keep my promise to Kate? How can I do what Ned wants?

I wanted Ali to wake and scream her bloodcurdling screams while she was still safe. Those imagined piercing wails forced me to put as much distance as possible between us and that open doorway. I turned, intent on saving my child, and practically threw myself into Tim's arms.

I'd never heard him enter the kitchen, yet there he was, pulling me toward him, wrapping his arms around us. It was the first moment of safety I'd felt since I'd scooped Ali up out of her crib and brought her to the kitchen with me.

"Hey. What's wrong? What are you doing down here?" His voice gravelly with sleep and confusion, Tim pulled us even tighter into his embrace. His presence broke not just the silence but also the terror that gripped my heart.

"Here." Pulling back, I thrust Ali into Tim's arms and turned, ready to run. Then Ali woke and cried out in hunger. At the sound of her cry, my breasts seized with the need to release the milk that filled them. For a moment, I hesitated and turned to look at both of them. Tim held Ali in his arms with a look of total confusion on his face, and Ali, whose little cries had moved swiftly from sobs to screams, demanded to be fed in the only way she knew.

"Emma?"

Ali's distress wasn't enough to stop me as I ran from the room and up the stairs with Tim following closely. Only the door I'd managed to slam shut and lock behind me stopped him. "Emma! The baby's hungry. You need to feed her."

My breasts throbbed from my race up the stairs, but I stayed silent behind our bedroom door. The stale smell of the basement clung to me, and the imagined sound of Ali's body thumping down the steep stone steps played over and over in my mind like a newsreel that never stopped. Thoughts were worse than words, I discovered. They got stuck in your head, and you couldn't scrape them out.

When Tim stopped yelling my name, and Ali's screams grew fainter, I knew he'd gone downstairs. I heard him pawing through the kitchen cupboards, looking for the infant formula, for the bottles, for all the just-in-case paraphernalia. When I heard him curse, I knew he was trying to screw the top onto the bottle without putting Ali down, yet I did nothing, just threw myself on the bed and imagined Tim's sigh of relief when he finally managed to get the all-important fake nipple into Ali's searching mouth.

And then I slept.

Eventually, I woke. Then I wished myself dead and slept again. I wished I would die without ever waking like Anne did all those years ago when she sat down to read her library book and Miss Maggie found her hours later. I wondered how I'd gone from the joy I'd felt when we discovered we were pregnant to imagining, if even for one second...? *Did I just imagine it, or did I almost do it? Does it matter? I thought it. Isn't that bad enough?*

It had been over twelve hours since Ali last nursed, and my breasts screamed for release. Wet, cold compresses did nothing to absolve me of the pain, and finally, in desperation, I expressed my milk into the bathroom sink and watched as it swirled, thin and watery, down the drain. Just one more travesty.

Tim never knocked on the bedroom door again that night, and other than dragging myself from the bed to use the bathroom and drink a few sips of water, I never left the room that once had been filled with the scent of fresh-cut flowers but currently smelled stale and sour.

I sealed myself off from my family, but my life revolved around theirs. The same grates that allowed heat to travel from room to room allowed me to hear both the wails of Ali's distress and the sighs of her comfort. Each time she cried out in hunger, my breasts pulsated in response.

"It's okay, baby girl. I've got you." Tim's voice, soft and soothing, would sometimes be swallowed whole by Ali's screams, then she'd calm, and the three of us relaxed into her silence.

I calculated the time without bothering to open my eyes simply by the cycle of my daughter's distress and Tim's soothing response. That was what took me from morning to night.

I SLEPT AGAIN, AND when I opened my eyes, Tim was sitting by my side, holding my hand and searching my face for signs of the woman he thought he knew. But that woman had disappeared. He just didn't know it yet. I tried to wriggle my hand loose, but he held tight.

"How'd you get in?" I whispered, knowing that any keys to the rooms in our house had long since disappeared into the history of the people who'd lived in it before us.

"With a paper clip and a tension wrench." Not even trying to hide the hint of wryness in his voice, Tim explained how he'd figured it out. He kept his voice low, so as not to startle me, maybe, or maybe because he'd gotten so used to whispering around the baby. "I was hoping you'd come out on your own, but when you didn't, I knew I had to get in."

He looked like he hadn't slept or eaten or taken even one moment to himself. His eyes looked tired, and his shoulders slumped. It hurt to look at him. It was the first I'd seen him in almost twenty-four hours, but I still closed my eyes. I still needed to block him out.

"How...?" I wanted to ask about Ali, but I couldn't. I couldn't bring myself to say her name, not out loud, anyway. But Tim knew; it was as if he heard the question in my mind.

Almost as proud of our calm daughter as he was at our unlocked bedroom door, he smiled. "She's sleeping."

I nodded. Sleeping. That was good. That meant she was happy. Full. "You look awful." I didn't know why I chose those words when so many other things were waiting to be said.

Tim agreed. "You don't look so hot yourself." He gently touched a finger to the gold bracelet that circled my wrist—the one he'd given me on our wedding day. The one that meant he would love me forever. No matter what.

We were silent. It wasn't the silence we had once been used to, the kind born from trust and love. Our silence was filled with confusion and hurt. How did we move forward?

"I don't know what to do, Emma," Tim whispered finally, his voice spent. "Tell me what to do." He held my hands in his, trying, I thought, to share his warmth, to force me to feel something. "I don't know how to help you. I need to know what's wrong."

I almost smiled. "So you can fix it?" No matter what the problem, Tim always thought he should be able to fix it. But some things couldn't be fixed. Like me. Maybe I couldn't be fixed. Maybe some things were meant to stay broken.

Tim was obviously thinking ahead, to a future of some sort for all of us, but I hadn't moved on from yesterday. "What made you...?"

I couldn't finish, couldn't put the words in my mouth and let them out again.

"I don't know what woke me." He yawned. "I was sound asleep, and then something startled me, I guess, and you weren't next to me. I sensed, I don't know, that something was wrong. That you were hurt. Or Ali." After releasing my hands, Tim scrubbed at his face while he talked, trying to wipe away his exhaustion.

"The basement door was open, and you were standing at the top of the stairs. And that made no sense to me. What did you need from the basement in the middle of the night? You hate the basement. I knew you must have been exhausted, and I don't know, I thought maybe you had started sleepwalking again. Your back was to me, and at first, I didn't even realize you were holding Ali, but then you turned and shoved her at me, and all I could do was grab her and hold on."

Tim's words brought it all back: standing in front of the open doorway with Ali in my arms. One split second of horror. I slowly drew in an uneven breath, and when I let it out, my body shuddered.

"Here, scoot up. Turn around." Once my back was to him, he pulled me in even closer, and I felt the warmth of his body.

We sat like that, close, not talking, for I didn't know how long. It was long enough for my shudders to stop, then he took my hairbrush from the table by my side of the bed and started brushing my hair. Long, smooth, slow strokes from the crown of my head all the way down to the tips of my hair where it rested on my shoulders. I closed my eyes, giving in to the rhythmic motion, lulled by the simple action of the brush moving slowly through my hair.

I was almost asleep when Tim broke our silence. "This could just be hormones." He cleared his throate. "I don't mean *just*. I mean, if it is hormones, or you're feeling the way you do because of exhaustion or something, then this can be fixed. Maybe Jamie can help you. Or give you a pill. Or something."

His words ended the first brief moment of peace I'd felt in twenty-four hours—no, since we'd come home from the hospital and I'd accepted that Ned had been right. I couldn't do everything. And my research had to come first.

My chest tightened. "Do you think a pill is going to fix this?" I grabbed the brush from Tim's hands and threw it across the room.

Tim's eyes widened, and he moved back to sitting on the edge of the bed. It might have been funny if we were just having a simple argument, but there was nothing simple about it, and a pill wasn't going to fix me. I backed up against the headboard, knees to my chin, putting as much distance between us as I could. I rocked back and forth and silently wondered what in the hell I was going to do.

Our silence grew again before Tim spoke. "Look, something's wrong. I know that." He didn't reach for my hand or move any closer, but I knew he wasn't done. "How about this. I'll take care of Ali while you get checked out by the doctor. It might be good for you to have a couple extra weeks of rest."

He was trying to be strong for both of us, and I thought about his offer. Could it be that simple? And then I remembered. "What about your book tour? Aren't you supposed to be in New York next week?"

"I already canceled it. I don't know why I agreed to a tour so soon after the baby." He lifted his shoulders. "There'll be other tours." Then he reached out and lightly touched my hand, testing the waters to see if I could handle his touch.

"Oh, Tim." My eyes filled, and my voice cracked when I spoke. "This tour is important. You said so yourself." I'd never seen him put so much of himself into one book. *This book.* He was sure the book had a shot at making the big lists. I turned my head away.

"Hey, it's going to be okay." He placed his hands on my shoulders and turned me toward him. "My time will come again. Right now, we have to figure this out. Right now, you and Ali are more important. Talk to me. Why are you hiding up here?"

Our hands were linked together again, mine slender and pale with long, delicate fingers that Ned had always said were the hands of a surgeon. Tim's were strong and golden brown, tanned from days of digging in our garden when he needed to work out a plot twist or a scene that didn't flow smoothly.

It wasn't that I thought he would understand, but somewhere deep inside, I thought if I could put my need into words, he might. Struggling to still my thoughts, I pulled myself up so that I could look into his eyes. "Remember my friend Kate?"

Tim nodded. If he was confused by what seemed a change of subject, he didn't let on.

I took a deep breath, and when I expelled it, I started talking. "I know Kate's dead. I remember her memorial service and everything that happened after she died. I do. But sometimes, it seems like she's *not* dead, and it's up to me to save her. Sometimes, I think I can never stop looking for a cure or an answer. Because I need to save her. Does that make any sense to you?"

Tim's face went blank, and he sat silently for a minute. His eyes searched my face. "No. That doesn't make any sense." He swallowed then continued, "Who is it you think you need to save?"

I was filled with certainty when I answered. "Kate. I need to save Kate."

I realized I wasn't making sense. Kate was dead. But I had to save her.

Chapter 12

Tim finally coaxed me from our bedroom. I hadn't showered, my pajamas no longer smelled fresh and clean, and I'd grown so accustomed to the dimness of our bedroom that the sun streaming in from the kitchen window made my eyes water. It was hard to believe that just yesterday, I'd stood in that kitchen and wondered if I'd lost my mind.

As if my every movement needed to be orchestrated so that I didn't wander out the front door, Tim led me to the kitchen table. He busied himself at the stove, and when he placed a mug of hot tea before me, I unclenched my fingers and wrapped my hands around it. The tea was too hot to sip, but I hungrily inhaled the scent of bitter orange, hoping it would remind me of a time in my life when I didn't wish— *What? That I could just disappear?*

My eyes roamed from the window to the stove to the fridge, anywhere but the basement door. When Tim saw me glance at the sink filled with empty baby bottles and rubber nipples crusted with dried formula, he shrugged. He threw a tea towel over the mess and made it disappear. "I don't know how one person alone can take care of a new baby and keep a house from not looking like a bomb went off." He looked proud. He *had* taken care of Ali; she was clean and fed and sleeping. He'd done his job.

"I would be the last person to judge you." My words unfolded in one long sigh while my eyes flitted from the overflowing kitchen sink to the kitchen window. The crocus and early daffodils were sneaking up from the ground. The earth was waking up. Life had moved on over the past two weeks since we'd brought Ali home from the hospital, and I'd been too caught up in my own worries to notice. Even while I lay upstairs in bed and wished for life to stop, Mother Nature had continued to work her miracles. I wrapped my arms around myself because suddenly, all I felt was cold.

Tim poured himself a mug of coffee and moved his chair close enough that when he sat, the length of our thighs touched. Tucking loose strands of hair behind my ear, he smiled. "It's going to be okay. *We're* going to be okay. I promise. Do you want to see Ali?"

Ali. *Her little mouth puckering, fingers splayed in contentment. Rolling. Thumping down into darkness. Thumping. Thumping. Thumping.* "No!" The word shot out fast and loud and harsh. I tried again, softer. "No. Not right now. Maybe... maybe later."

If Tim noticed my panic, he didn't comment. Instead, a smile lit his face, and the dark shadows that rested under his eyes like bruises seemed to disappear. "Wait until you see her. I swear, she's grown in just a day. She misses you. *I* miss you." He leaned in as if to drop a kiss on my forehead, but I stiffened, and his kiss—if that was what he'd intended—evaporated in the air.

"Hey." Tim was careful not to reach out to me, but he hadn't moved his chair, and our legs still touched under the table. "It's time we talk. Don't you think? Why did you lock yourself in our bedroom?" He looked at his hands wrapped around his mug of coffee, and he seemed to wrestle with himself before he finally spoke again. "Please tell me what's wrong."

I drew in my breath. He deserved answers; I just didn't have any. Not that I wanted to share. I willed myself not to think. Not to remember. "I don't know." I willed myself not to cry.

"Emma, please. Don't cut yourself off from me. We need to talk about this. There isn't anything you can't tell me. Remember? We talked about this in the hospital. I love you. Nothing would make me stop loving you."

Yes, there is something I could tell you that would make you stop loving me. And I can't tell you.

He was so earnest, and I'd put him through hell. He'd told me once that when he opened his eyes in the morning and looked at me, he thought of the day he first told me he loved me. He said he remembered the way my eyes lit up when he had asked me to marry him. If he knew what I'd thought, what I might have done if he hadn't been standing behind me last night, that was not what he would see when he opened his eyes in the morning.

Tim had thought he meant what he said, but he had no idea how easy it would be to stop loving me.

"Can you at least tell me what you were doing down here? Was there something you needed from the basement?"

I stared straight ahead, drew in my breath, and once again, let it shudder out. "I can't talk to you about this right now. I just can't." I bent my head and tried to sip my tea, but instead of the milky sweetness I expected, my mouth filled with bile. I placed the mug carefully on the table and pushed it as far back as I could so I wouldn't be tempted to pick it up again.

"I don't understand. Look at me. Will you please look at me?" Tim lifted my chin; I had little choice but to look into his eyes.

"Remember the very second I woke up after having driven for hours the night Ali was born? I wish you could have seen your face. You glowed. As if you'd just done something no one had ever been able to do before. I'd never seen you so happy. It was like there was a star inside you. You were radiant, and I will never as long as I live forget the look of joy in your eyes when you asked if I'd seen Ali. What happened to all that joy? You've been unhappy since the day we came home from the hospital."

Tim's words brought back every word Ned had said to me before we'd been discharged.

How can I tell him what changed? How can I tell him what I thought? What I almost did?

Chapter 13

Susan was our deal. If I was unwilling or unable to talk to Tim, then I had to talk to someone else, someone who could help me.

Susan's waiting room was much like my own, designed to offer comfort to the patients who walked through her door. The walls were a soothing seafoam green, and the chairs and couch, covered in fabrics that reminded me of all the random colors of sea glass, had deep cushions meant to encourage patients to sink in and relax. To take a breath.

Current magazines were displayed on the butler's tray coffee table for those who just couldn't sit and be still, and a carafe of water on a side table with drinking glasses next to it completed the scene.

Maybe it took another doctor to appreciate that comfort was essential when patients needed to wait their turn. We knew waiting wasn't easy. Susan's waiting room spoke volumes about how she'd managed to pull off both comfort and style, but when I perched on the couch, I felt like a bow stretched tight before the arrow released.

My first sight of Susan was when she opened the door from her inner office into the waiting room. She was maybe ten or so years older than me with short-cropped silver hair and a tan that told me she liked the outdoors. Tall, with animated blue eyes not the least diminished by her black-framed glasses, Susan wore a smile that started with her lips and easily covered every part of her face. I'd never been partial to tall women, and women who glowed with good health made me wonder what they did for a living, but I'd made a deal with Tim, and I needed to give the woman a chance.

I stood, and we faced each other. I wondered if she'd also been evaluating me as she held out her hand, but I supposed I'd find that out soon enough. Susan's grip was strong. Firm. I liked that. Women with weak handshakes annoyed me even more than men who didn't understand the value of a solid grip.

"Good morning." Susan's voice lifted with her smile; it sounded more like a melody than a simple greeting. She stepped aside so I could walk into her office and indicated I should take one of the two identical club chairs set to the side of her desk. She waited while I chose one and sat, then she took the other. The chairs faced each other with a small round table between them. I thought of the setting as a substitute for the theatrical version of the big leather couch that played center stage in a sitcom psychiatrist's office.

Susan looked as if the only thing on our agenda was to swap cookie recipes, while I felt unable to lean back and give my body permission to relax.

If the hardest step was admitting you had a problem, next in line must have been waiting for all the unknowns to show themselves. I had just enough time to take in Susan's clothing before our session began: a cream-colored V-neck sweater—cashmere, I'd bet—and tailored brown pants.

Susan looked as if the only thing on her mind was whether I used margarine or butter in my snickerdoodle recipe, but I gave her the benefit of the doubt and smiled while I waited for the session to begin. Then I recognized my intake evaluation in her hands, and I felt at a disadvantage. All I knew about her was where she went to med school and that she specialized in women's issues. I felt naked sitting across from her and silently cursed Tim for making me agree to come.

"I don't want to be here." I hadn't realized I'd actually spoken the words out loud until Susan responded.

"No?" Her voice and face reflected no surprise at my words, and maybe she'd heard them before.

My eyes darted around her office, as if someone would jump out of the closet and save me, before they finally landed back on her. "It was my husband's idea. I finally agreed."

"Oh? And what made you agree?"

I felt my face heat up. "Because I promised him I wouldn't go back to work until I... we get this straightened out. And I need to get back to work."

"Okay. That's a start. And I appreciate your honesty. It won't do either of us any good if you don't want to be here, but before you make that decision, let's just get to know each other. What do you think?"

Nodding, I shifted my purse from my lap to the floor next to my chair, but then I had nothing to hold on to, so I picked it up again and placed it on my lap. Susan watched, but whatever she might have thought about my actions, she kept it to herself.

"I see you're a surgeon."

"Yes, and a researcher." I leaned back just the slightest bit. Medicine, unlike motherhood, was my comfort zone. "I'm a neuro-oncologist. Right now, I'm researching the glioblastoma tumor and its incidence in children."

Susan gave me her full attention while I talked, then she responded in a way that let me know she understood how important my field was to me. "That's got to be difficult, working with critically ill children." Susan flipped through the file in her lap, my file, and I wondered what else was in there other than the forms I'd completed.

We went back and forth. Susan asked simple questions, much in the same way a hostess nudged a shy guest at a dinner party. She was polite and sincere, wanting only to know me a little better. I began to relax even more.

"What brings you here today?" Her voice hadn't changed tone, but her question took me by surprise.

I sat up straighter. We had moved on to the reality of the visit, and I wasn't sure I was prepared. I took a deep breath and exhaled slowly. My answer was exactly the way I'd rehearsed. "I'm here because I'm not bonding the way I think I should with my infant daughter."

Even to my own ears, that sounded too simplistic. I wanted to tell Susan how much I loved children. I wanted to tell her all the things I'd thought when I'd stood at the top of the basement stairs with Ali in my arms. I wanted to tell her I was terrified. I wanted to tell her I needed help.

But I didn't tell her any of those things. Abandoning my purse, I clenched my hands together to stop from picking at the callus on my thumb before the pain shot the whole way up my arm like poison racing to my heart. I told her other things. "I'm confused by my reaction to my daughter, and I seem unable to discuss my feelings with my husband. He thought—*we* thought—it would be best if I found someone I could talk to."

While I waited for Susan to respond, my eyes traveled from the couch to the chairs and the antique chest then up to the schoolhouse clock on the wall. I was mesmerized by that clock as one slow minute after another passed. Finally, when Susan spoke, I wasn't surprised by her response.

"That happens sometimes. It can take a new mother by surprise."

I could see already that she'd pigeonholed me as having postpartum depression. But that was not what I had. What I had was uglier and darker. It had to be. And I'd been a fool to go there and think she could help me. I had to leave, no matter what I'd promised Tim. I could never talk about what I'd thought. What I'd almost done.

"This was a mistake..." My voice tightened until finally, my words dwindled into silence. I fumbled my way upright, but Susan reached over and placed her hand on my arm as if she saw my darkness and refused to turn away. Her gesture was enough to allow me to sink back into my chair again.

"Why don't we just take a minute and relax? You're doing fine." Susan leaned toward the small table between us and poured a glass of water. She started to hand it to me then stopped. "Or would you rather have a cup of tea?"

In different circumstances, I might have smiled. I guessed I wasn't the only doctor who used a cup of hot tea as a way to comfort a patient.

I reached for the water. "This is fine." I held the glass with both hands and tried to think of what to say next. "I don't think I was meant to be a mother." I was nowhere near the truth, my truth, but I had no place else to go.

"Why would you say that?"

"Because... because I don't *feel* the things mothers are supposed to feel." It seemed so obvious to me, the difference between going through the motions and knowing in your heart that you would kill with your bare hands anyone who would dare harm your child.

Susan nodded as if she knew exactly what I was talking about. "What do you think mothers are supposed to feel?"

"That's the thing. I don't know. All I know is that I don't feel anything. I feel like I'm standing with my back against the wall and watching while another woman goes through the motions of caring for my child."

All of which was true. I felt like I was pretending. I wanted to love Ali, but I couldn't nurse her or hold her and not worry about my research. My patients. I couldn't look at her and not think of that early morning.

I placed my glass on the table before I spilled it, and in my sudden movement, my purse fell. My car keys and used tissues and a half-eaten candy bar emptied all over the floor. "I don't *feel* anything!"

I leaned forward to retrieve my belongings, again cursing Tim for forcing me to go there.

"What's wrong with me? I know everything's not supposed to be perfect, but..." I sat back, exhausted from everything I'd said, even though it was nowhere near enough.

"But?" Susan prompted as if wanting me to complete my statement.

"Mothers are supposed to look at their child like she's some gift from God."

"And what do you feel?"

"I don't believe in God."

"You don't need to believe in God to love your child." Susan's lips turned slightly upward, as if I'd just said I didn't believe in the Easter Bunny.

I nodded. Tears that I'd tried so hard to keep inside rained down my cheeks.

Susan placed several tissues in my hand and continued, "You're not the only mother to worry about bonding with your baby. I know right now you think you are, but you're not. Having a baby can be overwhelming. Terrifying."

I swiped at my tears. "No, you don't understand." I wanted to say more, but I couldn't.

"Tell me. What don't I understand?" Susan offered me a small smile; her eyebrows drew together as if she actually understood my pain. Still, I couldn't tell her.

I stuffed my latest batch of used tissues into my purse. "I need to leave."

"Wait just a moment. I have your medical records from your GP. I've looked at all your test results, and they rule out any physical issue. It's possible you're suffering from postpartum depression. It seems to be a good place to start." Susan looked up from my file. "Why don't we meet again and see if I can help you?"

Susan had wrapped my words up in a nice little package and put a bow on it. Except it wasn't my package. I wanted to make her understand, but I knew I couldn't.

Chapter 14

I chose the same chair I'd picked on my first visit. It was closest to the door, and every step counted if I felt the need to leave early. Susan recapped our last visit while I settled in my chair, determined to stay calm. *Our last visit.* Those were her exact words. As in, "It's a journey, and we're traveling it together." A road-to-Santiago kind of pilgrimage in which, once we reached our destination, I would feel whole again. *Will I ever feel whole again?*

"Based on everything we discussed last week, I'm suggesting we start with a diagnosis of postpartum depression. If we find, as we move deeper into our conversations, that that's not the case, we'll regroup and go from there. How does that sound?"

I nodded. *That neat little package that she thought fit me.*

"Tell me how you've been since the last time I saw you."

"I don't feel any differently, if that's what you're asking." I tried to remember why I'd thought, after leaving Susan's office the last time, that she might be the person I could talk to. I was there again but had nothing to say.

Susan's left eyebrow rose in a familiar tic, and right then, it seemed to suggest I might want to elaborate.

"I'm exhausted. Everything I do is an effort. Lifting my dinner fork to my mouth is an effort. When I do feel hungry, I'm so exhausted I practically fall asleep at the table. But then, when I climb into bed, I can't fall asleep. And then I want to cry, but I don't. I want to go back to work, but I can't do that either. Because I'm exhausted and because I promised Tim I'd try to find out what's wrong with me."

"Why don't you cry?"

"What?"

"You said when you go to bed, you're exhausted, but you can't fall asleep, and that you want to cry, but you don't. Why don't you cry?"

I did say that. "I rarely cry. It's a sign of weakness, and I'm supposed to be strong."

Susan nodded, made a notation in her notebook, and encouraged me to keep going. I'd said a lot, and maybe she hoped for more, but even the effort it took to get those words out was too much, and I shut down.

"What you've just described is perfectly natural." Susan reached over and squeezed my icy fingers. "Having a baby is emotionally and physically draining. You're not alone, Emma."

Maybe her words were meant to be a gift, but they didn't make me feel any better.

"Many mothers feel overwhelmed. They feel like their life is no longer their own. It's understandable. Everything goes by the baby's timetable now. It's important to take time for yourself, even if it's just to take a bath or read a magazine."

What Susan didn't know was that I had all the time in the world for baths and magazines. Tim took care of Ali, from middle-of-the-night feedings to baths to walking her in her stroller.

"Does your husband help with Ali?"

I nodded, half convinced Susan had just read my thoughts.

"How about family? Friends? Can they help too? Maybe give both of you a break? Even simple things, grocery shopping, or maybe helping out with the laundry. People like to be useful. Most times, all a new mother has to do is ask."

"Tim and I, we'd rather do things ourselves," I told Susan, blinking rapidly. I kept the unsaid to myself. Neither of us wanted anyone to know I spent most of my time in bed, and my family had visited only once.

"You might want to rethink that. People really do like to help. It might do you both some good."

Again, I nodded. It was easy to agree with Susan when I knew I wouldn't take her advice. But what was the point of being there if I wasn't going to at least try what she suggested?

"It wasn't the right time to have a baby." My words slipped out like they'd been greased with Crisco.

"No? Tell me why." If Susan was surprised by what I'd said, she hid it well, but her smile told me she was pleased to see I'd volunteered information instead of her having to wrestle it out of me.

"My work. I'm involved in a research project. I don't have time to take care of a baby right now. I made a mistake." I thought about what I'd just said. *Is it true? Was Ali a mistake?*

"Oh?" Up went the eyebrow. Susan sat and waited for me to continue.

"I didn't know she was a mistake. Not at first."

I remembered waiting for Tim to read the results of the pregnancy test. Every second had felt like an hour, and I thought my heart would beat out of my chest. It was a mistake to hope, yet I hadn't been able to stop myself. *A baby! Let there be a baby inside of me.*

The memory of that morning almost made me smile. "When I was much younger, I was told I would never conceive due to some severe internal injuries I'd suffered from a car accident. Birth control was never an issue because we assumed we'd never get pregnant. And then, and then I *did* get pregnant. It was... *she* was a miracle."

"So you were happy you were going to have a baby?"

"Yes, we were very happy," I answered honestly, fingering the gold bracelet on my wrist. "It was as if we'd received a gift. My period had been late, and I'd been feeling 'off.' You know what I mean? Even the smell of Tim's coffee first thing in the morning sent me racing to the bathroom."

My fingers rubbed the etched detail on my bracelet while I re-layed what it had felt like to find out I was pregnant. "When I brought home the pregnancy test, we'd joked about it. You know, thinking we'd rule out pregnancy before we started looking else-where. But then when we were waiting for the results, we both got caught up in the possibility of a baby, and we... and we were just..."

I remembered every second of that day. It had been a miracle. *How did I get from then to now?*

"I'd held my breath till that damn stick told me I was pregnant." Remembering, I couldn't help smiling as I thought of sitting on the lip of the tub, waiting for Tim to tell me the answer.

"We had talked about adoption, but even adoption was for later, once I'd completed my research. But the day we discovered we were pregnant, Tim's eyes had filled with want and need. There was no hiding his feelings."

"And how about you?"

"Me?"

"Were you happy when you discovered you were pregnant?"

I couldn't lie. "Yes." It was probably the most honest thing I'd said. But even so, I glanced at the clock, and when I saw how little time had elapsed since I sat down, I wondered if I would make it through the entire session.

"Did you have any complications with your pregnancy?"

"No, just morning sickness that sometimes turned into after-noon sickness. I was fine. Healthy as a horse." I smiled, remembering how each month, Tim would snap a profile photo of my belly and paste it into our baby album.

"I didn't think about anything my entire pregnancy except that we were having a baby." That wasn't true, but just like with Tim, I couldn't begin to tell Susan how my life at the hospital had changed once I'd told Ned I was pregnant.

"We'd no sooner danced our way out of the bathroom that morning when we went in search of a calendar, intent only on calculating the date of the baby's birth."

Susan glanced down at my intake form. "March fourteenth, 2003?"

"Yes. We were spot-on."

"So when did you start to feel differently?"

"Differently?" I knew what Susan was asking: when did I begin to feel Ali would affect my research?

"I don't remember." To hell with honesty.

Susan let me think about my answer, and although she seemed comfortable with our silence, I shifted in my chair, suddenly unable to sit still.

And the answer to her question was: about an hour after I'd learned I was pregnant. Yes, I'd been shocked by Ned's reaction when I'd finally told him I was pregnant, but he hadn't said anything that I hadn't already thought: I didn't have time for a baby. But I'd wanted him to convince me I did have time.

I *wanted* to have time.

"At first," I started, "I was very happy." I stared at my hands while I spoke. I watched as my finger dug into the callus on my thumb. I made it hurt. I made me hurt. I tried again. "We were thrilled to be pregnant."

Susan's eyebrow shot upward.

I backpedaled. "I have a lot of responsibilities with my job. My research. My boss... my boss thinks I won't be able to handle my responsibilities and take care of Ali. He thinks..." I swallowed. "He thinks..."

I kept going. "Ned thinks I should have waited to have a baby."

"Ned?"

"My boss. Kate's father."

"Kate?"

"Kate was my friend. She died when we were kids." Again, I looked at that damn clock.

"I see. That must have been difficult, losing a childhood friend. What did she die from?"

"She had a brain tumor." I stared at Susan's shoes, unable to lift my head.

"Is that why you chose your specialty?"

"Yes." I hadn't realized how far forward I'd leaned until I leaned back.

Susan shook her head slightly. "I didn't see anything in your intake evaluation about Ned or Kate, yet they seem to be an important part of your life."

The turn of our conversation scared me, and I tried to put us back on track. "I'm not here to talk about them. I'm here so you can help me bond with my daughter." My hands were fisted tight as if they held a secret.

Susan looked at her watch and stood. "I'd love to continue this conversation now, but I have another patient in ten minutes. We will talk about Ali and ways for you to become comfortable in your new role as a mother, but I think both Ned and Kate are an important part of your story. Especially Kate."

I also stood, relieved that I'd made it through another session. But if I hadn't been able to make Tim understand that something inside me made me believe I needed to save Kate when I knew I couldn't save her, when I knew she was dead, how was I going to make Susan understand?

Chapter 15

Susan's words played over and over in my head. *How can I talk to her about Kate?*

Tim's steady in-and-out snores told me a train could crash through our bedroom wall and he'd sleep right through it while I stared up at the ceiling and wondered if I'd ever fall asleep. I wanted to shove an elbow in his side. But then he'd be awake, and I didn't want to talk to him about Kate either. At least not right then.

Besides, he needed his sleep. After a day of caring for Ali and writing—who was I kidding; mostly caring for Ali—he deserved sleep more than I did.

I flipped my pillow over to the cool side. I rearranged the sheets and kicked the blanket to the end of the bed. But it wasn't the pillow or the sheets that kept me awake. It was Kate and her last hospital stay and how I'd hoped she wouldn't die.

The ride to the hospital had been quiet and fast with everyone—even me—praying. Ned had followed the signs to the designated ER parking but completely ignored the empty spaces between the painted white lines and instead headed directly to the entrance of the building.

I'd squeezed my eyes shut, certain we were all going to die, but at the last second, he'd stomped on the brakes, and the car had shuddered to a stop. He'd flung open his car door and grabbed Kate while Laura followed him toward the ER entrance, where the automatic doors had opened as soon as his foot triggered the sensor. I'd trailed closely behind, still half asleep after being wakened by Kate's screams of pain.

I'd made a fool of myself and burst into tears when I was finally let in to see her, and Kate had insisted I climb into the hospital bed with her if for no other reason than to stop me from sniveling like a baby.

It was then I'd first noticed the difference in our height. Kate had always been taller, yet with our heads on the same pillow, side by side, her feet reached only somewhere between my knees and ankles. Somehow in that last year, I'd grown taller. Somehow I was first when Kate had always been first. The first to jump from the high dive, the first to break a bone. The first to die.

Tim turned in his sleep and mumbled something about helicopters and training missions, and I imagined he was working out plot points. When he finally settled, he had thrown off his end of the sheet and snored even louder.

Back then, the walls in Kate's hospital room were some pasty-green color that could best be described as god-awful ugly, and the one window looked out onto a brick wall. The ceiling held more interest, and we'd stared at it—anything to avoid looking at each other. Wondering what came next.

"Look at all the cracks," I'd finally ventured, but Kate wasn't interested. "No. Really, look at them." I couldn't take my eyes off that damn ceiling.

"Maybe your dad needs to do something about them, you know, before it caves in." Even then, I'd thought Ned could do anything.

That had finally gotten her talking. "You do know he doesn't *own* the hospital, right? And anyway, I think he's probably got a lot on his mind right now. More than just ceilings."

I could still hear the strain in her voice. We'd stared at that ceiling so hard my eyes had started to water, and I'd rubbed at them, hoping Kate hadn't thought I was crying. Right about then, Kate realized the cracks made a design like a maze. Like those corn mazes farmers built in the fall where visitors needed to follow the right path to find their way out.

The cracks in Kate's ceiling became eight-foot-high stalks of corn—in her head, anyway. It took some convincing before I saw them. Kate had always been the one with the vivid imagination, a pro at seeing what wasn't there. The overhead light—the one nurses flipped on before the sun came up to take blood pressure and temperatures or to make sure the patient was still alive—became the sun shining on our faces. We played what turned out to be our last game of make-believe while staring at that ceiling.

We passed the same imaginary clues over and over as we laughed and pretended to walk through that maze. We refused to give up because we were so sure we'd find our way out. I'd almost forgotten the sound of Kate's laugh, the way it started up slow and kept building until that final snort exploded out of her mouth. Her whole face grinned when she laughed.

Then she'd stopped, and her eyes had grown big. She'd pointed at the ceiling. "The maze? There's no way out."

I'd thought she was exaggerating. Kate was nothing if not dramatic. I'd reminded her of the maze we'd visited last Halloween. It had been so hot that day, and we'd forgotten to bring water. We'd thought there was no way out then, because every turn we'd made sent us right back to the middle. But there was a way out. We'd just had to keep looking for it.

I'd looked at the ceiling one more time to prove my point. Because logic told me if there was a way in, there would be a way out. I located what had looked like the entrance with my finger and slowly moved it through the air, looking for what must be the exit. Again and again, I ended up back in the middle and had to start over.

Kate had been right. There *was* no way out.

FRUSTRATED BY MEMORIES that wouldn't let me sleep, I went down to the kitchen and made a cup of tea.

Before long, Tim traipsed into the library, where I sat curled up on the settee with a quilt thrown over my feet and my hands wrapped around my mug.

"Can't sleep?" Tim yawned, stretching out his arms. "What time is it?" He yawned again and sat next to me, rearranging the quilt so it covered both of us.

"It's early. I'm sorry. I was thinking about Kate. These past few weeks, Susan and I've been talking about her. It's brought back a lot of memories."

"Hmm. What kind of memories?" He shifted closer, careful not to jostle my tea, but his question made me slide down a little, not eager to repeat what I'd already told Susan.

"Oh, you know, mostly stupid stuff." I cleared my throat and decided to share a memory I hadn't shared with Susan. Maybe then I'd be able to sleep. "I'd never been one of those flighty girls who was best friends with one girl at the beginning of the week and by Friday had dumped her for some other friend. I didn't even think 'best' friend. I thought 'only' friend." I shook my head. "Kate wasn't like that."

I swallowed. "And then—and then Kate got cancer, and kids stepped away from her like she could look them in the eye and her tumor would jump ship and end up in their brains. And suddenly, I had what I'd always thought I wanted: Kate. All to myself."

Tim reached over and nuzzled my hair. "You were just a kid. That's how kids think." He yawned again, his body melting into mine.

I nodded, even though I'd never been convinced of my innocence. "You know what? You need to get some sleep. Before you know it, Ali will be up, and I'll need to get to the hospital. This can wait for another time."

"Obviously, it can't. Not with you sitting down here, worrying. Just tell me. What else has you upset? It'll make you feel better to talk about it."

It hadn't made me feel better to tell Susan, but there was no point in telling Tim that. He thought Susan was the answer to all my problems.

"All right, but then we're going back to bed. Kate and I fought a lot before she died. No one knew, I don't think. Not until I told Miss Maggie, anyway. Sometimes, I had to leave the room when we fought because I was afraid I'd say hateful things to her and she'd die while I was still screaming." My throat tightened. "And then I wouldn't be able to take it back. And my last chance to tell her I loved her would be gone."

I took a final swallow of tea and told Tim the rest of that memory. "I told her that once, and she said, 'You mean when I'm having one of my *tirades*?' And then she'd gone on to explain what *tirades* meant, as if I didn't know. We were always trying to best each other with new words."

Even half asleep, Tim was a good listener. "It must have been hard. To be Kate's friend."

I reached down to put my empty mug on the chest in front of us and laughed. "Sometimes, I pictured her flat on her back in some pearly pink coffin with her arms flat against her chest and a lily clutched firmly between her stone-cold fingers." I'd never told that to another person.

Tim laughed and pulled me closer. "Why am I thinking the last color casket Kate would want is pink?"

I felt the flush in my cheeks. "Exactly."

"What did Miss Maggie have to say about your fights with Kate?"

"Oh, she would have none of it. When I'd told her I hated Kate because she wasn't nice, her eyes had widened, and her lips had disappeared just enough to let me know I'd not lived up to my full potential. I knew right then I'd made a mistake. I'd thought she'd make everything better, but that's not at all what happened."

"No? Wait. Let me guess." Even half asleep, Tim did a fairly good imitation of Miss Maggie. "Don't be silly, Emma. Good girls don't hate. Maybe you're *angry* with her, but you shouldn't be. Kate's sick. She can't help herself."

I nodded. "I'd listened to what she'd said and then mumbled something about being *mad* at her, but she'd shot back with her usual 'only dogs get mad,' and that was the end of that."

Chapter 16

S usan didn't waste any time digging in on our next visit. "I know we've talked a lot about Kate these past few weeks, and I know how difficult that is for you, but our discussions have helped me understand how much she meant to you and how hard it was for you when she died. As difficult as this might be, I'd like to continue with Kate a little longer."

Before I could even nod, Susan changed the subject. "But before we start, fill me in on how things are going at home."

How things are going at home? Should I tell her that Tim is so exhausted he started the coffee machine the other morning without adding the coffee? Maybe I'll stick with something a little more positive.

"Ali rolled from her back to her stomach the other day."

Susan smiled. "That's wonderful! Did you see her?"

"No. I—I wish I had. I was sleeping." But I'd seen the look of disappointment in Tim's eyes that I'd missed what he considered Ali's greatest achievement so far.

Susan glanced at the notebook lying open on her lap. "That's too bad. Maybe next time."

"That's what I told Tim."

Again, Susan looked at the notebook she occasionally referred to while apparently reviewing some of our earlier discussions. "So, let's quickly summarize our last meeting before we move on. You were eleven when Kate died. Kate was also eleven?"

I sat up straighter in my chair. "Yes." While I waited for Susan's next question, I wondered if I would ever have the guts to tell her the real problem: what had made me imagine, if only for one second, that I'd be capable of hurting Ali. I wanted Susan to tell me I'd never think it again. I wanted her to promise me I wouldn't hurt my baby. But she didn't know I'd thought about hurting Ali. No one knew.

I dreaded the memories that came from talking about Kate and those last few months of her life. The limo we'd taken to New York so Kate would die at her grandparents' home because the Bennetts knew that if she died in her own home, in her own bed, they'd never want to live there again. The sunrise that Miss Maggie had always said meant new beginnings, but all I thought when I saw those first shadings of pink in the sky that morning was that when someone was dying, each sunrise only brought them closer to the last one.

"Emma?"

Susan's voice tore into memories I'd long thought dead. "What were you just thinking?"

Caught off guard, I told the truth. "I was thinking that there had been plenty of room for all of us in the limo we took on that last trip to New York before Kate died, but I'd felt as if I'd had to fight for each breath."

"That must have been an extremely difficult trip."

"I'd promised Kate."

"That's a pretty big promise for a child to make."

"I guess it was. That's the kind of friendship we had. We'd been friends for a long time." *We'd been friends for practically Kate's whole life.* "It seemed like a long time, anyway. It seemed like I'd known Kate forever."

I shifted in my chair, repositioned the pillow against my back, and waited for the next question.

"Were your parents with you?" Susan looked down at her notebook, turned a couple of pages, then flipped them back as she waited for me to answer.

I shook my head. "Just the Bennetts and me. And Kate."

Susan's eyebrows shot toward each other. If I'd had to guess, I'd have said she had a hard time with my answer. "Did you want them with you?"

I didn't need to think how to answer. "No. I had Ned. I told myself it was no different than all the trips I'd taken to the emergency room with them except... except this time was different. We all knew it was the last trip."

"I'm confused. How did you know it was the last trip?"

"Ned told me."

"Ned told you? How did Ned know?"

I shrugged. "I don't know. I'd just assumed that as Kate's father, he knew. Now, of course, I know there are physical signs to watch for, but at the time, I didn't question it. Ned knew everything."

"Do you remember seeing any of those physical signs of impending death before you left for New York?"

Shaking my head, I added, "But as a kid, I really wouldn't have known what to look for."

I was weary with the weight of my memories, but still I talked. "It rained that entire trip. Well, really, it started right after we'd passed Medford—a hard rain, with buckets of water pinging off the rooftop. Never-ending sheets of water sliding down the windows. And all I could think about was miracles and the people who believed in them. I thought how lucky they were to hold on to something bigger than themselves, bigger than their families, bigger than anything else in the world." For once, Susan hadn't had to pull every word from me.

"What kind of miracle would you have asked for? If you could have?"

I looked at my hands. I knew the memory would hurt, but I let it come, anyway. "I wanted the rain to stop and the sun to shine. I wanted Kate's God to let her live."

My words seemed to hang between us before Susan switched gears as if she wanted to give me a break from thinking about Kate's death. "What did you and Kate do for fun?"

"Fun?" I could barely remember fun. I remembered tears and screams and fights and promises. But fun? Then I thought about the puppies.

"My dad's puppies, I guess. They weren't my dad's. They were the puppies and dogs he rescued, but I always thought of them as belonging to him because he saved them. Each time Dad brought more home, to either acclimate them to life outside the laboratory, teach them socialization skills, or nurse them back to health, Kate and I helped. The older we got, the more responsibilities he gave us."

Then I laughed. "We did plenty of stupid kid stuff that got us into trouble, too, but what we loved best was working with the dogs my dad rescued."

"Tell me about the dogs."

I shifted in my chair again. I crossed my legs. "Beagles, mostly. From laboratories that used them for product testing. If my dad was passionate about anything, it was those dogs. He told me once what it was like when he and the people who worked with him entered one of those labs. The first thing they noticed was the smell. He said it was close to three-dimensional. A substance to be cut through rather than some elusive stench you could only hope would dissipate. He said the air was redolent with feces. Only he didn't say *feces*. He said *shit*. He said there was no better, or nicer, way to put it."

"What did your mom say?"

I laughed. "Mom got mad when Dad said *shit*. When Dad and the people who came with him to collect the dogs were finally able to focus away from the smell, the shock of what they saw was just as disgusting as the very first time they entered their very first lab. Crates piled on top of crates, stacked almost to the ceiling. Crates so small the dogs caged inside them barely moved. Turning around didn't come close to being a possibility. He said the crates were piled high with feces, water bowls were dry, and there was little evidence of food."

Susan's eyes danced with laughter. "Except he said *shit*."

"Yes. Except he said *shit*." That moment was the closest I'd felt to Susan. Like she was a real person and I was a real person. "We helped care for the dogs until they were ready to be adopted to what Kate and I always called forever homes. We always fell in love with those dogs. We named them. Wanted to keep all of them. Cried every time one of them was adopted."

Susan smiled again, and I had relaxed enough to allow the tension to begin a slow melt from the back of my neck.

"It must have been hard for you when Kate got sick."

"Hard?" As fast as I'd let down my guard, I stiffened. Kate, and her cancer, and my guilt over her death had set in motion a series of events that had come close to destroying me, so yes, I guessed I could agree with Susan. It was hard. There had to be a reason a brain tumor that preferred middle-aged men burrowed into Kate's eleven-year-old brain. There had to be a reason that tumor chose her brain and not mine.

"Sometimes," I whispered, "I'd almost forget Kate was dying, and I'd feel happy because the sun was shining or because it was Saturday and there was no school and I could spend hours playing with the puppies and helping them get used to the real world. Once, my crazy aunt Jane canceled her visit, and I'd been saved from enduring humiliating comments about my prepubescent figure. I couldn't wait to tell Kate, but when I got to her house, I hadn't been allowed to see her because she was having what she and I always referred to as one of her bad days."

Shaking my head as if I still couldn't believe I'd been so thoughtless, I added, "How could I even think about being happy? I had nothing to smile about. Nothing to feel happy about."

Ashamed all over again at those fleeting moments of happiness so long ago, I leaned forward in my chair. "You wouldn't think I could forget, but sometimes I did. And it was wonderful and horrible all at once. And I hated myself when it happened."

"You felt guilty that Kate was dying, and you weren't?"

My finger dug relentlessly into the callus on my thumb, and I didn't answer until the pain shot into my brain. "I wished it were me instead of her. And then—" I couldn't tell her what I'd thought.

"And then?" Susan prompted. She looked at me straight on, the way people looked at their dogs when they wanted them to know they meant business.

I looked past Susan at the photographs on her desk. All the frames were different shapes and colors, yet they looked like they belonged together, matched in an odd way that made them look casual yet correct. One big happy family. And a dog. I tried to concentrate on those pictures while I spoke. "And then... and then I saw how she suffered, and I was... I was glad it wasn't me."

I'd only ever said those words out loud to one person. No matter how many times the thought had gone through my head, I'd kept it to myself. Except once. Once, I'd told Ned.

Susan stayed silent for so long, I thought she hadn't heard me. And then she spoke. "How did that make you feel?"

I drew in my breath, and when I let it out, I released a lot of what I'd carried around since I was a child. "I made excuses to stay away. I pretended I was sick so her parents wouldn't want me there. I gave up precious hours and days because I felt like I was no friend to her at all." I stopped then took another deep breath and looked into Susan's eyes. "That's how it made me feel."

I looked up at the clock, hoping our time was up. I still had fifteen minutes, and it seemed that Susan planned to fill every one. "You must have felt very alone. Did you have anyone to confide in? Your family?"

"No, not my family. I guess I could have talked to my mom, but she was always with my dad, and they were always busy."

"Busy?"

"With the dogs. My dad's whole life revolved around the dogs he rescued, and my mom's life revolved around my dad. Mostly I talked to Ned. Back then, of course, he was Dr. Bennett."

"So you two were close?"

"Yes, very close. We're still close."

"What else did you talk with Ned about when you were young? Anything?"

I thought about that. "Sure. Religion was a big topic. The Bennetts were believers, and I, well, I mostly thought that if God existed, he'd sure made a mess of things. Sometimes, we talked about Kate's cancer, how it affected her mom. I think he didn't have anyone to talk to either."

Susan's eyes widened. "Surely Ned didn't talk to you about what his wife was feeling?"

"Sometimes."

"Did that seem odd to you?"

"As a kid? No. Now, I would find it odd, but not then."

"What kind of things did he tell you?"

I remembered how he'd once described Laura's pain. "I think Ned forgot he was talking to a kid. He told me Laura's pain caught her by surprise, as if she'd stubbed her toe, only when she looked down to see if her toe was bleeding, there was no toe, no foot, just the stump above her knee where her leg had once been."

Susan sucked in her breath.

"He expected me to understand, but I didn't. Not at first, anyway."

"How did you feel when Kate told you she was sick?"

"She didn't tell me she was sick. She told me she was dying."

I didn't need to stop and think about how I'd felt because I'd never forgotten. "I felt like I'd been sucker punched. I thought she was lying. I thought a million things all at once because I didn't want to believe her. She was telling the truth, though, because I saw her fear, and Kate had never before been afraid. Never."

"Were you with Kate when she died?"

"Yes. No! Only her parents were in the room with her when she died." *One more promise I hadn't kept.*

The last fifteen minutes finally passed. Susan took off her glasses and placed them on the little side table, the one that held tissues and water and occasionally a pot of tea. She almost visibly shifted gears, readying herself for her next patient. Or maybe the afternoon off.

I needed to say the thing that had haunted me for years. "I know Kate's dead." Haltingly at first and then furiously fast, I spewed it all out. "I do. I know she's dead. But I also know that I need to save her. It doesn't make sense to me, and I can't explain it to you. I *want* to. I want to make you understand. I want to make Tim understand."

I took a breath then looked at my hands as if the answer waited for me there. "But I can't. All I know is, this is why I keep searching for a way to stop the tumor that killed her. Because I can't let her die."

"Can't let who die?"

"That's just it. I don't know. I've always thought it was Kate."

Susan stood and walked over to her desk and looked briefly at her calendar. Then she turned back to me. "I'd like to see you again tomorrow. Will that work for you?"

Without even saying goodbye, I nodded quickly and left.

Chapter 17

"**I** know something's wrong."

I pulled the phone away from my ear and hit the speaker button. "Mom, don't be silly. Ali's fine. Tim's back to writing. Everything's good." I put the phone on the kitchen island and grabbed a sponge to swipe at the sticky granite. *Honey. It must be honey from breakfast.*

"And what about you?"

"Sorry, Mom. What did you say?" I heard her sigh from halfway across the kitchen, where I'd gone to the sink to rinse out the sponge.

"I said, what about you? How are you?"

"Me?" I couldn't help the snort that flew out of my mouth. I grew up in a family where there was little need for parental concern. If I wasn't standing before them with blood running down some part of my body, there was no need to interrupt their lives.

Damn! I grimaced as a splash of dirty water hit my shoe when I squeezed out the sponge. "I'm *fine*, Mom. Everything's good."

"You don't sound fine. And when I stopped over yesterday, Tim wouldn't even let me in the house. Said both you and the baby were sleeping and you'd call me later, but you never did."

I tuned out her voice. Tim had made me promise to return her call, so that wasn't his fault. But I'd forgotten. Maybe I hadn't forgotten. I'd had nothing to say. And I hadn't been sleeping either. I'd been cleaning. In the past few weeks, I'd gone from having no energy to cleaning everything that wasn't nailed down just to get rid of my nervous energy.

"And Miss Maggie told me Tim did the same thing to her the other day. What in the world is going on? Daddy and I are worried about you."

"You're worried about me?" I almost snorted. "*Daddy's* worried about me?"

"Don't be this way. Your father and I love you."

I wasn't sure my father ever expressed his love. That was never his way. That was what Mom always said. Even after the car accident that had left me tethered to a hospital bed with pins and rods holding me together, the best he could do was stand at the foot of my bed and squeeze one of my toes, staring over my head at something only he could see.

Arguing was pointless. "I'm sorry, Mom. Really. I meant no disrespect." I paid for that lie almost before the words left my mouth. Pulsating pain gripped the back of my neck and bit down, clenching and unclenching in a steady rhythm that matched the beat of my heart.

Tossing the sponge in the sink, I closed my eyes and massaged what felt like a block of wood lodged dead center in my neck while my mother's words filled the room. Her voice echoed against the cupboards and bounced off the walls; her words mocked my memories. Mom painted pictures of a happy childhood, and I remembered an empty house and silent rooms. I remembered unlocking the door and not stopping until I reached my bedroom, where I could slide a record onto the player and fill the silence.

How could our memories be so different?

"Seriously, Emma, let me take Ali for a few days so you can get some rest. Having a baby takes a lot out of a woman. You need to take care of yourself, you know. It's important you stay healthy, for the baby."

My eyes flew open, and out slipped words that I regretted immediately. "You've only seen Ali once. She doesn't know you. I can't leave her with you."

The only sound I heard after my outburst was my mother's silence.

Damn. "I'm sorry. Maybe you're right. Maybe I am tired." I searched for the right words, the right tone. She was my mother, but I needed to get her off the phone. Conflict was not my friend, a lesson I'd learned well from Kate, who had taught me that if I chose to argue, I might win the battle, but it wouldn't make me feel any better.

"I know what Ali needs, and I'm perfectly capable of giving it to her. But thank you."

"Maybe you need different vitamins. Maybe you need to check in with your doctor. Maybe..."

As if I hadn't said a word, she went on and on about what the baby needed. I *knew* what the baby needed. "Mom!"

"What, honey?"

"Nothing." *Let sleeping dogs lie. Isn't that what Daddy always said?*

"I'm only trying to help."

"I know, Mom. I know."

I wanted her off the phone, but I couldn't stop seeking reassurance that—I didn't know what I was seeking or why. I just knew I was desperate. "Mom? When I was a baby, what did you think about when you took care of me? What did you feel? Do you remember?"

She giggled as if I'd just asked about her sex life. "Well, mostly, Miss Maggie took care of you—feeding, bathing, those sorts of things. You know I was always busy with Daddy. And Miss Maggie was willing to help. She practically lived with us after you were born."

She paused, and I thought she was done.

"This isn't more about you thinking we were never around for you, is it? Because really, I don't have time to rehash your memories of what I feel was a wonderful childhood."

"No, I just wanted to know what you remembered. That's all." I continued massaging the back of my neck, my personal barometer of how well I handled any situation.

"Miss Maggie told me once she loved to inhale the scent of you after a bath," Mom finally offered as if she'd dug deep to locate a memory. "She made me sniff the back of your neck so I'd know what she was talking about, but when she handed you to me, you were slippery as an eel, and I gave you one quick sniff and handed you back. It was so quick I'm not sure I remember smelling anything except a wet baby."

"Didn't you want to take care of me?" I'd picked up the sponge again and moved on to swiping at the stickiness on Ali's baby carrier, sorry I'd brought up the subject. My mother's memories—really, Miss Maggie's memories—told me more than I needed to know. Maybe there was something wrong with both of us. Maybe my inability to "mother" had gotten handed down, like some genetic mutation, and each generation of us grew more and more distant.

"Don't be silly, Emma. I took care of you. Maybe I didn't bathe you every night, but your dad and I were good parents."

The quiver in Mom's voice told me I'd touched a sore spot. Maybe I wasn't the only one to question her mothering instincts.

My earliest memory was of standing on a chair in the kitchen with a tea towel wrapped around my waist and a big wooden spoon in my hand. I was maybe four and mixing flour and sugar in a big bowl.

"Hold the egg firmly in your hand and give it a good whack against the side of the bowl, then pour the yolk and white out of the shell and into a small bowl. Don't be afraid of the egg. It's just an egg.

If it falls on the floor, we'll clean it up. And don't fret about any shells falling into the bowl. We'll scoop them out later."

My mother would never have said "fret." The voice was Miss Maggie's.

"By the way," Mom said, switching gears and knocking aside my memories, "your dad's wondering if you're feeling up to going with us and the rest of the team to North Carolina for the rescue next weekend. I told him absolutely not, but he insisted I ask. You know men. They have no idea what it takes out of a woman after she's had a baby. I'll just tell him you can't go."

I'd forgotten about the trip. I'd forgotten about the dogs held captive in one of the largest product-testing laboratories in the country, who were now, for reasons known only to the people in charge, willing to release a few of the puppies. I'd forgotten, but it wasn't too late. I could still go. I needed to go. Needed to know I could do more than just stand with my back against the wall and watch while a woman I no longer recognized went through the motions of caring for a child.

"Ali wasn't born yesterday, Mom. Tell Dad yes, I'll go." I could barely say it fast enough.

"Don't you need to check with Tim first?" I imagined my mother's cheeks sucking in as she pointed out that I had other responsibilities and couldn't just go traipsing off without a worry for my daughter. Not that she hadn't done the same thing.

"No, I don't. Tim can take care of Ali for the few days I'm gone."

"But, Emma—"

"*No*, Mom." I blew out my exasperation in one big sigh, and I didn't care if she heard it. "You don't understand. This trip is what I need right now. Being there when those dogs are released, watching them find the courage to leave their cages, is *just* what I need. Besides, I missed the last release."

"Well, of course you missed the last release. You were almost seven months pregnant. If you're so determined to go to North Carolina, maybe I could take Ali. Maybe Tim could go with you."

"Mom? I've got to go. Someone's at the front door." I tapped End Call and set the phone on the island. She didn't need to know I'd gotten up and rung the damn bell myself.

Chapter 18

My car's headrest was at just the right height to cradle the pain emanating from the back of my head, and I leaned against it gratefully and closed my eyes.

But I still couldn't turn off the voices in my head: Mom telling me what I needed. Tim asking me what was wrong. Ali screaming for food and comfort and for no reason at all. And Ned. Ned's voice was the loudest. "Why are you sacrificing your research to stay home and play mother to one child when you could save hundreds, thousands of children?"

"Was that your mom on the phone?"

Startled, I opened my eyes. For one split second, I couldn't place the person who had slipped into the passenger seat beside me. If Tim noticed my blank stare, he chose to ignore it. Instead, he rubbed his chin, and when he spoke again, his voice was so soft it was as if he were murmuring his prayers in church. "Hey, what are you doing out here?"

I pulled myself back from any hope of solitude. "I don't know." I looked around, not even remembering that I'd gone to the car. I sat up straighter. "It's quiet out here." I barely remembered leaving the kitchen. "I like to sit where it's quiet."

"You can't hear Ali out here." Tim's almost imperceptible nod and his slumped shoulders told their own tale, and the sadness that crept into his voice made me want to cry. "You need to be able to hear her when she wakes up."

We'd had that conversation before. And I was just as guilty as I was every other time Tim found me hiding in the garage.

Nodding, I leaned my head back, hoping to drown out the sound of his disappointment.

But he wasn't done. "Emma? We agreed weeks ago that when I went back to writing, you would be responsible for Ali." Tim shifted in his seat as if he meant to move toward me, and my body shrank in response. It surprised even me, that reflex-like action—as if I'd thought he'd hurt me.

Instead, I'd hurt him. I could see it even though he'd shuttered his eyes. I could see it in the way he slumped farther down in his seat as if the weight of my problems was too much for him to bear.

"I don't know why I came out here. It's quiet. The quiet relaxes me."

"But the baby monitor was on the island in the kitchen." He reached into his pocket, removed the monitor, and placed it on the dashboard as if I needed proof. "I picked it up on my way out here looking for you. You can't hear Ali if she cries when you're out here without the monitor."

"I *know* that! I'll remember. I promise." The familiar stab of pain struck my chest, the same one I always got when we had that conversation. *Why can't I remember?*

I came close to being able to think in the dim light, but I couldn't tell Tim that, because I thought that was not what he wanted to hear. Instead, I promised again to remember the monitor.

I had no explanation for why I found the outbuilding we'd converted into a garage so comforting or, for that matter, why I went out there when Ali was asleep and forgot to take the baby monitor with me. I just forgot.

We were each lost in our own thoughts. I wanted him to go back into the house and leave me alone. I wanted everyone to leave me alone.

"Emma? I'm sorry about all of this."

"All of this?" I wanted him to spell it out. Suddenly, I wanted to punish him, and I didn't even know why.

He waved his hand around the inside of my car as if my sitting there and hiding were so completely unacceptable that he needed to apologize for it. "All of this. I thought we'd be happy."

I listened to the creaking of hundreds-year-old wood as the breeze gently brushed tree branches against the sides of the building's gray-washed walls, and I thought about when I was last happy. I wanted to explain what that was like—not to remember happiness. But I couldn't find the words.

Susan and I had talked about the importance of communication, but I couldn't talk about what I didn't understand.

Tim took my hand in his and rubbed my cold fingers between his warm ones. "Remember how happy we were when we found out we were pregnant? Remember thinking if we could have one baby, maybe we could have more? And you said you wanted six because only children always want more? What happened to all our happiness? What happened to wanting more?"

Tim was right. I'd felt completed, *brimming* with hope, before that little plastic stick had even hit the bathroom floor. I'd had no words to describe the wonder of a baby inside me. But I didn't have an answer for him. I didn't know where my happiness had gone.

Chapter 19

I noticed, not for the first time, Susan's collection of folk art. Each piece was naive and straightforward. She had a signed Grandma Moses titled *Apple Butter Making* that hung on the wall directly across from the schoolhouse clock. I was intrigued; the picture was a great advertisement for the shops in Intercourse. A patient could leave Susan's office and simply go across the street to purchase a jar of what was considered a staple in our part of the country.

Looking at the artwork helped me focus on something other than my problems and other than the schoolhouse clock, where one slow minute followed another until my time was finally up. I wouldn't have been surprised to learn that that was why Susan filled her office with so many objects to admire and examine. Sometimes, we all needed a break from ourselves.

"We covered a lot of ground the other day, and that's good," Susan said as we settled in. "The more you open up to me, the more we can figure out, together, how to get you where you want to be."

Where do I want to be? I tried to prepare myself for Susan's questions. Instead, I got sidetracked by her blouse. It was the exact same shade of blue as her eyes, and I wanted to ask if she'd known that when she bought the blouse, then I realized she was talking but I wasn't listening.

"Let's move on for a bit. Tell me—"

"What? Sorry." I laughed, embarrassed. "I'm distracted this morning."

Susan paused and smiled. "Tell me about the morning Tim found you standing at the top of the basement stairs with your baby in your arms. What were you doing?"

I'd been prepared to talk more about Kate. Anything. Just not that morning. Could I say no, that the subject was off limits? Unsure, I sat mute until Susan offered me possibilities.

"I know this is difficult for you, Emma, but we both need to be able to understand what you were thinking, what you were feeling that day. Was there something you needed in the basement?"

I crossed my legs. Uncrossed them. What could I possibly have needed in the middle of the night with Ali in my arms? If I made up a reason, could I avoid telling the truth? Was that what Susan was offering? A way out?

I wiped the palms of my suddenly damp hands against my slacks. "No, I didn't need anything."

"Was it cold standing there?"

I shook my head.

"Do you remember what you were wearing?"

"Pajamas." *Pajamas I'd worn for three days because I couldn't bother to get dressed.* "I wasn't wearing a robe."

Leaning forward, Susan picked up the carafe of water on the small table between us and offered me a glass. Grateful for the interruption, I accepted and drank as if I'd been talking all morning when the truth was that she had had to pry each word from me.

"Why did you take Ali down to the kitchen with you?"

I looked at my hands. "I don't know."

Again, Susan offered me possibilities. "Was she fussing? Was it time to feed her?"

Shaking my head at each easy question, I began to think I could get through the session.

"Do you remember what you were thinking?"

Susan had slipped that one in fast. As if throwing out a few easy questions first would lull me into answering the more difficult ones.

"I don't know! I don't *know* what I was thinking," I answered, wrapping my arms around myself, suddenly cold.

But I do know. That's the thing. I do know. "Tim stopped me before I could figure it out," I whispered.

"Stopped you? Stopped you from what?"

I heard the urgency in her voice. A curtain was about to rise, and when it did, I would reveal all. But I kept silent. I'd said more than I could explain.

"Stopped you from what?" Susan repeated, quietly.

And I couldn't... I needed help. If Susan was going to help me, I needed to answer her. "From *dropping* her. No! Not dropping her. From opening my arms and letting her slip from my grasp, from opening my arms and..." My voice grew louder with each word I spoke. Grabbing a handful of tissues from the table, I understood, finally, why they were there.

I didn't know what I expected. Maybe for Susan to gasp in shock or jump up and order me to leave or to call the police. Scenarios rushed through my mind in which men charged through her office door and took me away to a place where I would finally be punished. And in a way, that would be such a relief, but she sat there as if what I'd said was as unremarkable as telling her I was going to the market to buy a chicken for dinner after I left her office.

"You know, Emma," Susan said finally, her voice soft and slow, "for any number of reasons, motherhood fills some women with despair. And sometimes, that despair leads them to believe their baby would be better off without them. Or they would be better off without their baby."

I bent over in my chair, rocking forward, back. Forward. Back. *Would Ali be better off without me?*

"These thoughts don't necessarily lead to infanticide," Susan continued, slowing her words even more. "Sometimes, most often, these thoughts lead to where they should, to the mother, or the family, seeking help. And that's just what you've done."

I closed my eyes to stop the rush of tears that threatened, but they slipped beneath my lashes.

"I know how difficult it was for you to be honest with me. We'll get through this. *You'll* get through this."

Nodding, I wanted desperately to believe her.

"Tell me what you felt the first time you held Ali in your arms. Tell me what you were thinking *then*."

One short bark of laughter escaped, the result, maybe, of complete exhaustion. Or relief. I'd finally confessed.

That time, I didn't need to guard my words. "It was unexpected. The weight of her, the warmth of her. When I shifted her slightly in my arms, I felt the flutter of her heart against mine. Her heart! She was, well, she was perfect." I laughed again. "I'd expected her to wear the stress of birth, but instead, instead her cheeks were the color of thick cream, you know? When it rises to the top? She was luminous, with just the slightest hint of pink to her cheeks. She was... she was beautiful."

I was babbling, but I couldn't help myself. It was such a relief not to be confused about what I wanted and what Ned had told me I should want.

"I loosened her blankets and studied her body. I counted fingers and toes, marveled at tiny fingernails that reminded me of the translucent seashells I'd searched out on the beach when I was a kid. I took my finger, and I slowly dragged it through the little folds of skin on her arms and legs."

I stopped and reveled in every second of that moment. "It was unbelievable how soft she was, how perfect. I placed my fingertip in the bow of her mouth, gently, just enough that her lips pressed against it. Like a kiss."

The tension in my body had found release. "And then—and then she opened her eyes, and she stared at me. And I fell in love with her, right at that moment. I swore, I *swore* I'd keep her safe forever." I stopped again. What I'd thought, what I'd almost done was too real, too horrific, and I could barely bring myself to remember more from those first few hours after Ali was born. When I'd been happy.

But I forced myself to continue. It was my penance. No, not my penance. When I was made to pay for my sins, the payment would be much worse than putting into words the love I felt for my daughter. "She didn't even blink. Just looked her fill as if to say, 'I know who you are. You can't hide from me.'"

I bent my head, feeling as if I'd just run a marathon or performed a twelve-hour surgery or opened my heart and let Susan dig around inside.

I had one thing more to say. "I was thinking that I was falling behind in my research. I needed to get back to the hospital, back to my lab. I was thinking that maybe I wasn't *meant* to be a mother."

We were right back to that morning, and I was the one who'd brought us there.

"Did you think Ali would die if you dropped her?"

My head snapped back from the question, but I knew the answer. "Yes," I whispered. "Yes. Yes. *Yes.*"

"Do you think you would have dropped her if Tim hadn't been there?"

I looked at my hands once more. At my finger as it dug into the callus on my thumb. And I looked into Susan's eyes. "I don't know."

Chapter 20

"You're going to the hospital now? It's not even light outside." Startled, I turned to answer Tim and bumped into the corner cupboard that held our everyday dishes. I'd hoped to slip out quietly. Instead, Tim's voice held me in place, and the morning silence I'd hoped for was broken by the sound of dishes rattling on their shelves.

"Yes." I kept my voice calm because I wanted to avoid starting my day with a confrontation. "I'm going to the hospital now. I want to be there before my first patient arrives. I still have a lot of paperwork to catch up on. I swear," I said, inhaling slowly, fighting to keep the rhythm of my words light and hoping to defuse the resentment I heard in Tim's voice, "no matter how much I get done, there's always more."

We'd agreed that going back to work would be best for me. I couldn't—or wouldn't, if I was honest with myself—stop my research or hand my patients off to another doctor. We both knew I wasn't much good at caring for Ali, even though neither of us came right out and said it. It wasn't an ideal situation for either of us. I felt constrained by obligations I was hard-pressed to meet, and I could feel Tim withdraw from me every time I left for the hospital.

Tim walked to the counter and yanked the container holding the coffee beans from the cupboard. I winced when he let the door slam shut. The last thing I needed was Ali waking up early. I watched as he poured beans into the grinder, then I waited to see where we were going with the early-morning quarrel.

"Want me to put water on for a pot of tea?" His voice was tight, and I was pretty sure that he meant I wasn't going anywhere until we'd talked things out.

My stomach clenched. "I don't—" What was the point of saying no? There was no way I was leaving early. Not then. "Sure, thanks." I pulled out a chair at the table and ran my hand through my hair, even though it would mean rebrushing it before I walked out the door.

Tim busied himself with mugs and spoons while I tried not to think about the files stacked high on my desk.

"How can you push yourself so hard when you, when *no one*, has found anything close to a cure? Don't you get discouraged?" Tim pulled the chair out across from me and sat.

Before I could respond, he continued, saying maybe what he really meant. "I know we decided you should go back to work, but you're always at the hospital. We need you here too."

The argument wasn't new. Before Ali was born, Tim was fine with the time I devoted to my job; he even seemed interested when I came home excited about some finding and needed to talk myself out before I could relax. That was one of the things he'd first loved about me, my commitment to my patients: my focus, my drive. *But now he wishes I'd stop.* That wasn't what he said, but it was what I heard.

"This is hard for me too." I wrapped my hands around the mug of tea he slid across the table. "I don't want to miss time with Ali, but I can't help it right now. I can't give up. We've talked about this. There are doctors all over this country, all over the world, studying this tumor. Do you think that just because their circumstances change, they just quit? I can't quit. And if we didn't have Ali, you wouldn't want me to."

"But we do have Ali. That's the part you seem to forget. And you need to take care of yourself." Tim moved his chair closer and traced the dark shadows under my eyes with his thumb. "Look at you. You're exhausted." His voice was smoky with emotion, and I wanted to lean into his hand, but I held myself stiff, afraid I would give in to him.

"I'm worried about you." He took a long pull on his coffee, and I thought our conversation was over, then his voice grew hard. "And I'm worried about Ali. You barely see her now that you're no longer nursing. Some days, you don't see her from one day to the next."

I sat still, angry that once again, my mothering skills were being brought to task, but I waited for my emotions to calm. "That's not true." I pushed up from my chair. "I can't help it if I get home after Ali falls asleep for the night, but I always kiss her good night."

"Do you think she knows that?"

"I don't know what she knows." I felt my cheeks flame, and I poured my tea down the drain without having had even one sip before I edged toward the door. "I promise I'll be home early tonight. I know you're worried, and I'm sorry. I'll do better. I promise."

IT WAS A LITTLE AFTER five when I locked my office door behind me; I *would* make it home early. It wasn't even dark. Just a quick good night to Ned when I passed by his office, and I would be on my way. My face relaxed, and I'd soon be grinning like a fool. I would keep my promise.

Ned flagged me into his office as soon as he saw me. "I've got Curtis Shuman from Stanford on the line. I want you to hear what he has to say."

My smile disappeared. "I'm on my way out, Ned. I've been here since six this morning. I'm beat, and I promised Tim I'd be home early tonight."

"Good, good. You need to get out of here. This will only take a minute, I promise. Curtis has some fascinating information about culturing cancer cells that you need to hear."

Before I knew it, I was in Ned's office and listening to Dr. Shuman, Curtis, talk about a patient he was treating, a thirteen-year-old girl recently diagnosed with GBM. Along with all the standard protocols used to treat his patient, Curtis detailed for us a process by which brain stem glioma cells had been cultured so they could be grown and distributed worldwide for research. Thirty different countries were probing the cells that had invaded the child's brain. Researchers around the world were attempting to develop more effective therapies in treating a cancer that had no cure. What Curtis was telling us honestly took our breath away.

I was hooked. I was hooked as soon as I'd heard his patient was a child. A child with her whole life before her.

The call went on for hours, and when it finally ended, Ned and I looked at each other, both of us trying to wrap our heads around what we'd just heard.

"Julie!" Ned's voice was still ringing in my ears when his secretary appeared in the doorway.

"Julie, get me two tickets out to Stanford first thing in the morning."

"Pack a small bag," Ned said, turning back to me. "We won't be gone more than a day or so."

A day or two! I can't leave for a day or two. "Ned! I can't take off to California tomorrow. I just promised Tim this morning that I'd spend more time with Ali."

Ned sighed. "Would you rather I take David?" Not even waiting for my response, he picked up his phone and began punching buttons.

David. Ned had lobbed David's name in my direction as if the idea of his taking David to California was merely an afterthought and not a threat. That wasn't the first time he'd used David as bait to get what he wanted from me. I shouldn't have been surprised, but Ned's spite always knocked the wind out of me.

"That's not fair. You know I want to go. I'd give anything to go, but I can't right now. I can't break any more promises to Tim." Even as the words came out of my mouth, I wanted to pull them back. Conferring with Curtis Shuman wasn't just any opportunity; it was *the* opportunity. And I knew it. And so did Ned.

After turning back to his phone, Ned punched in the remaining numbers, and we stared at each other for the few seconds it took for the connection to be made. I was determined not to back down, but when I heard the ringing on the other end of the line, I grabbed the phone and slammed it on the receiver. "I'll go!" There was no way I would let David have that data before me.

I couldn't help myself.

Glancing at my watch, I saw it was well past Ali's bedtime, and I'd done it again—broken my promise. "I need to go. I'll be ready in the morning." Furious with myself, and with Ned, I gathered up my things, knowing that I somehow had to make Tim understand.

Ned, having gotten his way, was conciliatory. "I'm sorry it's so late. Let me take you out for a bite to eat since I messed up your plans for the evening."

"No, I've got to get home." All I could think about was Tim and how upset he would be with me. "I'll see you in the morning."

Ned moved from behind his desk and walked me to the door. "Are you sure you don't want to get something to eat?"

Each word he spoke slowed me down. "I have to go!"

"I know, I know. You won't be sorry about this trip. I promise you."

WHEN I TIPTOED INTO the family room, Tim was where I thought he would be, sound asleep on the couch, clutching one of Ali's little bibs in his hand.

"Hey," I whispered, leaning down so I could kiss the top of his head. "Come to bed. It's late."

Tim opened one eye and smiled. He looked up at me with eagerness, then his smile slipped away, and I knew then that he remembered I was supposed to have been home hours ago.

"What time is it?" Visibly shaking off weariness, he sat up and tried to focus on his watch.

"It's late. I'm sorry. I was on my way out the door when Ned asked me to join him on a conference call. We're flying out to California in the morning to meet with this doctor we were speaking to tonight. He's been culturing cancer cells so he—"

"Emma? Enough." Ali's bib fell from Tim's fingers as he stood and turned toward me. "I don't want to hear it. You're leaving tomorrow? How long will you be gone?"

"Just a day or two, I promise." *Please! Believe me this time. This time I mean it.*

"Do me a favor." Tim's lethargy was gone, and he was wide awake.

"Of course, anything." I felt the weight I'd carried home with me begin to dissolve.

"Don't promise."

Chapter 21

Ned even whispered like a kid, well deserving of the baleful looks from passengers seated near us who were trying unsuccessfully to read or nap. "Emma? Emma, are you awake?"

Feigning sleep on the flight home from California didn't save me from Ned's incessant talking. He was wired like a five-year-old on Christmas Eve. Not that I wasn't excited too. I was. But my enthusiasm was curbed by what I would face when I walked in my front door, days later than I'd said I would be.

"Ned, people are trying to read! Why don't you take a nap?" But when I looked over, he was sitting upright, no pillow or blanket in sight. His eyes twinkled.

"Can you imagine what this means?" Not bothering to lower his voice, he kept going. "Determining the best therapeutic approach to a patient's care based on his own molecular profile? This is what we've been looking for. This could mean the difference between an eleven-month life expectancy to maybe months more. Maybe years."

"I know." I yawned, careful not to rub my eyes, even though the dry air in the cabin made them itch like fire ants on a mission. "And we can talk about it tomorrow. Tomorrow."

"And then, who knows what that extra time could buy us? A technique to remove the entire tumor?"

"Ned. Stop."

He went silent, and it was almost a blessing. It would have been, anyway, if I hadn't known that his silence meant he was thinking of Kate. Thinking, I felt certain, that if only we'd known then what we knew now, Kate might still be alive. No matter what we did, or how many years had passed, Kate had always been right between us, reminding us both of all we'd lost when we lost her.

Kate's cancer took everything from Ned: his daughter, his wife. *Everything.* Everything he'd loved had been ripped away when the cells in Kate's brain went rogue. But his new enthusiasm had him spouting off possibilities that had seemed, not so very long ago, far beyond our wildest dreams.

They were my dreams too. I'd promised Kate I'd find a way. But I broke promises all the time, or so Tim said. Why was my promise to Kate more important than my promises to him? He'd asked that too. I didn't mean to break any of my promises, and then I would be pulled in other directions and forget about responsibilities that, in Tim's mind, at least, should have been as important as curing cancer.

After the shuttle bus dropped us off in the airport parking garage and we got into Ned's car, I checked my phone for messages. I had one from Tim, a picture of Ali with a great glob of drool caught mid-roll down her chubby little chin. No text, just a heart. Ali looked adorable and happy, and the message was Tim's way of calling a truce.

Again.

Pictures of Ali always made me smile, but within seconds, that smile was gone when Ned's voice broke into my thoughts of a happy homecoming.

"I need to stop at the hospital for a minute, and then I'll drop you off."

Ned put the car in drive and started to pull out of the parking area, but I reached out and put my hand on the steering wheel to stop him. "What? No! Let me out, and I'll call a cab. I just sent Tim a text and told him I'd be right home. He's waiting for me."

I didn't want to stop at the hospital. Not that night.

"Don't be silly. I'll only be a minute. You'll waste more time waiting for a cab."

He was right. I knew he was right. We weren't at LaGuardia. Cabs didn't line up at the curb. They had to be called. And if we didn't stand outside, regardless of the weather, and flag them down, they kept going. Plus, they would more likely than not turn down a fare all the way to Lancaster County in that weather—we were caught in a torrential downpour, and the weather forecast called for major flooding in a few hours.

After a five-hour flight—not counting the three-hour layover in Chicago—Ned was blessedly silent on the drive to the hospital, which gave me time to think about everything that needed to be said once I got home.

Tim needed to understand that I couldn't give up. My job *had* to come first. We were so close to a breakthrough; if he would be patient a little longer, we could make it through. We could! Then I'd be a proper mother to Ali. I needed more time. Just a little. Ali was barely a toddler; she wouldn't even remember that I was the person she waved bye-bye to every morning and sometimes didn't see again until the following day.

Before I realized it, we'd pulled into the underground parking garage at the hospital, and Ned pulled into his assigned spot. One hand already on the door handle, he smiled. "Come on up for a second. Curtis said he was faxing me some patient records, and I want to take a quick look."

Exasperation slipped into my every syllable while I avoided looking into his smile. "*No*, Ned! I need to get home. Just get what you came for so we can go. Please."

"I promise. This will take five minutes, ten at the most. Come up, just for a second." And there was his voice, the one that always made me say yes.

I was furious with Ned and furious with myself, yet I gave in. "Five minutes! Promise?"

"I promise, I promise. Five minutes." He walked around to my side of the car and opened my door. "Come on." And I went. Because he asked me to. Because I also wanted to see what Curtis had faxed. Because I couldn't help myself.

The moment he flipped on the light, we saw the files on Ned's desk. Julie must have placed them there before she left for the day. Ned picked up one folder and handed me another.

The minutes passed, then Ned broke our silence.

"Look at this." But before I could focus on what he pointed at, he gave me the gist of it. "With the latest grant Stanford received, they're using molecular imaging to improve early detection. This is fantastic. The sooner we identify the tumor, the longer survival rate we can anticipate. Next time we fly out there, we need to stay at least a week, maybe longer."

Leaning against Ned's desk, I read about the care required in re-secting and handling the tumor tissue. There was only one opportunity, and the pressure to do it correctly was enormous. Just thinking about the logistics filled me with trepidation. And absolute, pure joy.

Only when I arched my back to shake out stiff muscles did I realize I was still standing, but I shrugged it off. I had so much more to read. It was like the bedtime book that made you tell yourself you'd read just one more chapter, and before you knew it, you heard the birds singing outside your window.

Hours later, I looked at my watch and sucked in my breath; I'd done it again, and that time, I knew Tim would never forgive me.

"Ned!" My voice rose with my need to get his attention. "We need to go."

Ned didn't look like he was anywhere near ready to leave. I doubted he even heard me. Slapping my folder down on the desk, I grabbed the one in his hand and threw it on the pile.

"Ned! Tim's waiting for me. I have to go."

For once, he didn't argue, and we quickly gathered our things and headed to the parking garage. I didn't want to think about what Tim would say when I finally walked in my front door.

Ned glanced over at me before he put his key in the ignition. "I know I've made you late, but Tim will understand. He knows how important our work is." When he looked over his shoulder to back the car out, he added, "At least you have Tim at home waiting for you."

I barely heard Ned's words. I was too worried about Tim. For once.

Chapter 22

When Ned dropped me off, I wasn't surprised that the house was dark. Sad but not surprised.

Old houses were never silent even when everyone was sleeping, but the noise I heard when I climbed the stairs told me someone wasn't sleeping and was about to announce her displeasure.

I slipped past our bedroom and crossed the hall to Ali's room in hopes of reaching her before she woke Tim. "Hey, little girl. What's up with you? You're supposed to be sound asleep." Leaning over the crib rail, I reached down to smooth the wisps of hair that stood straight up in pointy little tufts.

Ali stared back—her emerald eyes a perfect match for Tim's except for the flecks of gold that twinkled in the glow from the night-light—with a look that told me she was about to let loose with a howl to shake the windows. Her lips puckered up to show she really meant business, and I reached into her crib and picked her up before she had the chance to do much more than whimper.

"There you go. I've got you now. What's the matter? Bad dream? Wet diaper?" A quick check told me she was dry, so I bent to put her back, and once again, her lips pursed in protest.

"I see. It's like that, huh?"

Tim deserved a break. And I wasn't much in the mood to get started on what I knew would be an unpleasant conversation if he had to get up with Ali. There would be plenty of time for that in the morning. I grabbed a blanket from the crib, wrapped it around Ali, and settled the two of us in the rocker—the one meant for me when Tim bought it but mostly used by him.

"Are you thinking about Thanksgiving? That your problem?"

We were all expected at Miss Maggie's the next day, even though I'd told her it was time for her to take a break from cooking all the holiday dinners. But she had an answer for that just like she had an answer for most things that didn't suit her: "I'll tell you when I'm too old, and until then, just show up when I tell you to. And you can bring some of that cinnamon bread Tim bakes."

"How about it, Miss Ali? Miss Maggie's stubborn as hell. And you don't need to be telling your daddy that I used a bad word either."

Ali burrowed into my arms, and the warmth of her little body filled up the spot in my heart that had been missing her while I'd been gone. "There you go. Just go on and close your eyes. I'll be right here."

I closed my eyes as well. But the stress of the long flight and Ned and what I anticipated would be a difficult discussion with Tim forced my eyes open. I didn't want to think about that. I didn't want to see the hurt and anger that would be in Tim's eyes or hear the recrimination in his voice when I had to admit that once again, I'd broken my promise.

Ali relaxed against me, and I let myself put tomorrow aside. "How about that, Miss Ali?" I whispered. "I'll worry about that tomorrow, just like Scarlett O'Hara."

Ali's little head bobbed up at the sound of my voice, and her eyes sparkled. "Not quite ready for sleep yet? That's okay. We'll just sit here and rock."

I looked around the room until I spotted my Scarlett O'Hara in all her glorious baldness. She was mixed in among all the stuffed animals and dolls we'd accumulated for Ali in the last eight months, and she reminded me of a Thanksgiving that I hadn't thought about in years. That crazy doll that I'd never been able to get rid of. "You want to hear a Thanksgiving story?"

I shifted Ali up so her head rested in the hollow of my neck. "The Macy's Thanksgiving Day Parade had been on mute—just like Uncle Ned liked it—when Kate and I headed upstairs to her room with the bag I'd brought from home. Auntie Laura was in the kitchen, and Grandma and Grandpa joined Miss Maggie and Anne and Uncle Ned in the family room. All afternoon, we heard the clanging of lids striking pots and spoons stirring sauces, and every time the kitchen door opened, the smell of turkey and mashed potatoes and gravy escaped, and the entire house smelled delicious—just like Miss Maggie's house will tomorrow. Maybe tomorrow you can have some turkey. Would you like that? Maybe even a drumstick."

The smallest of sighs escaped from Ali, and I knew it wouldn't be long until I could put her in her crib, but I was in no rush.

"This turned out to be Kate's last Thanksgiving. I'll explain that to you another time, but for now, the only thing you need to remember is that this was the Thanksgiving where people realized your mommy was more than just a little kid who followed Kate around like a lost puppy."

Will I ever talk to Ali about Kate? Maybe by the time she was old enough to be interested, I wouldn't have to tell her about the friend who died from a brain tumor. Maybe by then, I'd have the cure, and there'd be no need for the conversation.

"So. Where was I? Kate. Kate was super curious about that bag. 'What's in the bag? What's in the bag?' And when I showed her, well, she was very excited, and she said some very bad words. Because she was so excited. Words I'm sure you'll never say."

Kate had laughed so hard when she'd peeked in that bag, she'd had to clap her hand over her mouth. It had been a long time since I'd heard her laugh, and I remembered thinking I'd do just about anything to get her to laugh like that again.

"Every doll I owned was in that bag, including Miss Scarlett over there. And they were all bald. I'd taken Grandma's sewing shears and cut off all their hair. So they'd look like Kate, who by then had lost her hair from the treatments she underwent to fight her cancer."

Ali was mostly asleep, but by then, I was caught up in the story.

"Thirty minutes later, we'd marched ourselves downstairs into the dining room with *two* big brown bags. Everyone was already seated, and the food was on the table. Showing up late to the dinner table was not the way things were done back then, but no one said a word because everyone was fascinated by the looks on our faces and those bags in our arms. Even Miss Maggie said later that we looked like we were full of piss and vinegar. I'll explain that to you when you're older. Better yet, I'll let Miss Maggie explain it to you."

The grandfather clock in the parlor struck three. The one in the entryway held off for another two minutes. Two more hours and my alarm would announce the start of a new day, but I was almost done with my story, so I kept going, even though by then, I was only talking to myself.

"Unlike Kate, who was my very best friend, I hated to be the center of attention, but that day, having the eyes of every adult in the room on us never even made me blink. I reached into my bag and pulled out one of my bald dolls, and I held it up until everyone had taken a good look, then I placed it on the table. I did this over and over until my bag was empty. No one said a word. Not even Miss Maggie. And you know Miss Maggie always wants to know the why of things. When I was finished, Kate opened her bag and pulled out each of her bald baby dolls and placed them on the table. No one took their eyes off that table and all those bald baby dolls."

I looked over to where I'd spotted that old doll of mine, needing reassurance that she was still there.

"Anne—I wish you'd had the chance to meet Anne—Anne had lowered her head but not before I saw her eyes grow big—huge, actually—and then she turned sideways in her chair and picked up her fork and studied it. Like maybe she'd never seen one before. Everyone else looked like they'd never seen bare-assed, bald baby dolls before. Don't tell Daddy I said bare-assed."

My story was over, and yet I rocked. Before long, the slight creak of either the floorboards or the rocker started to lull me to sleep. *I really should tell Tim so he can fix that creak, but then I would have to explain the many times I sat here at night with Ali in my arms, and that would only confuse him.*

"So, Miss Ali"—I was sure by then that Ali was sound asleep, but I had one more thing to tell her—"that day was my first and probably only act of bravery. It was a show of defiance from a kid who was never defiant. Anyway, sweet girl, that's the story of Kate's last Thanksgiving."

Chapter 23

I never did get any sleep that night. By the time I'd put Ali back in her crib, I had just enough time to turn my alarm off and jump in the shower.

"Aren't you late for the hospital?"

My heart raced at the sound of Tim's voice—I knew he would be angry because I didn't come home last night when I said I would. And I knew we would argue. Before I looked up from the stack of phone messages I'd been thumbing through, I took a deep breath. "It's a holiday, remember? Unless there's an emergency, I'm not going anywhere but to Miss Maggie's for one of her traditional Italian Thanksgiving dinners." And because I hoped to defuse what was yet to come with a little humor, I added, "And good morning to you too."

Dressed in an old Yale sweatshirt and a pair of jeans, Tim poured himself a mug of coffee and leaned against the island. His hands were wrapped around his mug so tightly his knuckles were white, betraying the casualness of both his stance and his clothes.

Aiming for my own sense of casualness, I nodded to the chair next to me at the table. "Aren't you going to sit?"

"I'm good." His gaze shifted to the phone messages I'd been leafing through, several of them already crumpled into little pink paper balls. "Susan's office called twice while you were gone. You've missed some appointments?"

I nodded. "I forgot to cancel before I left for California. I'll call her office tomorrow." I looked down at two of the crumpled messages. "Although I'm not sure I'll reschedule."

"Oh?"

"It's been six months. I don't see that it's helping." *And I still don't know the answer to her question. Would I have dropped Ali if Tim hadn't been standing behind me? I'd give anything to be able to say no. No, I wouldn't have dropped her! I can't go back if I can't answer her question.*

"I don't think that's a good idea."

My head swiveled in Tim's direction. He shifted from one foot to the other, and when he finally spoke, his words were flat, and that struck me as odd. I felt the heat of an argument brewing, but Tim showed no more emotion than if he were listening to the weather report. "Look, this isn't working. *We're* not working. If you're not going to continue to get help, I'm not sure I see the point to this."

"This?" A pang of nausea gripped my stomach.

"This." He looked around the kitchen as if that explained everything. "Our marriage. I can't keep waiting for you to put us first."

"What are you talking about?" My voice rose, and I forced it lower. I didn't want to wake Ali. "You know this is temporary. As soon as Ned and I—" I stopped and swallowed. I hoped to still the bile that rose in my throat. "Look. I'm sorry. I'm sorry I was late last night. We just had to stop at the hospital for a minute, and then Curtis's files were there and—"

Tim slammed his coffee mug on the island, and I winced. "Sorry only counts when you make an effort to fix what's wrong. But you don't make an effort. You just keep doing whatever the hell it is you do."

"You know what I do. You act like I'm off having fun. This isn't fun. I know things are hard right now, but it won't always be this way. I meant to be here. I did. But—"

"But what?"

"I'm sorry." I looked at my hands, equally frustrated by the pockets of time that were swept away whenever Ned and I were together. "This is hard on me too." I lifted my eyes and caught the shadow of doubt that clouded Tim's eyes. "Don't look at me like that."

"Like what?"

"Like you don't believe me."

"I'm not sure I can believe you."

"Why would you say that?" My voice shook, but I fought to control it. "I love you. You know I love you. And I love Ali." I sounded desperate even to my own ears. "This isn't forever. Soon my research will be over, and I'll have time. Maybe we'll even have more children." I felt like I was dangling a carrot of hope, willing Tim to grab hold. But he stayed silent. "I just need..." I faltered, unsure what more I could say. "I'm sorry."

"It's not enough."

"What does that mean?"

"It means it's not enough. It's not enough that you're sorry. It's not enough for me. It's not enough for Ali. When was the last time you spent even a few minutes with her? When was the last time you held her? Talked to her? Do you even remember you have a child?"

I blinked and wished I could put my head down on the table. *Last night. I held her last night.* I could have told him about last night. Or all the other nights. *Why didn't I tell him?*

Chapter 24

"**I**'m sorry," I told Susan the moment I walked through her office door, apologizing for missing last week's sessions. "I've been in California on business."

It was the second trip to California that month, and most likely, there would be more. Stanford's Curtis Shuman didn't come to you; you went to him. He was the one who'd received the ten-million-dollar grant to improve the GBM detection and management process. And I was the one Ned insisted go with him. It was an honor that Ned chose me. I didn't need anyone to tell me that.

I had a patient of my own to see in a little over an hour, so I chose the chair facing the schoolhouse clock when I sat down. Smiling, smoothing my skirt down over my knees, I continued. "I know I've missed our last two sessions, but I'm here now, and that's what counts, right?"

The pupils in Susan's eyes dilated a smidge. "I think continuity is what's most important in your treatment right now, Emma."

I sat up a little straighter. Her response wasn't cold, exactly, but it wasn't what I'd expected either. If anyone understood the importance of grabbing an opportunity, I would think it would be another doctor. Especially when that doctor was a woman. Women in the medical community were not routinely selected over our male counterparts for plum assignments. It was important to grab what we could.

Susan was right, though, about continuity. I nodded. "I understand. I'll try to make sure it doesn't happen again." *Especially since*

Tim insists I don't let it happen again. I didn't promise her, though. No matter what I'd promised Tim. If I needed to be in California, I would go.

Even if I hadn't been to California, I might have canceled our last two visits. I wasn't ready to answer her question from our last session: Would I have dropped Ali down those basement stairs if Tim hadn't appeared? *Why, after all this time, do I still not know the answer?*

Susan handed me a cup of tea then added some cream to hers. "Why is what Ned thinks so important to you?"

My hand jerked involuntarily, and tea sloshed into the saucer. "What?"

Susan ignored the confusion on my face and in my voice when she repeated her question. "Why is what Ned thinks so important to you?"

I stirred some cream into my tea, buying myself some time, and tried to think of the best way to explain my relationship with Ned. And maybe second-guess where she was going with her question. "Ned's my boss. And my friend. So yes, his opinion is important to me, but no more so than that of any other friend or colleague."

"Oh? Many of your conversations begin with 'Ned thinks' or 'Ned says.' Haven't you ever noticed? I don't think it's unfair for me to conclude that what he thinks means a great deal to you."

"Well, maybe when I was a kid but not now."

I was higher than I'd ever climbed in that old apple tree but nowhere near high enough not to hear Ned when he called out to me. I'd thought I could ignore him, but I've never been able to ignore him.

"I need you, Emma."

"No," I'd said. "I'm not going to her memorial service. If I go, it means she's really dead, and I need her not to be dead."

And he'd looked at me with eyes brimming with sadness. "Sweetheart, she's dead whether you go or not. I know you know that."

"I can't do it. I can't walk into church and pretend Kate's in a better place. She's not in a better place."

"I get that. I do. But I need you to do this for me. Just for me."

And really, that was all he'd had to say.

I shifted in my chair and recrossed my legs. Then I quickly looked at the clock.

Susan's eyebrow shot up. "No?"

"No." The rattle of the teacup in its saucer as I placed it on the table only rattled me more.

"How does Ned feel about your baby?"

"You don't have time for a baby." That was what he'd said. It would be a mistake to tell Susan. She'd think he was an awful person, but he wasn't. He was Kate's father.

Only after my thumb started throbbing did I realize I'd been digging at the callus. "I think Ned wishes I'd—we'd—waited to start a family."

"What do you think?"

I thought about the best way to answer her question. "It would have been easier if we'd waited, but that's not the issue. We didn't wait."

I wanted to reach for my tea, but I was afraid I'd never get the cup to my lips, so I left it on the table and tried not to look at it.

"Has Ned ever convinced you that something you wanted was not in your best interests?"

"You don't get to where you want to be without a price." Ned's words jumped into my head as if he'd stood right next to me and whispered into my ear.

By then, Susan was on her second cup of tea while my first still sat on the table between us. I longed for just one sip. "Why are you asking me about Ned?"

"I'm asking you about people in your life. Ned's just one of them."

"There's always a price for what you want." That was what he'd said. *Tell her, tell her what he said.*

"Once, maybe. But I don't see where you're going with this."

Susan picked up my cup of tea and offered it to me. "Just trust me."

I looked at that cup and tried to convince myself I no longer wanted it. I shook my head, afraid to trust my hands, and watched as she placed it back on the table. "Once, we were at the library compiling lists of possible academic scholarships for college. I was sixteen, I guess. There'd been this group of girls. They were giggling, seated around this big round table next to the magazines. They had all these teen magazines spread out on the table. You know the kind I mean? *Seventeen?* That kind of thing."

Susan nodded, and I went on.

I laughed at the memory. "Those girls annoyed me. They had nothing better to do than pick out prom gowns and wait to be asked out, and I'd been so busy planning my future, I'd barely noticed that it was prom season. Anyway, I noticed them. It was hard not to. They were making so much noise. And that's when Ned caught me looking at them."

I'd thought I could pull that off as a young girl's silly memory, but even though it had been so long ago, I remembered how awkward I'd felt, thinking those girls were laughing at me when really, they'd probably never even noticed me.

"And... and I guess the look on my face told him more about why those girls annoyed me than I'd wanted to admit, even to myself."

Ned had set about erasing my brief flash of envy that had taken even me by surprise. Lifting my chin and redirecting my gaze from where it had settled so that I was looking at him instead of that table where those girls sat, he had spoken so softly I'd had to lean toward him to hear what he said.

"Ned reminded me that I'd been selected as the delegate from Pennsylvania to attend the Congress of Future Medical Leaders of America. He reminded me of how proud I'd been, how proud *he'd* been. He asked me if I thought those girls would ever have the opportunity to speak with a NASA astronaut or two Nobel Prize winners. He wanted to show me, I guess, that what I gave up was worth what I got in return."

"And was it?"

"Was it worth it? I don't know. Maybe that's part of my problem. I just don't know."

Ned had been right. I'd never been prouder, but that didn't erase the stab of wistfulness I'd felt that day in the library. More than wistfulness if I was honest with myself. Watching those girls, hearing their laughter, had made me wonder if I would always have to give up what other kids took for granted: proms and boyfriends and parties. It was never that I didn't want those things, just that there was never time.

If Susan was surprised by any of what I'd said, she didn't comment. Instead, she went in another direction. "Tell me about your father."

I stiffened. "My father and I aren't close." I said it like that was all I needed to say.

"Oh? Why not, do you think?"

My eyes flicked from that damn schoolhouse clock to Susan's face. "I don't know," I answered truthfully. "He was always busy, I guess, so I never really spent much time with him." I sat motionless. *What would it feel like to say we had been inseparable?*

Susan nodded, and I imagined "father-daughter issues" flashed through her mind. I wondered what that might bring to our future conversations.

"Do you love him?"

My fingernails bit into the palms of my hands. "Of course I love him. He's my father."

"But you were never close? You're still not close?"

"No, not really." I loved my father, but he was rarely approachable. "My father—my father filled his days and nights with saving dogs from medical testing facilities. And he continues to. Those dogs, what he did to save them, that's what he talked to me about on those rare occasions when he talked to me about anything."

"What was that like, listening to your dad talk about those dogs?"

I didn't need to think about my answer. I remembered how I'd felt then, how I still felt when he talked to me about those dogs. "I had to watch his lips and concentrate on his words when he told me rescue stories. Especially when there was no rescue."

Her head tilted slightly to the left; she stopped me. "What do you mean, no rescue?"

It was easy to forget that unless someone was involved, they might not understand how rescues worked. "Sometimes, the labs wouldn't release any dogs. They'd notify Dad that dogs were available, but then when he showed up, the people in charge had changed their minds, and they wouldn't release the dogs."

"So what happened to them?"

"To the dogs? They were euthanized." I sounded like those words meant nothing, but what I fought to forget was how I never wanted to look straight into Dad's eyes when he came home empty-handed. His eyes would be heavy and glassy, and I was always afraid that he'd cry. And I'd never seen him cry.

Susan's eyes took on a glassy stare as she listened to me explain about the dogs.

"Every dog Dad saved, worse, every dog he *didn't* save, sliced away at him. It still does. The laws need to be changed. It's bad enough that it's legal for laboratories to use animals in product testing, but it needs to be illegal for them to dispose of those animals like yesterday's garbage when they're done with them."

I looked at my watch. I knew our time was soon up, but I told Susan the rest of it.

"It made me wonder if the people who ran those labs had ever been kids with puppies that had slept in their beds. I wondered if they owned dogs and if they were able to look them in the eyes when they walked in the door at night. It made me wonder why *those* people didn't get cancer, but Kate did."

My mouth felt dry from all the memories I'd unfurled. I poured a glass of water from the carafe on the table, no longer caring if my hands shook.

"Did it hurt you when your dad so easily saw the pain those dogs were in but never saw yours?"

I drew in my breath at Susan's question, but before I could protest, she asked another.

"Have you ever considered that you replaced your father with Ned?"

That time, she paused long enough for me to answer. "No! What does all of this have to do with why I'm here?"

"Let me ask it another way. Have you ever felt that *Ned* replaced Kate with you?"

"Don't be ridiculous." I stood and grabbed my purse. "Ned did what my dad never thought to do—he held my hand and listened. He made me feel I had worth."

Susan remained in her chair, seemingly untroubled by what she had to recognize as my anger. "So Ned has always had your best interests at heart? I'd like you to think about that for our next session."

Chapter 25

Three Years Later

Ali tried desperately to get what was in the box into her bowl. But it just wasn't working.

"It's okay, sweetheart. Mommy can help." I attempted, again, to wrest the cereal box from Ali's little hands, but she was having none of it.

"No! Daddy do it!"

"Ali. Let Mommy help you." But every time I tried, she pushed my hand away.

"No!"

At the sound of Ali's voice, Tim looked up from his newspaper. "What's going on?"

I waited a moment to see what Ali would say, but when she remained silent, I filled Tim in.

"Apparently, I don't pour cereal correctly." My eyes went from the box in Ali's hands to her empty bowl, expecting Tim to tell our daughter that she needed to be nice to Mommy.

Instead, he smiled at Ali, took the box from her hands, and poured the cereal, after which he sliced a banana that, apparently, always went on top. As each slice hit the cereal, Ali scooped it up and into her mouth. It was a game, and Ali was winning. When she was done, she rewarded Tim with a grin bright enough to light an airplane runway.

I refused to acknowledge what had just transpired. "You'd think you were the one who pushed her out almost four years ago." I was going for humor, but Tim's response was silence. "Too early in the morning for jokes?" Seated between my husband and daughter, who both seemed to find me lacking, I saw that I had failed miserably at easing the mood that hung like a dark cloud over our breakfast table.

Tim finally acknowledged my words. "What do you expect? Just because you changed your game plan for the day doesn't mean you can expect us to alter our routines." Then he looked over at Ali, stole a Cheerio out of her bowl, and popped it into his mouth. "How about it, sweetie? Daddy pours your cereal in the morning, doesn't he?"

I'd tried to defuse the situation, but Tim seemed to enjoy pouring oil on the fire.

"You're so busy with your cancer trials and your patients, Ali barely..."

"Ali barely what?" I squared my shoulders, but I struggled to keep my voice even. Each word rose higher than the last. *What the hell just happened here?*

"Nothing." Whatever Tim had planned to say, he apparently thought better of it, but Ali's little head swiveled left and right as she inhaled more than just the cereal she stuffed into her mouth.

I tried to remember why I'd thought taking a day off work was a good idea.

Tim didn't need to say what he was thinking for me to understand. *Ali barely knows me.* That was what he'd meant to say. And it was the truth. That was why I was home today. That was why I'd garnered Ned's contempt by asking for the day off, which was something I rarely did. I had also rescheduled three patient appointments so I could take Ali to the children's museum in Harrisburg. And then, after I'd scheduled everything, Ned changed the latest clinical trial meeting to late that morning, so I'd been forced to agree that David should fill my spot there.

Which meant I would be the last to see the data.

I knew that Ned was punishing me just as well as I knew I'd taken the day off to make up to Tim and Ali for extending my last trip to California.

I tried like hell to block out what I'd given up to be home that morning. "Hey, I was joking," I told Tim, referring to my sorry attempt at humor by suggesting he should try pushing a seven-pound baby out of his private parts. "I get it. It's okay."

Maybe I was half joking. I'd thought Ali would want to spend time with me, just the two of us. I never expected her to say she didn't want to go.

I deserved it, though. Tim was right. I put patients and research before family. Always. I had to, but still, I needed to defend myself. "I want to be here. I do! I just can't right now." It took a moment before I realized he'd left the room. He'd heard all that before. He was tired of hearing *someday* come out of my mouth. As far as Tim was concerned, Ali would be in college by the time I was ready to be a proper mother.

"I wish you had more faith in me!" I yelled, even though he couldn't possibly hear me.

My cereal grew soggy while I thought about what Tim had said. It wasn't that Ali didn't know me. She knew me. But I was well aware of what he meant: I was the person who came home and offered little more than a momentary distraction in her day. She would wrap her arms around my legs and give me a quick squeeze, almost always with some small gift in her hands. A leaf or a rock or a picture she'd colored. Tim was behind those daily offerings. He nudged her to greet me at the door, but I thought there was some part of her that somehow understood that all of that was temporary. I was confident she loved me. And more importantly, that I loved her even if I was the person who always went away.

"Here. Let me help you with that." Trying to simultaneously climb down from her chair and hold on to her bowl, Ali had managed to get the corner of her pajama top hooked onto the arm of her chair. The image of her tipping one way and the bowl flying the other brought me abruptly back from feeling sorry for myself. I removed the fabric and helped to steady her, then I leaned in and hugged her. "You know I love you, right?"

Ali nodded and smiled, hugged me back, her earlier momentary displeasure apparently forgotten. I leaned over to kiss the top of her head and marveled at how closely she resembled Tim. He really could have pushed her out. Their hair was the same raven-black; the only difference was that Ali's fell in curls around her shoulders. She even had his smile, the one that started in his eyes and came straight from his heart.

They were both fair-skinned, too, living up to Tim's family surname of MacMurchadha.

"Go on now. Go get dressed," I told Ali while I rinsed her bowl and dumped the contents of mine down the garbage disposal. I placed our bowls and spoons in the dishwasher even though Tim would come back later and rearrange them.

Okay, now, what am I going to do with the rest of my day? It wasn't often that my time wasn't micromanaged down to the minute. I stuck my head in Tim's office so I was sure he heard me. "I'm going to the hospital." Without waiting for a reply, I headed upstairs to our bedroom and changed out of my jeans and into a pair of the tailored black slacks I favored on days I wasn't seeing patients. If I hurried, maybe I could still slip into the clinical trial meeting. If not, I had plenty of overdue paperwork that needed my attention. I did then what I always did; I put thoughts of Tim and Ali behind everything else.

"I'll be home later," I announced to no one on my way out the front door.

Chapter 26

"What are you doing here?" Gail, my secretary, looked surprised when I walked through the door to the reception area of my office.

"Nice to see you too." I hung my jacket up and provided an altered version of my morning, leaving out all the parts that hurt. "Ali and Tim already had plans today, so I've postponed my day off. Is the meeting still going on? I'm hoping to slip in and catch the tail end of it."

"Oh, I'm so sorry. Dr. Bennett rescheduled it for first thing this morning. It just broke up. If I'd known you were coming in today, I would have called you."

I bent over to pick an imaginary piece of lint off the cuff of my slacks. I'd counted on attending that meeting once I realized I wasn't going to spend the day with Ali. I'd counted on hearing the findings and pressing forward with my research.

"No problem. I didn't know myself I was coming in until just a little while ago." My smile was weak, but it was the best I could offer. "Can you bring me the patient files that need to be updated? Might as well get some paperwork done since I'm here." I headed toward my office and shut the door behind me. *When did Ned decide to reschedule? How long will it take his secretary to distribute the minutes? How long until I know the findings?*

Soon I had a cup of hot tea and a piece of pound cake on my desk. And more files than I cared to see, every last one requiring updates. It was probably just as well I came in today.

"What's with the cake?"

I already knew the answer. Gail had a lifelong struggle with her weight. At four foot nine—"and a half," as she was always quick to add—not only was she several inches shorter than me, but she was also about thirty pounds heavier. Whenever she felt the urge to go off her diet, she baked something delicious then gave it all away. According to Gail, she felt fulfilled when everyone else enjoyed her goodies.

"Just you never mind about that cake. Enjoy it. I was in one of my moods."

I laughed because Gail's moods were always to my benefit.

Gail handed me the last stack of files. "So how is sweet little Ali?" Effectively changing the subject, Gail's question pulled me back from thoughts of that damn meeting and which patients in the trial had received conventional radiotherapy and which had received temozolomide. Even the doctors didn't know, not until it was over. Now everyone knew—except me.

I mentally pulled out a fresh Ali story. "She's wonderful. She turns four in two weeks. Can you believe it? Tim's busy planning her birthday party. I just stay out of his way and do what I'm told."

I sounded like I was laughing at myself. I was good at that. "The weather's so nice," I continued. "Ali's still riding her little tricycle. They go searching for treasure. That's what she tells me. Last night, I went home to a beautiful bouquet of wildflowers. Ali was very proud of herself when she gave them to me."

I almost believed there had been flowers when I got home last night.

"You're lucky Tim works at home," Gail said before closing the door behind her.

"I *am* lucky," I agreed, even though Gail was no longer there to hear me. *I am lucky*, I told myself again, wondering who I was trying to convince.

It wasn't that I never saw myself the way Tim did—as a fake. I painted pretty pictures for others, pictures made of pretty words. Pictures made of bubbles. But all someone needed to do was blow on them and those pictures disappeared.

I'd never once gone exploring. I didn't know whether Ali's little tricycle was red or blue, but if I'd had to guess, I would say it was red. Or maybe pink. I thought pink was her favorite color. Did they make tricycles in pink? Or yellow?

I'd missed every childhood milestone so far. I never meant to. I *meant* to be there, yet somehow I wasn't. And Tim's patience was wearing thin. We barely spoke because by the time I walked in the door at night, he was sound asleep. I couldn't remember the last time we smiled at each other. Or laughed. When was the last time we laughed? Made love?

AFTER GAIL CLOSED MY office door, the files stared me in the face. I lifted the first one off the pile, opened it, and immediately slammed it shut. *Fuck it.* I tossed it on my desk and stormed out of my office.

His door was open, and for once, I didn't hesitate in the doorway like some timid little mouse. Instead, I strode into his office and slammed the door shut behind me. In ten steps, I was in front of his desk. "Why did you reschedule that meeting?"

Ned looked up, quickly shuttering the look of surprise in his eyes. "Good morning. What meeting are you talking about?

"You know damn well what meeting I'm talking about. The clinical trial results."

A look of artificial confusion crossed Ned's face. "You weren't there? Oh, that's too bad. David did a great job. Sorry you missed it. Julie should have the results out to everyone by the end of the day—at the very latest, tomorrow morning." Ned smiled, clearly satisfied he'd relayed all pertinent information. "Anything else?"

"Ned!" I felt my throat close, and my eyes filled with tears. My morning. Ali. All of it. It was too much. Without even thinking, I dropped into the chair in front of Ned's desk. "Why are you doing this?"

"What? You were scheduled off today. It shouldn't concern you if I reschedule a meeting when you chose not to come to work. You're supposed to be a dedicated doctor. If you want to stay home and play mommy, do it. If you want to work for me, then you damn well better be here."

His words were stones thrown to make me bleed. "It was *one* day—"

"Yes. And it turned out to be the day I rescheduled a meeting. Without checking with you first."

He was right. There was no reason to think I should receive special treatment. I swiped at my eyes and nose with the sleeve of my lab coat then sat up straight in my chair.

"You're right." But my words fumbled over my memory of the day I'd told him I wanted to be a doctor. We'd been out in the garden on the old swinging bench when I'd told him I wanted to find a cure for GBM. I'd been so afraid he would laugh at me, pat me on the head, and tell me what a good girl I was, just like my parents had when I'd told them, but he hadn't. He hadn't laughed at all.

Ned seemed caught up in the same memory. "Remember when you told me you wanted to do what I couldn't? You wanted to save kids like Kate?"

I cringed. "I was a kid."

"No. You were right. You wanted to be better than me. And I'm still trying to show you how to do that. You don't get to quit or slow down or—or take a day off. Not until you're done. If you're not willing to do that, then you'll never be better than me."

"So you're punishing me for something I said as a kid?"

"No. I'm teaching you."

Chapter 27

"*You don't get to quit.*"

Ned's words followed me back to my office. He had to be wrong. No one could sacrifice more. *Except Ned. He's sacrificed everything.*

I flipped open the first file on my desk: Mary Grace Anderson. Brain stem glioma, malignant. At six, she was just over the cusp for a decent prognosis, but even if she were younger, there wasn't much hope. The tumor had spread throughout her brain.

I made a note to call her parents and see how they were holding up.

Next file. Next file. Next file. I added notes where needed then verified lab report results. The mess was my fault. I refused to take copious notes and complete forms while a patient was in my office. Eventually, though, I had to take the time to catch up.

Hours later, I stood and stretched. Then I grabbed my purse. "I'm going down to the café..." But I was talking to an empty room. Gail must be at lunch. I left a note and ran down the stairs, my only nod toward physical exercise for the day.

My attention drawn by the vibration of voices coming from the ER, I swung left instead of heading to the cafeteria. "Multiple traumas. Mass shooting. Children! Amish school!" The voices rose, but the resolve of the head nurse never wavered as she barked out orders.

The room went silent for maybe a second. Then it exploded. Ten, twenty voices at once. Words needed to be said, maybe for no other reason than to try to make sense of them.

"Little girls! Ten of them!"

We were, geographically speaking, the closest local trauma center. We'd learned many of the victims would arrive shortly via helicopter before transport to pediatric trauma centers in Philadelphia and Hershey. It was our job to stabilize them first before sending them on.

The shock was palpable as it wound its way quickly through the examining rooms and nurses' stations. "There's never been an Amish school shooting. Who would do such a thing?" That was what everyone wanted to know.

Within minutes, a team of doctors and nurses moved up to the hospital's helipad to wait for the first arrival. My feet were glued to the floor. I couldn't just slip back through the double doors of the ER and return to my office. Every hand was needed.

While we waited, news dribbled in. "Two confirmed dead."

And then, "Shooter dead!"

And someone, I didn't know who, put into words my very thought: "Well, at least that's done."

After the first helicopter landed, the ER erupted with even more activity. Adrenaline surged as gurney after gurney arrived and the triage process started. Every available doctor helped.

"You!" Someone grabbed my shoulders and spun me around. "Assess quickly. Best chance of survival. Won't make it another hour. Put them in order. Best to worst. Now!"

I blinked.

"Just do it."

While I walked from gurney to gurney, the orders of others echoed around me. "Gauze. Chest tubes. Faster. Faster!" Synchronized, it was. A horrible dance, really more of a ballet from hell. First with steps fast and furious, then when the action slowed and everyone waited, it became a beautiful diorama. Or it might have if the performance of the nurses and doctors hadn't been so crucial.

Jaws were clenched tight from the execution-style head wounds covered in blood; each girl was also, sadly, a Jane Doe. I searched pockets and looked for purses and bookbags. Nothing.

"There's no identification."

I thought I'd muttered it to myself, but the nurse assisting me answered, "The Amish don't carry identification, mostly because they refuse to get their picture taken." *Of course, I knew that. I'd just forgotten.*

The girls who survived were sent on their way without anyone even knowing their names. And somehow, that made it all the harder.

It was a long and bloody day. When I finally left the hospital, the sun was no longer shining as it had been earlier. The beauty of the sugar maples I'd admired hours ago—the yellows and golds and burnt siennas, the raging reds, their colors splashed across the hospital campus—had disappeared into the night sky.

Nothing tragic should have happened on such a beautiful day.

I'D NEVER BEEN SO THANKFUL that Tim was able to care for Ali at home. I hoped she would never witness a day like that one. I hoped she'd never be told to line up and stand still and wait to be shot.

When I pulled into our driveway, Tim was standing outside our front door, his face a mask of pain and worry.

"Are you okay?" I'd barely dragged myself from the car before he reached me and pulled me into his arms. Then just as quickly, he pushed me away as if he expected to see the horror of the day smeared all over my lab coat. Satisfied that I was at least in one piece, he pulled me in again and whispered, "It's on the television. Are you sure you're okay?"

"I'm..." I didn't know what I was. For the first time in hours, I allowed myself to feel the pain of everything I'd seen. "Oh my God, Tim. Those little girls!" We held on to each other, neither of us quite believing what had happened.

Before we could say another word, the front door opened, and Ali stood there, perfectly still, one little hand on the doorknob, unsure maybe whether she wanted to step out onto the porch. I couldn't take my eyes off her. She was whole and alive, squeaky clean from her bath, her dark curls pulled up into a little topknot on her head.

Ali looked like she didn't know whether to smile or cry, perhaps sensing the tension I'd carried home with me. I walked up the steps slowly and knelt before her so that we were eye level. I probably would have crushed her to me, scaring her senseless, if Tim hadn't stepped in close to take the brunt of my hug.

In one chubby little hand, she clutched a piece of orange construction paper. Orange. My eyes narrowed at the sight of the paper. I couldn't look away from it. *Orange. The paper is orange. Was there an orange spark from the gun when he fired it?*

Wanting to wipe that vision from my head, I took a deep breath, and gently, I touched Ali's paper with one finger, almost anticipating the heat. Finally, I took the paper from her and held it firmly in my hands. "Is this a bird?" By the look on her face, I could see I'd guessed wrong. "No? Ah, an ant. I see that now."

We moved inside and tried to make sense of a day that made no sense.

After Ali went to bed, I told Tim what I'd seen, what I knew. What I didn't know. "I don't know why the victims were all girls. We heard that he made all the boys leave the school, and then he boarded the windows shut. One little girl left with the boys. Somehow, in the confusion of the killer screaming at the children and the children screaming in terror, she got away."

Tim had already heard some of that on television, but he let me talk, and he listened. The only way I could get the horror out of me was to give it to him. He gladly took it from me so I would be free of it.

"At least two of them were sisters. I know one died. I don't know about the other one. It was—it was awful, Tim. Imagine lining up, facing the blackboard, and waiting your turn. Imagine hearing the first shot." I swallowed. My heart was breaking with every word I spoke. "Imagine being last."

The vision was all too real, but when I squeezed my eyes shut to block it out, I imagined, instead, the sharp report of the gunshots. The space between each shot precise. Anticipated. When I finally stopped talking, Tim placed a glass holding an inch or so of amber liquid in my hands. He wrapped my fingers around it so that it was secure.

"Here, drink this. It might help." He watched as I took one tentative swallow then gulped the rest.

He fell asleep holding me, and for the first time in what seemed like forever, I felt as if we belonged together, but every time I came close to relaxing, the vision of that first child wheeled into the ER stole any thoughts of sleep I might have had. She looked so small lying on the gurney, a little girl of maybe five or six, her face the color of paper or chalk, her life's blood draining from her body. I couldn't stop wondering whether she lived. We'd done what we could and sent her on her way to Hershey, where they were better prepared to care for her injuries.

The not knowing ate away at me. The not knowing forced me from the comfort of Tim's arms to stand just inside Ali's room, close enough to watch her little chest rise up and down but not so close that my presence would wake her.

It didn't take much imagination to picture her little body laid out on a gurney, the blanket covering her stained red.

"What are you doing?" Tim whispered, wrapping his arms around me, his strength providing the assurance of safety I craved.

Leaning back into his warmth, I whispered, "Nothing. I was just standing here."

My words reminded me of that other night so long ago, the one I tried so hard to purge, yet always the memory of it lurked in the dark recesses of my heart. The night I stood in front of the open basement door with Ali in my arms.

Chapter 28

"How could your God let this happen?"

"God doesn't let things happen. They just do."

"Then who do we blame when hell opens up and spits out evil and the person responsible lies in a pool of his own blood, unable to answer for his sins?"

"I don't know, Emma. God doesn't answer to us."

Tim and I went round and round on the subject. Not just us. People at the hospital argued the same points. Some were lucky enough to have their faith to hold on to. Some, like me, floundered, lost in the abyss of a world gone wrong.

An act of violence in an Amish school was impossible to wrap our minds around. Guns were for hunting animals, not for killing innocent little girls. That was what the Amish believed. School shootings happened, yes, tragically, but it was unheard of for a mass shooting, or any shooting, to occur within the wood-framed walls of an Amish school. Yet it did, and the world came to scrutinize those people who believed in compassion even while they dealt with the travesty that had been thrust upon them.

Suddenly, our little piece of the country became fodder for the reporters and television crews that swarmed our streets in the name of news. They'd come to write a story of horror, and they were hard-pressed to understand the forgiveness the Amish community extended to the family of the man who had killed five of their beautiful little girls.

I tried and failed to understand it myself.

I WAS CURLED UP ON the couch with my mug of tea when Tim wandered downstairs that first Saturday after. "After." That was how everyone referred to the shooting. "Before" was when everything had been whole. "After" was after the shots had been fired.

Tim walked into the room and sat on the stool near my feet. "And what are you up to this morning?"

I smiled and stretched. "Absolutely nothing."

"No? No hospital? No lab?"

"Nope."

Ali was sleeping, and for just that moment, we had the house to ourselves. Other than that first night, I hadn't been able to talk much about the shootings. I still didn't want to, but I did want to talk about my hopes for a better us. "You know why I married you?"

"Because I'm incredibly handsome? And rich?"

I laughed. "Well, sure. Both those reasons. Especially the rich part. I always did want to marry rich."

Tim took my hand and held it in both of his. "I knew it."

"I married you because the words you write fill me with laughter and hope."

"And money. Don't forget the money."

"Oh, I could never forget the money. Be serious." I giggled. "I'm trying to be serious. You need to be serious too."

"Okay. Look. I'm serious." Tim swiped his hand down his face, and it changed from smiling to stern, which made me laugh all the more.

I swallowed, wanting to say my words just right so he would understand. "I love that you're a writer because no one dies. No one dies unless you want them to, and even then, they're not truly dead because they were never real. There's no blood. No real blood, anyway. There's no clock ticking where every second that passes is one less second until the patient takes his last breath or, worse, turns from a living, breathing person to a vegetable."

"Whoa. You really are serious this morning."

I nodded. I was serious. "Just once, I want to choose my own ending. I want to choose the patient whose tumor turns out to be benign rather than be stuck with the one whose disease is so far ahead of medical technology that other than numbing the pain, there's little I can offer."

Tim moved from the stool and slid next to me on the couch. He wrapped both arms around me. "I don't know how you do it. I hate that you do it. I hate that every day, your patients steal a little more of you. I'm afraid that someday, I'm going to wake up and you'll just be gone."

I squeezed his hand. "I won't be gone. I promise." I doubted we'd had a conversation that serious in, well, forever. We were long overdue. "If anything good has come of this, this tragedy, maybe it can be us. Maybe we've been given a second chance. A chance to smell the roses. You know what I was thinking when I drove home that—that night? I was thinking—this is so simplistic, but it's what went through my mind. I was thinking that just because you crawl out of bed in the morning, you don't necessarily get to crawl back in at the end of the day. And we forget that. We forget that it can all just disappear." I looked down at my hands, wishing I could say something that didn't sound like a sympathy card.

Tim leaned his chin on my shoulder, and I felt him draw in his breath. Still, he stayed silent.

"That terrifies me. I don't want to not come home some night and the last thing we said to each other was..." I stopped and thought about the number of times I walked out the door and neither of us had said 'goodbye' or 'I love you' or even 'see you later.' It was too many times. Way too many times. "I don't want to not come home some night and the last thing we'd said to each other was *nothing*."

So things changed. Slowly.

Dinnertime was no longer a sandwich picked at while reviewing patient charts at my desk. It was warm food and conversation. Laughter. A physical ending to a day that wound down slowly rather than stopped abruptly, only to be revisited in exactly the same way the next day.

Tim didn't believe me until I'd shown up by dinnertime three nights in a row. One night, I was even home in time to set the table.

"You really are cutting back your hours."

"I really am."

I was long overdue to smell my fucking roses.

Chapter 29

 eople don't change." Ned leaned against the doorjamb of my office door and watched as I picked up a file, started to shove it into my briefcase, thought better of it, and returned it to the file cabinet.

"Of course they do. There was a time I wouldn't dream of going to New Hampshire for the weekend. And here I am. Off to New Hampshire. I'll be back on Monday."

"But David—"

I looked up from my briefcase, certain there was nothing that needed to be added. In fact, I would leave it right there. No need to take it with me if I wasn't going to open it. "David's a fine doctor." I no longer felt threatened by David. If Ned was going to choose him over me, we both knew he would be making a poor decision. At some point, David's skills would equal mine. He just needed time. "David is qualified to handle anything that comes up this weekend. Besides, you'll be around."

"THE FIRST TIME YOU see New Hampshire should be in the fall."

"But why?" Ali was in the "but why" stage of childhood, where every statement or fact or opinion was met with a question. Tim's comment about the best time to see New Hampshire started her off for the day.

147

"Because it's lovely in the fall. The leaves are spectacular." Catching sight of Ali's eyes in the rearview mirror of the car we'd rented once we landed, he explained. "*Spectacular*. It means really beautiful." Tim refused to use vocabulary suitable for a four-year-old, and I grew accustomed to the continual explanation of words between them. It reminded me of the word game Kate and I had played when we tried to one-up each other by throwing new, bigger, more obscure words into our conversations.

"Look out the window. See all the pretty colors?" Tim pointed out the reds and golds and every shade of orange from amber to vermilion, and before long, Ali was suitably impressed with New Hampshire. Of course, we could have gone anywhere, and she would have been thrilled. That was just how unusual it was for us to take a weekend trip.

Ali looked left and right through the windows, taking in the leaf colors and the mountains in the distance. "I think I love New Hampshire."

To be fair, she fell in love easily. Only recently, she'd fallen in love with the garden gnome at Miss Maggie's, and she'd become enamored of the deep-cushioned wingback chairs at the library, where she and Tim sat for hours while he read to her.

"Did you know that instead of four seasons, there are actually five seasons in New Hampshire?"

Ali thought about that for a minute and laughed. "No, there aren't, Daddy." She knew her seasons, and a fifth one had never been mentioned.

"Yes, there are, baby girl. There's spring and summer and fall and winter." Tim stopped for a minute so she could think about that. "And then there's mud season. It comes between winter and spring after all the snow melts off the mountains. The streets become covered with mud, and instead of all these pretty colors everything is... what color?"

"Brown?"

"Yes, brown. What do you think that might look like? A brown town?"

Ali's laughter filled the car. "Yucky!"

"Or maybe," I added, wanting to join in, "it looks like a town of chocolate! What do you think?" But she'd already turned back to Tim, and my comment got lost in their conversation. It would take time for her to become accustomed to my presence. I knew that. I'd spent years holding myself apart from her, and she would need to learn to trust in my presence, and I promised myself I'd be patient.

That weekend, Ali fell in love with maple syrup and the trees that produced maple syrup and the sap buckets that held the syrup as it dripped from the spigots jammed into the trees. And I fell a little bit more in love with her.

Once we returned from New Hampshire, we settled into a routine where no one was surprised when I came home on time, and my place in our home became more deeply established.

"I know I shouldn't say this," Tim whispered one night after he'd found Ali and me playing a game of hide-and-seek in the kitchen. "Hell, I shouldn't even think it, but you're different."

His comment surprised me. How quickly I'd forgotten how different I'd been. "Different? Am I?"

"Mm. Since that day. You know—"

I did know. Maybe I *was* different. I still handled my full patient load, but I'd cut back on my research. I was losing ground, but I ignored—or tried to, anyway—the pointed looks Ned gave me every time I walked past his office at the end of the day. I didn't forget Kate, but I tried hard not to put her first.

And I thought I was happy. I thought I could make myself happy with what I had. Tim and Ali. My patients.

But I was wrong, and reality crept back in. Referrals for new patients came in, and I couldn't turn them away. How could I? Those people begged their doctors for help, and their doctors begged me to take them. And one of them might lead me closer to the answer I sought: stop the GBM tumor from growing back.

And suddenly, I wasn't different anymore. I told myself Tim and Ali would wait for me, and I was right back to sneaking into my house long after Tim had given up and gone to bed. I didn't change. No matter how much I wanted to.

Ned was right. People didn't change.

Chapter 30

"Things are right back to where they were."

At the sound of Tim's voice, my keys slipped from my fingers and fell to the floor. "What? Oh, Tim! You scared the crap out of me." I bent to pick up the keys and placed them in the pewter bowl on the little table right inside the door. "What are you doing up this late?"

I'd just walked in the door from another long day at the hospital. When Tim switched the light on in the library, I could see him sitting in his favorite leather wing chair. But instead of leaning back relaxed, he sat stiffly, and his feet were planted firmly on the floor.

I wanted to deny his accusation, but that would mean I'd have to lie, so I willed myself to meet him halfway. "I know. I'm late again. I'm sorry." I walked into the room and offered my explanation. "There was an emergency at the hospital. I couldn't leave. I should have called."

"What about last night?"

"What?"

"What's your excuse for not coming home until after midnight last night? And the night before?" He paused, his voice like steel. "Do you have an excuse for every night?"

"No, of course not." Tim was right, and if I could deny it, I would. It wasn't that I'd forgotten my promise to him. Or to Ali. It was just... how did I make him understand how important my work was? I couldn't put us first. Not yet. I'd been wrong to think I could.

"I'm sorry." I moved toward the settee next to his chair and sat, wanting somehow to make things right. When I reached out to take his hand, his fingers curled tight, keeping me from even that small comfort. Still, I tried to defuse the conversation. "It's late. I know you're upset, and I'm sorry. I don't want to fight about this. Why don't we talk in the morning?"

"Will you be home in the morning?" His question came from experience, and it took only a minute for me to remember I had an early consult in the morning.

"I..."

"That's my point. You're never home." He spoke so softly it was as if I'd imagined he'd said anything at all.

I wondered at my own naivete, thinking he would never notice how I'd stretched the hours of my schedule until I was right back to working twelve- and fourteen-hour days. I should have anticipated the conversation, prepared for it, but like so many things, if it wasn't directly related to my patients or my research, I lost sight of it.

But that night wasn't a good time to get into it. "I'm tired. We'll talk about this later."

"When?"

"I don't *know* when." Each word rose higher in volume than the last. "When I have more time."

I was exhausted and frustrated and guilty as charged. "I'm going to bed."

"Do you know what Ali asked me today?"

I'd been halfway out of the room, and I stopped and turned to face him, the beginnings of a smile touching my lips. I expected him to relay some cute question, like "Why do people poop?" Her current interest was the mechanics of the human body, and she'd become fascinated by bodily functions. I might not be there much, but I still knew what kept her mind busy.

I looked forward to him saying something that would help us forget the harsh words we'd just exchanged. Something that would allow us both to agree that an argument that night was pointless. I thought I could listen to Ali's story and feel joy at how perceptive and bright she was, and then we could go to bed so I could get some sleep before I had to get up again. I was expecting that kind of question.

"What did she ask you?" I prompted, moving back to the settee, willing to spend a little more time in the library. Eager even to hear something that would give a happy ending to the day.

But Tim stayed silent while several minutes went by, and my chest grew tight. "Tim?"

Tim exhaled as if he'd needed to push something evil from his body. When he spoke, his voice was flat. He could have been reciting the grocery list. "She wanted to know why you don't love her."

Each word slipped softly between us as if he'd just shared a secret that wasn't his to share. His words had jagged edges, and they took my breath away.

The pain in my chest took me by surprise, and I shut my eyes, willing it to pass. "What? Why would she say that?" When I opened my eyes again, the expression on Tim's face was no different than if he'd just told me the goldfish died.

"Of course I love her!" I pulled myself up and knelt next to his chair, willing him to look at me, forcing him to listen. No matter what problems we had, he had to know I loved Ali.

"You told her that I loved her, didn't you?"

Instead of answering my question, Tim explained that Ali had had a playdate with Hannah, a little girl who lived in Eden, and sometime during the afternoon, Hannah had asked Ali why she didn't have a mommy.

I sucked in my breath. "What did Ali say?" I wasn't sure I wanted to hear the answer, but I couldn't not hear it either.

"She said she didn't know. And then she asked to come home."

My body slumped forward until my head rested on the arm of Tim's chair. Again I reached for his hand, but again he refused to relax his fingers.

"Oh, Tim. I don't know what to say." I thought about Tim's explanation, and it didn't make much sense to me, and I felt my face grow warm. "Kids don't say stuff like that. Obviously, Hannah overheard her parents talking. They should mind their own business."

Tim stared straight ahead. If he focused on anything, it might have been the fireplace directly in front of the settee. Maybe the family photo resting on the mantel was what held his attention and allowed him to pretend I was no longer in the room. It was taken last year at the beach at one of those places where we dressed in costumes and posed as someone other than our true selves, caught for eternity as patrons of some Wild West saloon. Ali sat on Tim's knee, dressed in a cowgirl outfit complete with fringed vest and cowgirl boots a size too big. The boots kept falling off her feet. We were all smiling.

And I thought, *See! We were happy.* As if that picture was the proof I needed.

"Can't you say something?" But Tim had no comfort to offer, and I could see how he'd sat with these words all day, needing to talk to me, and I'd come home late, and Ali's question had festered in his heart. I could see how he had no words to ease my guilt.

He refused to look at me when he finally spoke. "What do you want me to say? You weren't here. You didn't see the look on Ali's face when she walked in the door. You didn't hear Hannah's mother tell me she wasn't sure what happened when Ali asked to come home, even though they hadn't eaten lunch yet."

"Tim, I—"

"Do you even know Hannah's parents' names?"

"What? For God's sake. What difference does that make?" Both grandfather clocks chimed two, and suddenly, I was no longer interested in sleep.

"Tim, please..."

"Don't say anything. Just don't."

Somehow, I need to fix this. I knew I could fix it. I needed Tim to be patient a little longer. I needed to find some way to make Ali understand the importance of my work. I needed her to understand that someday, my hours of working late would be over and I would have all the time in the world.

Tim got up from his chair. I thought he was going to leave the room without saying anything more, but at the last minute, he stopped and turned.

"Someday, Emma, you will regret this. You have this need, I don't know what it is, to play God or save the world. I begged you to get help, but you couldn't even do that. You stopped seeing Susan. You don't listen to what I'm telling you. You barely pay attention to Ali..."

"You don't understand. I'm doing what I have to do."

"Ignoring your family? Is that what you have to do? Making your child feel as if she doesn't have a mother? Is that what you have to do?" Tim barked his questions, giving me no chance to answer, to explain.

"No, I... no! I just need a little more time." But Tim wasn't listening. He'd walked out of the room.

I needed to save... I was no longer sure who I needed to save. But I couldn't stop.

Chapter 31

I did what no mother should. I avoided my daughter. Twelve- and fourteen-hour days at the hospital made it easy. Weekends at my research lab made it easy. Fulfilling my agreement to be the keynote speaker at a medical conference in Phoenix allowed me to avoid both Tim and Ali and not face the reality that the last few glorious months of smelling my roses had just been an emotional reaction to a tragedy.

It was the wrong time to leave town, but for me, it was perfect. I had no choice. The arrangements had already been made. Barring an emergency, it would have been unprofessional to back out. It never occurred to me that my marriage and my daughter could constitute an emergency.

The only good thing about the trip—and I needed to find something good because guilt was eating away at my heart in tiny little bites—was that I planned on meeting Laura, Kate's mother, for lunch. Laura had moved to Arizona after Kate died. I could barely blame her, although it had devastated Ned.

Friends and neighbors and complete strangers had made it their business to crawl through the crevices of their life while they'd waited for Kate to die, and they'd walked around with pain that made just about anyone look anywhere but into their eyes; she'd needed to walk away from the memory of it all.

Her leaving had been one more blow to what once was Ned's family. One more cancer casualty—the kind rarely cited in the cancer statistics.

Other than sending Christmas cards, we hadn't kept in touch. I'd been a kid when she'd left Ned, and by her own admission, it had taken her years to think of me, her dead daughter's best friend, without resenting that I'd been healthy while cancer had felled Kate.

At Laura's recommendation, we met for lunch at a table on the patio of the Mix Up Bar at the Royal Palms Resort and Spa. When I arrived, I had just enough time to lift my face to the sun and breathe in the scent of what I soon learned was desert willow when the waiter led me to the table where Laura was already seated.

"Look at you!" Laura's eyes lit up as she grasped my hands in hers and held me away from her then quickly pulled me in close for a hug. "You're all grown up!"

My cheeks grew warm. "It's been a long time since anyone's said *that* to me."

Emotions quickly washed over Laura's face. Mostly happiness, but I caught a tinge of sorrow that lingered for a moment before we sat. The waiter adjusted the sun umbrella so we were gently shaded before he went off for two glasses of water, then we set about reconnecting.

Laura couldn't seem to take her eyes off me. "Look at you, with your perfect hair and makeup! Your parents must be so proud of you!"

"Because I have perfect hair and perfect makeup?" I laughed—short and fast, since compliments of any kind made me uncomfortable, especially compliments about my looks. "Thank you, but when I look in the mirror, I still see the gangly kid with the bad haircut."

"Of course, I didn't mean your parents should be proud of your looks, although I will say that linen shift you're wearing is stunning. I'm talking about your cancer research. Ned told me. You're making quite a name for yourself in the medical community."

I felt my eyes widen at how easily Ned's name came into the conversation.

"What? Don't look so surprised. We keep in touch."

"What do you two do, swap sections of the newspaper while drinking your morning coffee?"

"Well, almost. Ned tells me you two are close to a surgical breakthrough? A procedure to prevent the GBM tumor from growing back?"

There was that sorrow again. She did a good job of hiding it, but it was there, under that smile she fought hard to keep in place.

I nodded. "We're nowhere near ready to go public with our findings, but yes, we're close. And really, Ned's the one who's gotten us as close as we are." That wasn't really true, but it was typical of me to deflect praise.

Kate was our connection. We didn't start with Kate's cancer, but it didn't take us long to get there; even after all those years, Laura could barely stand *not* to speak of her. And that quickly, the atmosphere surrounding us changed, and I nearly regretted my call to meet her before I flew back to Pennsylvania.

Laura pushed away her half-eaten lunch as if her thoughts filled her belly in a way her sandwich never would. "Imagine if someone had been this close"—her chin dipped slightly, and when she looked up, she seemed to look at something only she could see—"Kate might still be alive."

It took my breath away, the thought of a Kate who'd lived.

Laura's memories were different than mine. I was eleven when Kate died; Laura was Kate's mom. She might have prayed for miracles, but she was old enough to know better than to believe in them.

"Sometimes, I think Ned was more honest with Kate about what to expect than he was with me." I said it as if Laura had been privy to the thoughts running loose in my eleven-year-old head.

Laura nodded. "Kate insisted on the truth, and Ned didn't hide it from her. You know how she was. She didn't want to die that way, and we didn't want her to die that way either." Laura looked to me, it seemed, for confirmation that what she'd said was true. There was no reason for Kate to suffer, but before I could question her, the waiter showed up holding a silver tray filled with goodies: cakes and pies and parfaits. We both chose lemon meringue pie, even though neither of us had eaten much lunch. That was the one good thing about being an adult, I guessed. We didn't need to clean our plates to get dessert. Ever.

I plunged my fork into toasted meringue piled up high on top of buttery lemon curd—and hauled out a mouthful. "It would be rude, don't you think, if we don't at least taste this?" A second forkful of pie headed toward my mouth when I remembered Laura's comment about there being no need for Kate to suffer, but before I could bring it up, Laura spoke.

"Imagine if..."

I looked up. But Laura seemed stalled. "Imagine if?"

"Oh, nothing. I was just thinking. Don't pay any attention to me."

If I'd learned nothing else, I knew that when someone said, "Don't pay any attention to me," they meant the exact opposite. I turned my back on my pie and placed my hand on Laura's arm. "No, really. Tell me."

"I guess I was thinking what it would be like if Kate hadn't had to die. If your procedure had been available when she was still alive."

I glanced at my hand on Laura's arm, then I looked up into her eyes. "That's an odd way to put it, if Kate hadn't *had* to die. She died because she had a brain tumor. It wasn't like she had a choice."

"Well, yes, of course. But she died that night..."

I watched as Laura seemed to pick and choose her words. "You didn't know, did you?"

"Didn't know what?"

"You were very young. Ned always meant to tell you, I'm sure of it, but you were only eleven, and then I suppose he just put it off. And I don't know, maybe he discovered he couldn't. He *should* have told you."

Eleven. When Kate died. Ned telling me it was time to say goodbye. Waiting outside the bedroom door, even though I'd promised Kate I'd stay with her until the very end. And then the next morning—

"He did tell me. He told me she died in her sleep."

Laura bit her lip and stayed silent. Over the years, I'd tried hard not to think of that night. But sitting across the table from Laura on that sunny afternoon, hearing the low patter of voices of the other luncheon guests surrounding us, I remembered some of what Kate had said before I'd said good night. About dogs and forever sleep and the responsibility of pet owners to know when the time was right, even though the truth was that no one was ever ready to make that decision. But it had to be made. And it was the pet owner's responsibility to be strong.

And none of it had made sense at the time. And that was how I knew. "You're telling me that Ned killed Kate?" My voice rose, and my words started to trip over each other. People twisted in their chairs, searching for the source of the drama while I struggled to get myself under control.

Laura looked like I'd slapped her. "Before today, I... I thought you knew. All this time, I thought you knew. I'm so..."

I turned my head and refused to look at her. Refused to hear her sorrow. I scraped the meringue left on my fork against the side of my plate. I did so long after the meringue disappeared. "No. No, I didn't know."

I recalled Ned's hand on my shoulder. "Everything will be okay," he'd assured me. The comfort he'd offered then, when I was a child, had just turned into something evil that needed to be shaken off and stepped on.

"I'm not making excuses for Ned, but I can understand how difficult this would be for him to discuss with you. This isn't why I left him. At least, it's not the only reason."

I thought I'd heard the worst, but it turned out to be only the appetizer for the worst.

"Kate begged her father to help her, and to be honest, I pleaded with him too. I just didn't realize that once she was gone, I could never touch him again." She stopped then, apparently lost in her memories of long ago. "I could never let him touch me. I'm so sorry. I thought you knew."

At that moment, my lifetime of trust in Ned disappeared. I didn't want to hear that Ned had given up, and I sure didn't want to know that Kate had kept her last great secret from me.

I motioned to the waiter for the bill. I needed to get on that damn plane and leave. But Laura stopped him dead in his tracks with just a look and turned back to me. "Please. Don't go. This is a shock."

"You don't give up." I bit each word off and spit it out. I'd grown up on those words. Even then, I whispered them to myself every night when I fell into bed, exhausted. From never giving up.

"What?" Laura's voice was hollow, her eyes wide.

"That's what Ned taught me. You never give up."

I knew Laura understood. She nodded. Ned had always preached those words to everyone. About damn near everything.

"Would you have wanted her to suffer? She would never have lived, Emma."

But I was done. Nothing Laura could say would erase the pain from the secret she'd spilled over that damn pie.

Chapter 32

Eager to confront Ned with Laura's words still beating in my heart, I pulled into Eden in record time, but once I sat in my car outside his house, I needed a moment. I knew even then that when I walked out of his house, I would never walk back in.

While all the other houses in the neighborhood slept, every window of Ned's house shone with a glow of expectancy. Obviously, Laura had warned Ned that I was coming.

I didn't wait for him to invite me in. I just dared him to tell me the truth.

"You killed Kate."

"What?" Even with Laura's warning, he staggered at my words.

"When you told me it was time for Kate to die, I thought you meant that as a doctor, you recognized the signs of approaching death. But I was wrong. Our trip to New York had nothing to do with Kate spending her last few days with her grandparents and everything to do with an agreement between you and Kate. You agreed with an eleven-year-old child that it was time for her to die?"

I'd seen what I'd wanted to see. I was a kid; I believed adults told the truth. I believed they were too smart to lie.

Ned stood in the doorway just long enough for my words to register, then he silently motioned me in. I stood there, the night air creeping down the collar of my jacket, furious and confused, unwilling to follow even a simple request from the man to whom I'd rarely said no. "What happened the night Kate died?"

Ned shook his head. "Come inside. Please. I should have told you myself. I owe you an explanation. Maybe an apology."

"Maybe?"

"Would that help? An apology?" Ned's voice was tight; he drew himself up and made himself big. But I would never look up to him again. "It won't bring Kate back. You're furious because you just learned something you seem to think you deserved to know before. Well, maybe you *did* deserve to know, but I never told you. Kate didn't want you to know."

Tears welled up in my eyes, and I turned away. I'd driven there because I needed to confront Ned and accuse him of murder, and then he'd told me the same thing Laura did: Kate wanted to die. And she didn't want me to know.

"Why?" Even I heard the hurt in that single word.

His eyes bright, Ned ignored my question; maybe he pretended that it didn't hang between us. "Let me pour you a glass of wine." He led me into the living room as if I hadn't practically grown up in that house, and he watched while I settled in the wing chair by the window. "Here, give me your jacket."

By the time Ned wrapped my fingers around a glass of wine, I'd almost decided I'd made a mistake in going there. *Why does this matter so much? Is it that he didn't tell me? That Kate didn't tell me? What didn't she want me to know?*

Weary of my questions, I lifted the glass to my lips and, when I swallowed, felt the first stirring of warmth in my body. I was determined to let it go. Kate had been dead for decades, and no good would come from our conversation. I took another sip, which followed the first and continued to warm me. I relaxed into the chair.

Then I sat up. Who was I kidding? I couldn't let it go. "What didn't Kate want me to know?" Before Ned had a chance to answer, I remembered a conversation from long ago.

"What if I'm wrong?" Kate had asked.

"Wrong about what?" Back against the wall, I'd sat across from her, knees pulled up to my chest. The floor was a poor substitute for her bed or even the rocker next to it, but at the time, I'd needed a little distance between us. Not that I'd thought her tumor was contagious; it was more that she frightened me. I hadn't known a Kate who felt fear.

"What if there is no God? No plan? What if there's nothing?"

It was the first I'd known Kate to question her religion. "Would that be so bad?" There hadn't been an ounce of I-told-you-so in my voice, but Kate needed to be prepared. What if she *was* wrong? I wanted to sway her. I wanted her to believe what I believed: that once you're gone, nothing and no one can ever hurt you again. "Would it be so bad to just go to sleep and never wake up? That's what I believe." And honestly, it *was* what I believed. It was still what I believed.

But Kate had wanted Heaven and angels and maybe even harps. She'd wanted a God who was in charge. *Was that what she was afraid of? Did I cause her fear?*

Before I could tunnel any further into my past, Ned nodded slightly, acknowledging my need for the truth. "She didn't want you to know how afraid she was of the pain. She tried to protect you."

Ned's voice, filled with the same empathy he reserved for bereaved parents when he told them nothing could be done to save their child, was no more than background noise as I let the grief of failing Kate, again, wash over me. It wasn't fear of what she'd find in Heaven or no-Heaven. It was what she'd feel before she got there. And she'd tried to shield me.

"I understand why you didn't tell me when I was a child. But what about later, when I was older? When I became a doctor. Why didn't you tell me then?"

"I—I couldn't." Ned downed his glass of whiskey in a single swallow then poured himself another while we sat and looked at each other, two strangers who'd known each other forever.

"You gave up," I told him finally, my words coated in bitterness.

"What?"

"You gave up when you helped Kate die. Why have you always insisted that I never give up? That even one detail might help us find the answer? You gave up. On Kate. On me."

His eyes little pinpricks of darkness, Ned's face shut down. "She was my *daughter,*" he whispered. "You have no idea..."

That wasn't what I'd gone there to talk about. But I did. "I have every idea. I have a daughter, and if you'd had your way, she'd be dead too."

Ned's face went white. "What are you talking about?" His words sounded thick. Strangled.

"You know what I'm talking about. The entire time I was pregnant, you told me I shouldn't be. That it was the wrong time for a baby. Every time I was sick or needed a break, you threatened to give my work to David. You locked me out of meetings. You held every promotion over my head so I would do what you wanted. Even when Ali was born, you intimated that I get rid of her."

Ned sat frozen. Was he remembering? My accusations rolled over him, and I wondered which, if any, he might address.

"I never forced you to do anything. If you chose to follow what you thought I meant, that was *your* choice, not mine."

My hand twitched, and the wine in my glass splashed onto my cream-colored slacks. The fabric sopped up the liquid but left a port-wine Rorschach-like stain that would forever be a reminder of that conversation. "What did you say?"

"You heard me. I never put a gun to your head."

I looked out the window rather than at the man I no longer knew. *The basement stairs. Ali's little body. The sound of her falling that*

I can't erase even though I never dropped her. I watched as a faint blush of pink touched the dark sky, and the long night would soon end. And I was glad because there was so much that needed to be said. Not to Ned. To Tim. There was so much I needed to make up for.

I turned back from the window, from the sight of Miss Maggie's house just down the street, her shutters closed tight against the early morning, and I stood to leave. "I used to see each day as a new beginning. I used to see each day as a chance to make right what wasn't. To make Kate's death right."

I couldn't help thinking I would probably never step foot in that house again when I asked one more question. "Do you believe in God?"

Ned laughed, a sound that surprised me, given what we'd just said to each other. His laugh was a sound I'd always loved. He wasn't a big man, but he had a big man's laugh. From the belly or, as my dad always said, from the gut.

"You haven't changed a bit, Emma. You are still so sure God is out to get you. Yes, I believe in God. And I already know what you're going to say, and the answer is still yes. I believe in God, even though I couldn't save Kate. I believe, even though I prayed for help and he didn't help."

It amazed me that even then, Ned sidestepped my question. "Do you believe God will forgive you?"

"For what? For helping Kate die? Everything I've done, I've done *because* Kate died. All I've tried to do is save other children from this disease."

He let me think about that for a minute, then he said his final words.

"Sometimes—sometimes, sacrifices are necessary."

I sucked in my pain at his words, but I couldn't leave. *Was Ali meant to be a sacrifice?* "I trusted you. I've trusted you my entire life. After Kate died, I stopped being a kid because, I don't know, because

I thought I *had* to, because I thought I had to make up for Kate's death. As if it was my fault she died. Even as a kid, I'd thought it was my job to figure it out. And you encouraged me and pushed me, and I thought it was because you loved me. But all along, it's always been about Kate's tumor. You may never have wanted to talk about it, but it's always been right there between us."

I left then, and I never looked back. My only hope was that I could undo my own mistakes.

Chapter 33

It was early morning when I walked in my front door after driving away from Ned's.

My gut told me to race up the stairs and wake Tim and tell him everything. Beg for forgiveness. Logic told me I had an early consult in two hours. There wasn't time to discuss everything that needed to be said.

Besides, it was no time for a rushed conversation. We were in the middle of an argument. Not the middle, because the argument was over, but Tim hadn't spoken more than two consecutive words to me in days because I'd missed Ali's graduation from preschool. I broke my promise. Again.

I was *unable* to attend, not unwilling. There was a difference, but Tim didn't see it that way.

"It's an *hour*," he had retorted when I'd told him I wouldn't make it. He couldn't comprehend that the specific hour of Ali's ceremony was when I had a conference call scheduled with Robert McGuinness, head of Oncology at UCLA. Between the time difference, Robert's schedule, and mine, it had taken days to set up a date and time when we could discuss his latest breakthrough. It was an hour I couldn't give up.

But Tim wouldn't let it go. It was inconceivable to him that I would willingly pass up an opportunity to watch our daughter walk across a stage to receive her diploma from preschool.

"Look, I get it," I'd told him. "I get that they made graduation caps out of paper plates and ribbons. I know this is a big thing, and I'm sorry, I am. I can't help it. Not this time."

"That's what you always say. 'Not this time.' Is there ever going to be a right time?" Then he'd stormed out the door.

There was truth to everything he said. I'd missed Ali's first words; the day she learned she didn't need to grab hold of a table or bench to inch her way from one end of a room to the other. When Ali was officially potty trained, Tim's mommy group learned before I did.

I'd missed all her firsts, and his reaction wasn't simply because of the graduation. It was everything I'd missed. But that was over. I had been so, so wrong. I wasn't responsible for Kate's death; I didn't know why I ever thought I was. Yes, I still wanted to be the one to find the answer, but it didn't *have* to be me. What mattered most was that the answer was found. What mattered most was my family. That was what I wanted to tell him.

Our talk would have to wait. But I could check to see if he was awake. If he wanted coffee. I stood next to our bed and watched him breathe, sound asleep. One arm pillowed his head, and the other stretched out toward my side of the bed, his fingers open and relaxed.

I slipped my shoes off and slid in beside him. I inched closer until our bodies touched. Closing my eyes, I concentrated on breathing slowly. I promised myself I'd get up in a second, but my breath caught when I felt him turn toward me. When I felt him reach his arm around my waist. When I felt his face burrow into my neck.

I was barely willing to draw another breath and risk disturbing the moment. "I love you," I whispered, even though I knew he couldn't hear me. And as I turned to lift myself up out of the bed, his lips curved gently into a smile.

Chapter 34

When Tim called a few hours later and asked me to meet him at the Cameron Estates Inn, I felt it was a sign of everything good that would come to us after so many years of promises broken and harsh words thrown like stones at each other.

I couldn't have picked a better place myself.

We had changed, but the room was still the same, comforting and intimate, with tables spaced far enough apart that no one felt obligated to respond to conversations from nearby guests and a wait-staff that provided service as if you were the only people in the room. Shuttered windows, brick walls, and flickering candlelight gave a glimpse into a different time while providing all the luxuries of the twenty-first century.

It was the best place for a reconciliation, and after last night, after what I'd learned from Laura, and Ned, Tim and I were due a fresh start. But only after I apologized for almost ruining our lives.

I unfolded my napkin, placed it on my lap, and smiled at Tim. "This is lovely." The dinner invitation clearly meant he'd forgiven me for missing Ali's graduation. Why else would he have asked me to meet him there, at the very restaurant where he had asked me to marry him?

Tim ordered for us, a Manhattan for him and a glass of Pinot Gris for me, a Domaine Weinbach Pinot. My favorite. The last time I sipped that wine and felt that hopeful was the day Tim brought a bottle home to celebrate the removal of the last drop cloth and the last sheet of plastic from our newly restored home. Right down to the slate-tile backsplash and the yellowware bowls filled with fresh vegetables in the pantry, the vision in our heads had become a reality. The wine had been the perfect accompaniment to that celebration, and it would be perfect for the current one also.

And the night was a celebration. The end of the craziness that had plagued me for almost my entire life. I couldn't wait to tell Tim my news.

Our glasses lightly touched when Tim tipped his toward mine. I wanted to make a toast to new beginnings. I wanted to tell him how wrong I'd been, but Tim beat me to it while the first sip of ice-cold wine released a hint of lemon into my mouth.

"Ned mentioned when I saw him last week that you were both pretty excited about a new drug that's hit the market."

One more sip gave me the patience to put aside my thoughts, and I launched easily into a response regarding the research to determine if Avastin would be successful in preventing the recurrence of GBM. "The drug isn't new," I explained. "It's just new for use with GBM patients, and we're still testing it. There are side effects that need consideration, so we're weighing the risks against any possible gains. But yes, it is pretty exciting. Anything that gives us hope these days is exciting."

For once in my life, I wanted to talk about something other than my work. Or Ned. The last thing I wanted to talk about was Ned. But Tim didn't know yet that my relationship with Ned was over. I didn't know if I could go it alone; the only thing I knew for sure was that Ned would never again be a part of my personal life, no matter how much that terrified me.

I needed to tell Tim what I'd learned last night, but looking around the room, letting the intoxicating aromas tease me, I suddenly wanted to enjoy a few more minutes of the lovely evening with my husband.

"Tell me about your new book. Ali tells me it's all about knights in shining armor and grand ladies in distress, but I'm pretty sure you only told her that because little girls love stories about knights in shining armor. So what's it really about?"

I expected Tim to weave a story that would make me hold my breath until I'd heard the hope-filled ending. I expected to hear beautiful words and feel my eyes well up, but he just looked at me and stayed silent. Only then did I realize that he had never unfolded his dinner napkin; it was sitting dead center on his plate. I couldn't seem to look away from it.

My glass was empty, but magically, another appeared, and even though I never had more than one, I welcomed the sight of that glass and the wine it held. I didn't know why that damn napkin bothered me, but it did, and I started to babble.

"Your call was such a pleasant surprise. Your suggestion to meet *here*, where we have so much history—it's, well, it's very touching." I reached out then, across the table, my eyes glued to his hand, expecting it to open and meet me halfway. Instead, his knuckles turned white where his fingers had wrapped themselves tightly around his glass.

And still I talked, choosing to ignore what my eyes told me. Instead of slowing down that evening to enjoy every second, I was suddenly anxious to blurt out how wrong I'd been. To tell him about Ned. "I'm very—"

But he interrupted me before I could say more.

"Emma." That was all he said. My name sounded flat to my ears, as if it were made of cardboard and headed toward the trash. He picked up his glass and downed its contents. It reminded me of last night when Ned had gulped his drink before talking about Kate's death.

I blinked at the sight of Tim's empty glass, at his voice so tight I could have walked across it. My hand crept back toward my side of the table, and I quickly lowered it from sight, an appendage that needed to disappear before it embarrassed me again.

Tim spoke my name again as if he thought I hadn't heard him the first time. "Emma!"

Then it hit me how people felt compelled to pinpoint exactly when something horrific happened. Something that turned out to be so pivotal to every part of the rest of their lives, they reeled from the effects for years. Maybe forever. Because—and I didn't know why—for some reason, we seemed to need to remember who we were before and how it changed us after. We needed to put a date to the thing that destroyed us. An exact month. A day. A year. We even went so far as to believe that if we had done one thing differently, we could have stopped the horror that was headed our way.

"Not just yet," Tim uttered to the waiter who had suddenly appeared at our table with a list of the specials for the night.

I watched the waiter head toward the next table, and I thought about how we all remembered where we were and who we were with and what we were doing the morning those planes slammed into the towers and destroyed our country's innocence forever. For our parents, it was the day they realized no man was safe: not JFK, or Bobby, or Martin Luther King, Jr.

"Tim?" I closed my eyes for a second. It was a delay technique I used when I knew bad news was headed toward me, but even with my eyes closed, I saw his napkin, crisp and untouched. When I opened my eyes and looked directly into his beautiful face, I saw how hard it was for him, too, and I wanted to make it easier, but I couldn't.

"Please. You're scaring me. What is it?" I would remember what happened next for the rest of my life. Whatever Tim said was going to be one of those moments, and by the time he finished saying what he had intended to say, I was going to wish I'd done one thing differently.

"I filed for a divorce. I'm sorry, Emma, but I can't do this anymore."

My hand jerked, knocking over my glass of wine. "What?"

Our waiter appeared immediately and sopped it up while I held my words inside. Another showed up with a fresh glass. Throughout those ministrations, I waited; it seemed an eternity until I could clarify.

"What did you say?" Each word quivered as it fell from my mouth. *He can't mean divorce. Not now.*

"I can't live the way we live, and I don't want Ali to live this way either. She's coming with me." His words flowed like syrup, smooth and slick, sickeningly sweet. They spread across the table and dripped silently onto my lap, where my hands clutched desperately at my napkin.

I should have prepared for it long ago—as if one could prepare for such a thing. I'd given Tim every opportunity to leave, and when he didn't, I thought he'd seen what I saw: my situation was temporary. The future could be everything we'd dreamt it could be.

"But Ali's not even six," I begged, not wanting to make a scene but unable to keep the hurt out of my voice. "She needs me. She needs her mother." I had no right to say that. All those years I hadn't been a mother. But I was ready. Once I told him what I'd learned, he would know I was ready. He'd understand.

"No," Tim said softly, his voice a rasp of pain. And the words that followed were just as soft. "She doesn't."

I turned away. *This morning. Just this morning, I saw you smile. I did. I felt you reach for me.* My eyes filled. I tried to focus on something other than his words. I couldn't cry. Not there. Besides, I never cried. I stared at the wavery glow of candlelight across the room; each flame seemed to bleed into the next.

Then I faced him. "Because I didn't go to Ali's graduation? You invited me to dinner here? Where you proposed marriage, where I accepted, where we were so happy? I thought... I thought..." I strove to keep my voice low, but with each word, it gained strength.

I could see by the look on his face that when he'd called and arranged for us to meet there, he never connected the restaurant with where our story had started. I could see that, for him, all the years since that night had turned our history of the place to dust.

"But... but I came here tonight to tell you I was wrong. I came here tonight—"

"Emma, stop! I don't want to know why you came here tonight."

"But it's important. What I have to say changes everything. Ned—"

"No!" Tim's words were brittle, his eyes little pinpricks of black. "I don't care."

I tried to strike back, like an animal who'd been poked, but even to me, my question was pathetic. "Why didn't you just have me served with the papers?" And somehow, when his head jerked upward at my question, I knew the answer before he even opened his mouth.

"You'll be getting them tomorrow. At your office."

He stood then and walked out. He never looked back.

What I learned that night was that once Tim stopped loving me, he just stopped. He no longer felt what I felt; he no longer cared what I felt. I doubted he meant to be cruel. Maybe he didn't think he was cruel. Maybe he was just done.

Again, I tried hard not to think of what would have happened if I'd done one thing differently. But the truth of it was, it was never just one thing.

Chapter 35

I held on to that damn napkin as if it might save me.

When Tim quickly stood and walked out of the dining room, people turned toward our table then just as quickly turned away, sensing, maybe, the angst of his hasty exit yet wishing to be respectful and overrule their need for a dose of drama.

Who knew? Maybe they also noticed his napkin still sitting dead center on his dinner plate. Maybe they knew he wouldn't be back.

IT WAS SNOWING WHEN I finally stood and walked out to my car. The first snow of the season, it was meant to make the world hopeful and pure, but all I saw was the sorrow in Tim's eyes when he told me he didn't want to hear what I had to say.

The windshield wipers swept away the flakes so I could see the road, but I never bothered to swipe at the tears that rolled down my cheeks. I kept both hands on the wheel and stared straight ahead.

A little less than two inches of white had fallen by the time I pulled into my driveway, but more was coming, and I should have pulled into the garage. Instead, I put the car in park, turned off the engine, and walked into the house without even bothering to take off my boots.

Oblivious to the little puddles of snow that melted behind me, I walked into the library to find Miss Maggie sleeping soundly in Tim's chair, a copy of her latest Agatha Christie propped on her chest.

"Miss Maggie?"

Just my hand on her shoulder brought her upright. She looked around as if to reacquaint herself with her surroundings, squared her shoulders, pushed my hand away, and fumbled for her watch. "I'm awake. I'm awake."

I knew as well as anyone that she considered it a personal affront to be disturbed when she was sleeping, but I didn't want her stiff in the morning from sleeping in the chair all night. "I see that. It's time for bed. You can tell me all about your evening with Ali in the morning." All I wanted was to crawl into bed and pull the covers over my head, but to do that, I needed to get Miss Maggie moving.

"Why are you home so early?"

"It's snowing." I felt like I did when Kate and I'd been caught doing something we shouldn't and hoped the shortest of answers would get me off the hook. As if those two simple words could explain why I found myself home at seven thirty on a night that I'd expected would be one of the best nights of my life.

"Come on. Let's go upstairs. If you want to read more, at least you can do it lying in bed, where you'll be more comfortable." I didn't have whatever it might take to make my voice sound normal. I just hoped she was tired enough not to notice.

Miss Maggie had stood to gather her things. "Where's Tim?"

I started to tell her he'd already gone upstairs. "He's—" The words caught in my throat. I couldn't lie. I picked up the coverlet she'd used to drape across her knees and started to fold it, but when it slipped from my fingers, I left it where it dropped. "He's not here." *I have no idea where he is. All I know for sure is that he'll be here in the morning. For Ali.*

"Well, I can see that. Where is he?" By then she was wide-awake. And as usual, demanding answers.

"He's leaving."

"Tonight? Where's he going? I thought you said it was snowing?" She moved to the window as if to reassure herself that I'd been right about the weather.

I drew in a breath then blew it out. "I don't know where he's going. He's leaving *me*. He's taking Ali. Divorcing me."

I curled up on the settee and drew my knees up so I could wrap my arms around my legs. I rested my forehead against my hands, curling into a little ball, needing to make myself small, and even though a fire roared in the fireplace and I could practically feel the flames lick at me, I was freezing.

Miss Maggie's eyes widened. "Emma." She reached up to the collar of her sweater as if to be sure it was still there, then she sat down beside me. "What do you mean?"

Do I even know what this means? My head rested on my hands, my words muffling into my body. "I know. You're shocked."

"Don't be ridiculous. Only a fool would think you two were happy."

"Well, then, I guess you could say my parents are fools." Her words had forced a bark of laughter out of me.

"Yes, well, we don't need to talk about that. Tell me what happened."

"It was that damn kindergarten graduation. I told you about it. No. That's not true. It's everything. He wants more for himself and for Ali, and... and I can't blame him. The thing of it is—"

When I lost track of my words, she reached out and put her hand on my arm. "The thing of it is?"

It all came out then. Everything I'd learned over the past two days. Ned and Kate and how I thought I had to be the one to find a cure because I'd lived and Kate had died.

"It's not that I thought he'd never leave. But when he didn't, I—I thought he'd wait for me. I thought he understood that all of this was temporary." My eyes felt gritty, and when I tried to focus, spots filled my vision. "I thought I could make up for everything. I thought I still had time."

I reached for a tissue in the pocket of the coat I'd never bothered to take off and found the damn napkin I'd carried home from the restaurant.

Chapter 36

Neither of us could walk past Ali's room without stopping to watch. Her chest rose and fell in that easy way of soundly sleeping children blessed with health and happiness—arms flung over her head, blankets tossed aside, the slightest smile lighting up her entire face.

"When is Tim coming to pick her up?" Miss Maggie's voice splintered the silence.

"Tomorrow sometime. I don't know. In the morning." I couldn't take my eyes off Ali. "Do you think I'll ever see her again?"

"Of course you'll see her. I don't know where they're going, but he's going to let you visit. He's not a monster."

FOR THE FIRST TIME in years, I wished I could pull the covers over my head and hide. And maybe things would be different when I finally reached for my robe and decided to start my day. Maybe last night had been a dream. A nightmare. Maybe Tim and Ali and I could begin the rest of our lives today.

I shook my head. I knew better than to believe in miracles. Flinging the covers aside, I pulled myself out of bed. I'd finally taken my coat off sometime in the middle of the night, but the cashmere sheath I'd worn for dinner was twisted around my waist.

Showered and dressed, I found Miss Maggie sitting on the bench in the hallway when I opened my bedroom door. She stood when she saw me and quickly launched into what had kept her up into the early-morning hours. "Let me talk some sense into Tim."

"No. This is my responsibility. I want you to stay up here until they leave."

"Don't be silly. I can help." She reached up and captured a lock of hair that had slipped from my quickly made ponytail, but I gently swatted at her hand.

"No. You can't fix this."

"You are a damn stubborn girl. Pardon my French."

Nodding, I walked past her, focused only on making coffee for Tim and tea for me.

Both the coffee and tea were set to steep when I was startled by a knock at the door. *Oh Lord, who can that be now?* Tim wasn't due for another thirty minutes. But when I opened the door without bothering to check, expecting to find some religious group eager to thrust a pamphlet into my hand, I found Tim. He'd meant everything he'd said last night. No one knocked at their own front door unless they didn't live there anymore.

Tim walked in and stomped his feet lightly, dislodging the snow he'd walked through to get to the front door. I watched as he sat on the bench to remove his boots and place them in the boot tray we kept for such things. Ali's red snow boots were already there, waiting for her.

I hadn't thought about the sidewalks covered with snow. The car sitting outside. Snow removal had always been Tim's job. I was going to need to think of those things.

Tim's voice broke the silence. "I'm early." He reached into his pocket, pulled out his house keys, and set them gently in the bowl we kept on the table near the door. The move forced me to suck in my breath.

"Here, give me your coat. Ali's still sleeping, but I've made coffee." My words came slowly, as if they were stuck somewhere deep inside me and I had to haul them out one by one.

Tim sat at his usual spot at the table, and I sat at mine, each with our fingers wrapped around a steaming mug. Again, I could almost pretend it was a normal day. I would promise to be home early, and Tim would pretend to believe me. *And that's exactly why you're sitting here this morning.*

I considered my options: begging for forgiveness, throwing myself at his feet, grabbing his knees and refusing to let go until he was forced to drag me along as he mounted the stairs toward Ali's room. I believed for one quick second that he would never turn away from me. That once more, he'd forgive me.

I couldn't imagine a life without him and Ali. Didn't want to. I wanted to explain how wrong I'd been in believing I'd needed to atone for Kate's tumor because it had struck her brain and not mine. Her death hadn't been my fault.

But I was too late. I'd broken too many promises. It must have been almost impossible for him to make his decision, but he'd made it. And somewhere deep inside, I knew it was in Ali's best interests for them to leave, no matter what Miss Maggie said.

We sat in silence for a few minutes until finally I asked what worried me most. "What will you tell Ali?"

Tim cleared his throat, and his words, once they came, were dry as dust. His eyes were glued to his coffee mug while he spoke. "I'm going to tell her we're going on an adventure. I'm going to tell her we'll build snow castles and we'll make snow angels. And when we come inside, we'll make hot chocolate."

He finally stopped staring at his mug and looked up into my eyes. "I'm going to tell her about her new school and her new home." His hand reached out toward me, and I stared at it. One finger gently traced my thumb as it rested on the handle of my mug. "I'm going to tell her that you can't come with us."

I held steady on to my mug and nodded. When Tim walked to the sink and rinsed out his mug, I didn't move. I felt his hesitation and could almost guess that he considered placing it in the dishwasher but then thought better of it.

TIM HAD ARRANGED TO take just a few of Ali's things, and I'd agreed to ship the rest when they were settled, so it wasn't long until I heard him helping her on with her boots and coat. Until the front door closed behind them.

Then the house was silent. Or as silent as two-hundred-year-old houses could be. I picked up my mug of tea and placed it near Tim's coffee mug. I would deal with them later.

I couldn't help myself. Once I reached the upstairs hallway window, I looked out, almost blinded by the whiteness. It reminded me of winters when Kate and I had wanted to sled down the Chadwicks' snow-covered hills and I'd been too afraid to ring their doorbell and ask permission.

I saw two sets of footprints, one large and one small. Tim had matched his stride to Ali's. The whoosh of air I sucked in clouded the window when I finally let it out. I wiped my palm over the cold glass and watched as the falling snow filled in the indentations from their boots. Within minutes, there was nothing left to see.

Something as simple as a footprint shouldn't have hurt so much.

"I NEVER SAW IT COMING."

I had begged Susan for an emergency appointment, even though I'd stopped seeing her three years ago. "That's not true." I shook my head. "I've seen it coming for years. I just closed my eyes to it."

She barely had time to sit before I started blathering, not the same patient she'd had to pry each word out of when I'd first started sessions with her. Today, I couldn't shut the hell up.

"Why don't you start—"

"At the beginning," I finished for her. She wasn't talking fast enough. "We argued over Ali's preschool graduation. I couldn't go. I *couldn't*, and I knew Tim was angry..."

I felt a need to fill the silence. "Tim hadn't spoken to me in days, but then he invited me to dinner." I left out the part about earlier that morning, feeling him curl into me, watching the slow smile that touched his lips even though he was still sound asleep. It was—it was too painful. "I thought he'd forgiven me. I'd wanted to tell him that everything would be different now, but he didn't want to hear it. He didn't want to hear anything I had to say." I drew in a deep breath and struggled to calm myself.

"Why did you think your life would be different?"

Her question stopped me cold. How much could I give up? "Ned no longer controls my life." I chose each word carefully, weighing its worth before I said it out loud. My cheeks drew in for a beat while I tiptoed around Ned's words until I found a pared-down explanation of the truth. "He... he's not the man I thought he was."

"No?" Susan's left eyebrow rose.

"I know you're not surprised." I looked at my hands clasped tightly in my lap. At the throbbing callus on my thumb. "I know you've long thought Ned had control over me." I looked up with eyes blurred with tears. "You were right. You were right about everything, and I should have listened when you wanted to talk about Ned. He's why I stopped seeing you."

"Emma." Susan reached across the small table between us and placed her hand on mine. "It's not a matter of right. Or wrong. Can you elaborate on why Ned is no longer the man you thought he was?"

No matter how I felt about Ned, I couldn't give up his secrets. I sat up straight and remembered what he'd said: *Sometimes, sacrifices must be made.* "No."

"No?" She seemed to consider the swiftness of my answer, but for whatever reason, she dropped the subject. At least for the moment. "Tell me what's most important to you right now."

"Now? My family's what's most important to me. But... they're better off where they are." *Stop lying. Stop lying. Stop lying. All I think about is opening my front door to find them standing there with smiles on their faces. Wanting to come home. If I let myself, I can feel the weight of Tim's body leaning into mine and the warmth of his arms when he wraps them around me. If I let myself, I can feel the hardness of the wooden floor when I fall to my knees in front of Ali and hug her. If I really let myself, I can feel Ali hugging me back. It's all I've ever wanted.*

"Why would you say that?" Hearing her question made me think she didn't know anything at all about me.

"I never got the chance to put them first." I paused and backed up. "That's not true. I had plenty of chances. I just never did. I never put them first. And now, well, now it's too late. Now I'll never get that chance."

Susan removed her glasses and placed them carefully on the little table between us. I recognized the habit and felt myself stiffen. Yet still I was startled. "Does that give you a sense of relief?"

"What?" My heart felt like it would beat out of my chest.

"Giving up is easier than fighting, and what I see right now is you giving up. Because it's easier." Susan's voice was calm. Careful. But her words forced me to defend myself.

"No! No! It's what's best for them. They're better off without me."

"Why do you say that?"

"Because. Because what if I can't keep my promise?" *Just the thought terrifies me.* "What if this time is like all the others? What if I go back to putting medicine first? To putting Kate first."

"What if you put you first? What would you want then?"

I didn't know.

Chapter 37

Miss Maggie looked around the library as if she'd spotted a rat in the corner. "You need to sell this place."

"Just because I need to replace the electrical panel doesn't mean I need to replace the entire house." I slammed shut the overstuffed bottom drawer of my desk and hoped that would settle the question. That wasn't the first time Maggie had brought up the selling-the-house subject.

"The entire house could go up in flames."

I nodded. "Well, that would take care of the mess this desk is in." The drawer was closed—barely—but crammed so full the damn stuff was trying to escape. Edges of papers stuck out, and when I tried to stuff them back in, I couldn't get the drawer open again.

"Damn!"

"What's wrong?"

"The drawer's stuck."

We'd been enjoying a glass of wine, a new Saturday evening habit, and I'd gotten it into my head that the paperwork the contractor had left with me was in that drawer, but when I'd searched, I found everything but. Including the original copy of my divorce, which should probably have been in my lockbox instead of the desk. Just looking at the divorce decree reminded me of how desperate I'd been for Susan to help me when Tim filed for divorce.

I spread the document out on my desk and traced my fingers over the seal that proclaimed us separate. If, as Miss Maggie suggested, the house were to burn down, the desk probably wasn't the safest place to store it.

It *was* ridiculous to stay there; the house was huge and always in need of repairs. And I'd never gotten used to the silence. To the echo of my footsteps when I moved from room to room. But how could I leave? That was our home.

My voice went flat, mired down with hope that seemed, well, hopeless. "I can't sell the house. You know that. I need to be here if they come back." Then, as if I'd found ammunition, I shot back, "Besides, you stayed in your house after Anne died."

"It's different when you lose someone to death. I *know* Anne's not coming back. I'm not wasting my life waiting for miracles." Miss Maggie's eyebrows drew together. "You should be out, not sitting around with me on a Saturday. You need to start dating again. You need—"

She looked around the library, searching for... I didn't know what, then she completely changed direction. "And what in the hell—pardon my French—will you do with seven bedrooms?"

I couldn't help myself. I laughed. "I'll open a brothel." I did my own looking around, wanting to dramatize my suggestion. "What do you think? This room could be the meet-up room. You know, where the ladies snare the man of their choice?" I had no idea how brothels worked. I wasn't sure that word was even used anymore, but it was worth watching the way Miss Maggie's lips disappeared.

"You shouldn't joke. And I don't think that's how it works. The men pick out the women."

"Really? Well, it should be the other way around."

Miss Maggie's eyes landed on the bookshelves where my medical journals resided along with a first edition of every book Tim had written. "Perhaps while they wait their, um, turn, they can peruse your bookshelves."

I never could best her. "Perhaps."

Chapter 38

Susan looked just as healthy and vibrant as ever, while I was well aware I'd lost weight in the last six months, and my eyes looked like I hadn't closed them in weeks. Fortunately, she kept any comments about my appearance to herself.

"So tell me how you're doing."

I laughed. "Since the last time I saw you?"

It helped to work into things. "Ned retired. Did you know? I was named chief of Oncology. David reports directly to me now."

"Well, that must make you happy."

I had the decency to blush. "It's not like that. At least, not anymore. Once my promotion was announced, we fell into a sort of partnership. And it works. We've become friends, and David's turned into a brilliant surgeon. It turns out he never really wanted my job. He knew Ned had used him as leverage against me. Ned being out of the picture removed the stress between us."

"So how is Ned?"

There was so much I could say, but still I kept his secrets. "I don't know. I don't see him, since he's no longer at the hospital."

There was so much I didn't say. How he'd shown up unannounced at my house with his need to explain. My refusal to let him in. How he'd stood on my front porch and said what he'd come to say, anyway.

"I was done the moment I heard your car door slam when you left my house. In that single moment, I saw what I'd done." His words were low, but I'd fought against leaning into them. He'd looked out over my

land while he talked, at the trees and the vastness of all that I cherished. He looked anywhere but at me.

"I didn't start out to be a bad man, Emma. I made wrong choices. And I kept making them." He'd shrugged when he finally brought his eyes to mine. "Until that was all that was left—my pile of bad choices."

I'd had only one question for him. "You're not talking about the night Kate died, are you?"

Ned's words burrowed into my head as I carefully answered Susan. "The only way Ned could accept Kate's death was to do everything in his power to eradicate the tumor that had killed her."

Remembering Ned's words, I added, "I think Ned started out like most of us, good and kind. Honest." I closed my eyes, remembered how much I'd loved him when I was a child, and then opened them again so I could look straight into Susan's. "Ned felt like he'd failed Kate. And it ate him up."

"There seem to be similarities between your story and Ned's."

I nodded, even though there was a time I would have taken great offense at her comment. "Kate's death nearly destroyed us both."

I'd never fully resolved the guilt I felt in both failing to put my family first and that one instant of insanity when I'd stood at the top of the basement stairs and considered a life that didn't include Ali, but I'd finally accepted that there was a place for me in the world.

"I think Ned and I just dealt with our guilt in different ways."

Susan's head tilted to one side. "Think of what you call your guilt as a wound or a scab. Maybe even a scar. It leaves a mark that never goes away completely, but it's not bleeding or infected either. It's survivable."

Again, I nodded. It was a great analogy. I repeated her words in my head in hopes I would remember them when the time came to give myself a pep talk.

"So, how *are* you coping without Tim and Ali?"

I thought about the last few years. It had gotten easier. Somewhat. "Better. I think? I'm busy. I work long days. Right now, my team has three case studies where the tumor progression has slowed enough that an additional six to eight weeks of life can reasonably be expected."

I'd always talked to Susan about my work. It was so much a part of me, it was hard not to. "That's an additional six to eight weeks to find an answer—not a *cure*. We've almost given up on a cure. Right now, what we're hoping to find is a way to remove the tumor whole so it doesn't grow back."

Susan looked suitably impressed. "That's wonderful."

"It is. We're nowhere near where we need to be to present formal findings, but we've received enough grant money to keep the research going. So we're really optimistic, even if I'm pretty much drop-dead busy."

The look that passed across Susan's face was one I'd seen before. "What?"

She laughed. "You know me too well. I just want to suggest you not cover up your feelings with work. So, what brings you here today? I was surprised when I saw you scheduled an appointment."

"I can't sleep. More like I'm afraid to sleep."

Susan's office was warm from the sun streaming through the windows, and the glass of iced tea I held was sweating. Droplets of water beaded up on my skirt, and I brushed them away, suddenly feeling foolish. "And I don't need to tell you that a surgeon who can't sleep can't pick up a scalpel and expect anything good to come from it."

"Afraid? What do you think will happen when you close your eyes?"

I shook my head. "Not afraid like a monster's going to get me. Just that I hold off closing my eyes because when I sleep, I dream about Kate. And I don't want to dream about her or think about her. That part of my life is over. Yes, I've dedicated my life to glioblastoma because of Kate. But Kate herself? She's dead, and I need to accept that."

Susan listened like she always had: full in. "How long has this been going on?"

I tried to remember. "It seems like forever. I don't know, maybe six months?"

I dug at the callus on my thumb while I talked, my finger rubbing against the roughened patch until little pieces of dead skin sloughed off into my lap. I stopped only when I noticed Susan watching, and I felt my face grow warm. "Sorry. One bad habit I've never been able to stop. Anyway, that's when I knew I needed to see you—when I looked in the mirror one morning and decided I can't stay awake forever." I sat on my hand. It was the only thing that worked.

"What is it specifically that you think about Kate?"

"Sometimes, I think about when we were kids, but mostly, I guess I think about the work I'm doing right now, the clinical trials, new medications. If only all of it had been available when she was diagnosed. There would have been so much hope for her."

Susan nodded. "That's a pretty normal feeling." Her left eyebrow rose slightly. "Do you still think you need to save Kate?"

I scrubbed at the sudden goose bumps that covered my arms. "I don't know. Maybe."

Chapter 39

"The median overall survival rate for GBM patients has increased only a little over three months in the last twenty-five years." I looked from face to face, wondering whether any of them had what it took to see past the failures and hang on until they identified the right procedure or combination of procedures to fight the tumor.

"That, ladies and gentlemen, is one piss-poor statistic."

Along with research and patients, because Lancaster General was a teaching hospital, I was also responsible for training each new batch of interns when they showed up on my rotation. Teaching pulled me out of myself; it stopped me from thinking, at least for a little while, about one of my last sessions with Susan. *Did* I think I still needed to save Kate? When she was already dead and couldn't be saved?

Mentally, I shook my head. I couldn't deal with my own fears, not then, anyway. Not with a class filled with soon-to-be doctors sorely in need of instruction. So I dealt with their fears instead. And it made me push them even harder. If they were going to become doctors, I wanted them to be good ones.

"Surgical resection is the standard treatment for GBM, but the recurrence rate of the tumor is high, and additional surgeries involve additional risk. This is why we are lucky to be involved with this new trial."

I came close to telling some of the most promising students that if they ended up choosing oncology as their specialty, they'd need to suck it up, because otherwise they'd never make it. And then I worried I was too tough. Those words were too close to Ned's "never give up," and I swore I'd never be like him.

"This trial is only phase one, which means we are coming in at the beginning. Which is where we want to be. Basically, what we're dealing with, first, is a dose-finding study. We need to determine the maximum tolerated dose of the LAG-3 antibody."

I looked out over the faces before me and wondered which of them had the balls to make themselves stand out in that group, where they had all been first in their class but suddenly found themselves only one of many. It was a position they were unused to, and many of them sank rather than fought for what previously had been a given.

"Who can tell me what the LAG-3 gene is?"

My eyes jumped from face to face while I waited for an answer. Not even one hand shot upward. "It's a protein." I spoke slowly, hard-pressed to hide my exasperation. "Right now, the estimated completion date for this trial is set for August of next year. And remember, this is only phase one. We need things to move faster, people."

"JUST BECAUSE I'M CRABBY doesn't mean I taught a class today." I poured a glass of wine and leaned against the kitchen island with my phone caught between my chin and my shoulder while I listened to Miss Maggie tell me how I felt.

"Did you teach a class today?"

"Yes, but—"

"Are you crabby?"

I took a long swallow then pulled the bottle back out of the fridge, knowing I'd need a refill soon. "Well, according to you, I am."

Miss Maggie laughed. "A perfect stranger could tell you were crabby."

"There are no perfect strangers."

"True enough. So what did they do wrong this time?"

Already, I'd lost track of the conversation. "Who? My students? They didn't do anything wrong. They just don't have any fire. They're too complacent. Doctors all over the world are trying to find an answer to stop the GBM tumor from growing back, and these people just sit there and look at me when I ask a question."

"Emma. Just listen to yourself. Not everyone's willing to work twelve, fifteen hours a day. Not everyone chooses to spend the night on the couch in their office instead of heading home to their own bed."

"I didn't—"

"Don't even start, young lady. Gail called me this morning to see if I could talk some sense into you."

I laughed and took another sip of wine that was more like a gulp. "Guess I'm busted."

"I guess you are. You're going to make yourself sick—"

"No. I'm not," I interrupted, which was pretty much taking my life in my hands. Miss Maggie did not take well to interruptions. It wasn't respectful. "Sometimes, I wish time would just stand still. You know? So we could catch up with this damn disease. Time is every researcher's enemy. There's never enough of it."

It was Miss Maggie's turn to laugh. "Time doesn't stand still. For anyone. Which is why you need to think about dating again. It's been three years since your divorce was final."

"Well, time should stand still, and I don't have time to date. Let's talk about something else. How was your day, and when are you going to consider moving in here with me?"

"To answer your questions, fine and never. But here's a new topic. I had lunch with Ned today."

I sighed, maybe a little too loudly. "I really don't want to talk about Ned."

"No? Well, that's unfortunate because I do. And it's going to take more than you groaning into the phone to get me to shut up. I know you think Ned should be punished to within an inch of his life, but he did what he had to do. He did what most of us, if we were honest with ourselves, wish we'd had the guts to do. And believe me, he doesn't need you to punish him. He's punished himself a thousand times over whatever you would do to him."

"Miss Maggie—"

"I'm not done yet. You need to let this go. If for no other reason than you could use his help. I would think you would look kindly on anyone who could help you with this bastard—pardon my French—tumor."

"Can I talk now?"

"No. Still, he would do it all again if he had to."

"You're going to make me regret I ever told you about the night Kate died."

"That might be true, but you already told me. Too late now for regrets."

"Trust me, Miss Maggie. It's never too late for regrets."

Chapter 40

I slapped at my alarm clock, but the damn ringing didn't stop. *The phone. It has to be the phone.*

"'lo?"

"Dr. Blake, this is Steve Henderson. Sorry to disturb you, but we had a patient come in last night with a head injury, and you're going to want to take a look at the scans."

I forced myself into a sitting position. "Talk."

"Christopher Charles, age fifteen, head injury from the ski slopes at Round Top. We did a CT scan that indicated a slight amount of bleeding in the brain. So I ordered an MRI."

"And?"

"The MRI indicates a mass."

I glanced at the clock. It was a little after five. "I had to get up soon, anyway." I yawned. "I'll be there in an hour." *It must be one helluva mass.*

GAIL HANDED ME THE file the minute I walked into the office.

I looked at my watch. It was six thirty. "How did you know to be here so early?"

"Henderson called me after he talked to you. He knew you'd want to see these scans ASAP. Just so you know, the family's here."

I nodded. "Awfully early."

"They never left. They've been here all night."

Being a parent can be hell. "Okay. Bring me a cup—"

Gail smiled. "It's just about ready."

I signed in to my computer, opened the image, and found myself eye to eye with a large mass.

I pressed the intercom. "Get me—"

"They're here."

One of these days, I'll catch her off guard. "Send them in."

When the door opened, I stood. "Mr. and Mrs. Charles. Please. Sit." Indicating the two chairs positioned in front of my desk, I smiled as warmly as I could under the circumstances. "Can I get you a cup of coffee?" The words were no sooner out of my mouth than Gail returned with two mugs of coffee and a basket of muffins.

Mrs. Charles wrapped her hands gratefully around the steaming mug. "We came as soon as they called us. We were sleeping, but we just threw on some clothes..." She looked down at what she was wearing, a pair of jeans with rips in all the right places and a turtleneck, thick and wooly. "We—"

Mr. Charles placed his hand on her arm. "It's okay, Bethanne. They know we got here as soon as we could."

It seemed a good place to start. "Mr. and Mrs. Charles—"

"Please. Bethanne and Christopher Senior. Big Chris."

I nodded. "Bethanne and... and Big Chris. I've reviewed the results of the CT and MRI scans, and I'd like to talk to you about what I see."

Big Chris nodded. "You're chief of Oncology. We're a little confused about why you've been called in."

"Yes. Well, let me back up a bit so I'm sure you're aware of everything. When Christopher was brought in last night, a CT scan was ordered because of the head injury. That scan reflected a small amount of blood on his brain." Bethanne's eyes grew round, and I knew I would need to explain, but first, I wanted to give them the results of the MRI. "Because of that blood, an MRI was ordered. The MRI reflects a large mass on Christopher's brain."

I stopped to let that sink in. Bethanne clutched at her purse as if she were about to be robbed. "What do you mean, mass?" Her words came out soft and feathery, yet they were obviously foreign to her.

Big Chris remained silent, his earlier outgoing demeanor apparently subdued when I threw "large mass" into the conversation. I imagined him mentally gathering all the information they'd been told between last night and that morning and attempting to reach a conclusion. But the look on his face told me that when he reviewed the data, he could do no more than back away from it. If I had to guess, I would guess he was a numbers man. Comfortable only when dealing with hard facts. Numbers didn't lie.

"I'd like to perform a brain biopsy to determine what's going on. But before I do that, I'd like to ask you some questions. Has Christopher experienced any severe headaches lately? Any nausea, vomiting? Vision problems?"

At each question, they shook their heads. Big Chris scrubbed at his face as if he could wash away what was beginning to look like fear. "Are you saying Christopher has a brain tumor?" Unlike Bethanne's, his words were flat. Hard.

"I'm saying I don't know. It's extremely rare that a mass this size would not produce symptoms. Are you sure he hasn't had any physical issues?"

Bethanne sat upright. "Of course we're sure. Christopher is our only child. We—"

I raised my hand. "Please. You don't need to defend yourself. I can see how concerned you both are. What I'd like to do is what's called an open biopsy. What that means is that I'll remove a small piece of the mass and have it examined by a pathologist to determine the status. If it's possible to remove the mass, I'll do it at that time rather than operate a second time. I'll need your permission to do this. If you agree, Gail will give you the necessary papers."

I had to hand it to them. They listened to every word. "Of course, you're going to want to talk about this. But I have to be honest. The sooner I see what's going on, the better Christopher's prognosis will be."

"Are you saying he might die?" They'd both uttered the question, almost simultaneously.

I took a deep breath. And another. "I'm saying that I'd like to perform the biopsy first thing in the morning."

Chapter 41

The biopsy revealed stage 4 glioblastoma multiforme. That meant two things: I wouldn't be removing the tumor. At least not that day. And most likely, Christopher would die.

When Bethanne and Big Chris entered my office, I directed them to the couch instead of the chairs. The chairs were for initial consultations and then again when I was able to give my patients and their families good news. Because sometimes, I actually was able to deliver good news.

The couch was different. Set against the far wall, it was positioned as far away from my desk as possible so that visitors could almost pretend they were there for any reason other than the real one. With its plump cushions, the couch provided a modicum of comfort for a moment or two when my news wasn't good.

Once again, Gail brought in mugs of coffee. I chose the chair adjacent to the couch and sipped my tea, giving them time to settle and myself time to find the right words when there were no right words.

"Mr. and Mrs. Charles—"

"Please. Bethanne and Big Chris."

I chose my words carefully and spoke slowly. "The biopsy revealed a massive brain tumor. Glioblastoma. I'll be honest. I don't know how a tumor of this size could have gone undetected for so long. If it hadn't been for the head trauma Christopher experienced on the ski slopes, I'm not sure when it would have been detected."

At first they sat perfectly still. What I'd just handed them was a lot to take in, and they needed time to process my words. I also knew it wouldn't take long for the room to be filled with questions.

"What do you mean? They said he had a head injury? Glioblastoma? Isn't that the brain tumor?"

Bethanne answered Big Chris's question before I could. "Teddy Kennedy. McCain. Didn't I just read John McCain was diagnosed—"

I interrupted, wanting to get them back on track. "Standard protocol is to remove as much of the center of the tumor as possible and then follow up with radiation and chemotherapy treatments to further reduce the size of the tumor. If we perform this surgery, it's possible Christopher will live another twelve months. If you choose not to allow the surgery, you can expect your son to live about three months."

There were times I hated my job. That moment was one of them. "If that's your decision, we will do everything possible to make your son as comfortable as we can."

I reached forward and put my hand on Bethanne's arm. "If Christopher has the surgery, it's possible he might live longer. Advances are being made every day."

"You're telling us at best our son only has a year to live? Because he hit his head?"

"Bethanne, the head injury didn't cause the tumor. The tumor was already there. I realize I've given you devastating news, but there is another option. There's an experimental procedure to remove the entire tumor. It's only available to patients with less than three months to live."

I stopped. It was a lot to swallow.

"Because of the size of Christopher's tumor, I would like to present his case to our review board for consideration as a candidate for the experimental procedure to remove the entire tumor. With your approval, of course."

"And then Christopher will be cured?"

I watched the glimmer of hope surface on Bethanne's face. Even when I gave her the odds, she didn't flinch. I guessed she was just so sure that God would climb down from his mountain and save Christopher. For no other reason than that he was her child.

"Mrs. Charles—Bethanne, I can't promise you that. This procedure is new. It's risky. We've performed less than a dozen surgeries."

Bethanne looked at Charles, then they turned to me. If they heard my words, they certainly didn't understand them. Bethanne's eyes begged me to explain the tumor to her. "But he never complained about anything. I don't understand."

I couldn't answer her question. I didn't understand either why Christopher had never presented any symptoms. Instead, I talked about Christopher's chance for a full life. "This surgery is the result of years of research by doctors all over the world. If you want Christopher to have this procedure, I need to take his case before the board immediately."

Big Chris never spoke. He listened while his wife bargained for their son's life. I would have never pictured her as the stronger partner, with her manicured nails and perfectly arched brows, but it seemed Big Chris's physical size and resounding voice were of no help to him in that situation.

CHRISTOPHER LOOKED like his father. He was just as big, with thick sandy-brown hair and bushy eyebrows. Big Chris was warm and friendly, at least until he'd been presented with his son's diagnosis. Christopher sucked in every bit of joy life offered, as if his body radiated sunshine.

"Good morning. I'm Dr. Blake. I wanted to meet the up-and-coming chef. Your parents"—I nodded to where Big Chris and Bethanne sat in chairs by Christopher's bed—"they tell me you have big plans, and I thought I'd let you know I have trouble making canned soup."

"Everyone should have trouble making canned soup," Christopher quipped.

Just those few words told me so much about my new patient. "So. Your parents talked to you about what's going on in that head of yours, and I hear you've convinced them to go for the experimental surgery, which, as I told them a short while ago, has just been approved. That's a pretty big decision for you to make. I'd like to talk to you a little about what we're facing. Okay?"

Christopher nodded.

"Without this surgery, you will never get better." While I talked, I never took my eyes off the boy. I wanted to see the second he displayed a flash of fear.

Christopher nodded again. "Mom said maybe I'd have three months. She said you insisted she be straight with me if they were going to let me make the final decision."

"It's a tough decision to make. But I need you to understand that even with the surgery, you might die. This procedure isn't a promise. It's a chance. That's all I can offer you now. A chance."

"I know." He never took his eyes off me. If anything, he seemed to lean in, to make sure he didn't miss any of what I told him. He was a remarkable young man.

"That's all I'm asking for. A chance. I have plans." His smile grew wide as he talked. "I'm sure my family's told you I'm going to the Vermont Culinary School?"

It was my turn to nod. What I noticed immediately was his word choice: He was going to one of the top culinary schools in the country. Not wanted to. Not hoped to. He was *going*.

"At some point, after culinary school and after I've had the opportunity to work in some important restaurants, I plan to open one of my own. Right now, I'm creating recipes for a cookbook I plan to publish. I can't do any of that if I die, and you're the only one who can give me a chance to live. That's what I want. My chance."

It was a lot for a mother and father to hear. Big Chris leaned forward in his chair with his elbows on his knees and his head in his hands. I wanted him to sit upright and look at his son, but he never did. Bethanne, on the other hand, never took her eyes off him.

While Christopher talked about food and the recipes he was creating for his cookbook, I could almost visualize his author photo on the back cover of his book. With that mop of hair falling into his eyes and his wide smile that showed off teeth so white it was hard to believe they were real, he would capture the heart of every cook who even glanced at that book.

"It sounds to me as if you have your entire life planned around food."

Christopher laughed. "That, I do."

"Since you like to plan ahead, let's talk about after the surgery. You'll undergo chemotherapy treatments as a precautionary measure against any lurking cancer cells."

"Okay."

"I'll explain more when the time comes, but I wanted to let you know what comes next. You seem like the kind of guy who needs to know."

When Christopher said he was looking forward to chemotherapy, Bethanne exhaled one strangled sob; it was the first show of pain she'd displayed in front of him. I knew what the boy meant, though. If he was undergoing chemotherapy, he was alive.

I couldn't help comparing his reaction to Kate's. When Kate suffered through chemotherapy, it was simply to keep her alive a little longer. Ned had enrolled her in every clinical trial he could just so he could continue his research and maybe find the answer that would save her.

Kate had dared the almighty hand of cancer to whack her a good one while she underwent chemotherapy. She'd acted as if the sky was her limit, and if she was going to die, she'd have some fun before she did.

I had the feeling Christopher would fight like hell. That was the difference between wanting to live and knowing you wouldn't.

Chapter 42

I knew from my years of medical experience—not from any first-hand parental knowledge—that it was one thing to be told your child would most likely die in three months and quite another to kiss him right before he disappeared into the OR for an experimental surgery and wonder whether you'd just kissed those three months goodbye.

On the day of Christopher's surgery, I imagined that Bethanne and Big Chris looked longingly at that three-month time frame I'd originally given them, thinking that if they'd not let Christopher convince them otherwise, three months would have given them that much longer to beg their God for amnesty.

But Christopher held them to their promise. He didn't want to live if he couldn't dream.

I MADE IT A POINT TO speak to my patients before they succumbed to the nirvana of anesthesia. It was a trust thing. It wasn't that I ever had a lot to say—just a word or two. Just to let them know I valued them. It was no different with Christopher.

"Hey, how's it going?" I smiled into dark-brown eyes fighting the effects of medication meant to help him relax.

I reached for his hand, squeezed his fingers, and tried to show him in every way I could that no matter what happened, it would be okay. I believed that. No matter what, it would be for the best.

He smiled back, his eyes fighting to stay open, and whispered, "When I get out of here, I will cook you chicken basquaise. It'll knock your socks off."

I laughed. "I don't know what that is. But I promise, if you cook it, I'll eat it."

I saw the slightest quiver in his lips; it was the only clue of how hard he fought to be brave.

"You'll love it," he assured me. "It's got es..." Christopher closed his eyes for a moment, opened them wide, and finished, "espelette pepper in it. Makes all the difference in the world."

"Deal." I wanted to think that he fell asleep planning that meal. I wanted to think he closed his eyes happy.

I COULD ALMOST TASTE that chicken... whatever it was called. Christopher's celebratory dinner. Mine too.

The surgery was textbook perfect. I removed the tumor whole, tentacles attached; nothing remained but healthy brain cells. I closed my eyes, and as I'd done with the previous successful surgeries, I mentally thanked every doctor whose name I knew for their part in allowing Christopher to follow his dreams.

There were smiles all around the operating theatre. The team had been with me for every one of those surgeries. They knew the importance of what had occurred there that day.

I turned to David. "Thanks for assisting."

He grinned. "My pleasure. How about we grab everyone later for a drink?"

I started to respond when the head OR nurse yelled my name. I turned from David and looked into a sea of red as she futilely tried to stanch the flow of blood. While David and I had discussed a celebration of another win against GBM, Christopher's brain hemorrhaged. Within seconds, he was dead.

The room went silent. Everyone turned to me as if I might possibly have an explanation. I looked down at the floor, searching for my own answer, and then up at the clock. "Time of death, one forty-five p.m."

I taught my students that if they hoped to become surgeons, they needed to remove their emotions from the equation of a patient-doctor relationship once they hit the OR. It was a rule I'd always believed in.

BETHANNE SAW ME FIRST. She jumped up, a smile on her face. That was how sure she was I'd brought good news.

The tone of my voice caught her attention, though, and instantly, her smile disappeared. "Mr. and Mrs. Charles, will you follow me, please?" I'd been on a first-name basis with their family, but it was important to give them the respect called for at the moment.

When we reached the room reserved for just such things, I opened the door and followed them in. "Please." I felt as if I were talking under water, every word heavy. "Have a seat." I indicated the arranged furniture, plush and comfortable, purposefully selected, just as the couch in my office, to offer comfort. A pitcher of water and glasses were already arranged on the side table.

"Please! You're scaring us. When can we see Christopher?" Again, Big Chris said nothing. But one look told me he'd already seen what Bethanne had not.

I looked directly into their eyes, another thing I taught my students, so that I was sure I had their full attention. I reached out and placed my hand on Bethanne's arm. "I'm so, so sorry, Mr. and Mrs. Charles." I kept my voice level and pain-free, and before either of them could do more than suck in their breath, I kept going. "I removed the tumor." Before that could even sink in, I told them the rest. The last thing I wanted was to offer false hope. "Christopher's brain hemorrhaged. It was unforeseeable, and we were unable to stop the bleeding. We did everything we could, but we couldn't save him. Christopher died a short while ago."

Died. I never wanted to become comfortable with that word. It was important for a doctor to hold on to the pain of death, to never take for granted the trust a family handed over when they asked for help.

I watched as my words sank in. Big Chris stared at his hands as he'd done much of the short time I'd known him. Bethanne retrieved her rosary from inside her purse and began to thumb through the beads, mumbling words I could only assume were prayers.

There was nothing more I could do for their family.

Chapter 43

Christopher had been different. He had touched my heart in ways I'd never seen coming, and I didn't know if I could continue to offer hope to others when, even when everything went perfectly, my patient died.

Ned would have asked me what I'd learned from the case. He would have pointed out that the hemorrhage might well have been caused by the head trauma Christopher had experienced. He'd tell me to get my emotions in check and move on. He'd remind me I wasn't God and that I had no business thinking I could hold a child's life in my hands. He'd remind me it wasn't always up to me.

FOR MONTHS, I CONTINUED to live my life as I'd always done: patients, research, home, sleep. Repeat. And then one morning, I couldn't.

"Good morning, Gail. I'm not coming in for the next few days. Please clear my schedule and see if David has time for anyone who needs to be seen immediately."

I waited while Gail digested words she'd never heard before. And when she finally spoke, I was reminded why I'd hired her in the first place.

"Will a week be enough?"

Right now, a month wouldn't be enough. "I'll let you know later."

I ended the call and decided to wash windows. I could hire someone, but I liked the physical labor. I liked the process: pulling out the screens, hosing them off, attacking all the grime that had accumulated in the windowsills during the months when it had been too cold to even think about letting in fresh air.

I liked the rhythm of dipping the sponge into hot, soapy water and wiping away the accumulation of life that had settled on the glass. I liked taking a clean, dry cloth and buffing the glass, making it sparkle so the view outside looked clean and fresh.

Even emptying the bucket at regular intervals and filling it with hot water and cleaning solution reminded me of fresh starts.

And that was what I needed. A fresh start.

It wasn't like I took a day off every time I lost a patient. I couldn't even remember the last time I took a day off, but I remembered the last patient I lost. I never lost sight of who came to me with hope in their eyes.

When the phone rang, I was almost grateful for the interruption. The up-and-down movement of cleaning grime from my windows kept my body busy, but my mind was free for thoughts I wasn't yet ready to face. But I let the call go to voicemail as my arm raised the sponge to the next window.

Only a few people had my landline number—that was the point of a private line—but the truth was, I wasn't much for talking on the phone. Invariably, I let calls go to voicemail; I might need to return the call, but I'd do it on my terms. When the ringing stopped, I briefly wondered if the marketer who thought I needed whatever he was offering would leave a message.

I moved on to the next window and gripped the soapy sponge. Then I froze. The sponge fell out of my hand and back into the bucket. When I heard Tim's voice, I barely noticed the splash of dirty water on my newly refinished wood floors.

"Call me."

What did he want? *What if he wants to come home? Don't be ridiculous. Why would he want to do that? But what if he does?*

My heart raced while I mopped up the soapy water from the floor and tossed the bucket and sponges and drying rags in the garage. There was no way I could wash windows then, not when Tim was waiting for me to call back.

I hadn't heard from him in three years, not since the last time he sat in my kitchen and told me he planned on telling Ali I wasn't coming with them.

Just those two words brought back all the moments that took me from the day we met until the day he walked away.

I kept hitting Replay so I could listen again.

"I CAN'T JUST CALL HIM back."

"Whyever not, for pity's sake? The man called you. Isn't that what you've been moping around waiting for all these years?"

I already regretted walking over to Miss Maggie's, but I'd needed to get out of my own house, where the phone and the answering machine begged for my attention.

"I can't call him. I don't know what he wants."

"*That's* why you call him. To find out." Miss Maggie looked at me like I was five. "All you do is hit Redial."

"I know how to use the phone. Maybe he's lost Ali's immunization records. Or maybe he can't remember her blood type and he needs it for a school trip." And then I took a real leap. "Or maybe he needs Uncle Ray's phone number?"

The more I thought about it, the more logical that sounded. "Didn't you just tell me when you saw Tim and Ali last week that he was writing a piece for the Rhode Island Historical Society? Uncle Ray's an expert on furniture restoration. Maybe that's what he needs?"

Miss Maggie shrugged. "Don't know." I waited for her to elaborate, to assure me that that was exactly the reason Tim had called, but apparently, that was all she was going to say about the subject.

There was little I knew about their lives. Only what Miss Maggie told me—and news from my family after their occasional visits to Tim and Ali in Providence. I knew he was happy. He liked living in a college town; he even taught a few creative writing classes at Brown, the school that had put him on a waiting list when he was in high school but grabbed him up quickly once he'd become a well-known author.

They'd found their own forever home, a small Victorian on Benefit Street in College Hill. I knew Ali was happy too. She attended the Moses Brown School, a Quaker school where students were encouraged to respect one another and value the truth.

"I'm pretty sure if you call him back, he'll tell you what he needs." Miss Maggie speared a pickle from the little dish on the table and placed it on her plate. "Are you sure you don't want some lunch?"

"Thanks. I'm not hungry."

"I guess not." My hand had just reached toward her sandwich when she nodded. "You keep picking the food off my plate."

Ignoring the laughter in her eyes, I swiftly brought my hand back to my side of the table. "The message is just so short. How am I supposed to figure out what he wants when all he says is 'Call me'?"

Miss Maggie sat there, eating what was left of her sandwich.

"Aren't you going to say anything?"

"No. I'm going to eat my lunch. Not in peace, mind you. But I'm going to eat it."

The longer I waited to return Tim's call, the stronger my hope grew. That was the real reason I was sitting there talking about what to do instead of doing it. It wasn't like me to hope. But I couldn't stop myself.

"If he calls again, I'll pick up. Even though I still don't know what he wants."

Miss Maggie said nothing.

"I will!"

The walk home took twice as long as usual, but once I got there, I knew what I had to do.

Chapter 44

He recognized my voice immediately.

"Emma?" My name was a question in his mouth, but it was followed by silence, and I understood quickly that none of the possibilities I'd imagined had been the reason for his call. Gripping the phone to my ear as if that would help Tim speak, I waited. I wanted to give him time to tell me what was wrong because I knew something was wrong, but I wasn't that good at waiting.

"Yes, I'm here," I urged. My voice grew shakier with each word. "What's wrong?" Again I waited, and finally, Tim spoke.

"It's Ali. She's..."

My breath caught somewhere in my throat. Immediately, my imagination flung itself down mountainsides while I waited for Tim to finish saying what needed to be said. Ali what? I imagined car brakes screeching and Ali left bleeding and broken on some street too far away for me to reach. I pictured her taken, picked up by some maniac in a panel truck, or at the bottom of a flight of stairs with her body twisted in a way no body should. That was how my mind worked in that moment of not knowing. My mind screamed, "Ali *what*?"

Seconds passed. When I thought my heart would burst, Tim spoke again but not before I heard his deep, shuddering sob. "Ali couldn't—didn't—get out of bed this morning. I went up to her room to get her moving so she wouldn't be late for school, and..."

His words were fast. Jumbled. "Tim! Slow down. I can't understand what you're saying."

He stopped and took a breath. He started again, slower that time. "I thought she'd overslept. I knocked on her door, but when she didn't answer, I walked into her room. She was still in her bed."

I tried to imagine Ali lying in a room I'd never seen, in a bed I didn't buy, and I understood, finally, that I would never be able to picture the life my daughter lived. I sank to the floor with that knowledge; my heart filled with remorse at all I didn't know.

Before I could utter even one word, Tim spoke. "I thought she was sleeping." His words were harsh against my ear. "But when I walked to her bed, she was staring into space. Into nothing. I'm not sure she even saw me."

Taking a deep breath, I willed myself to loosen my grip on the phone. "Where is she now?" And even as I spoke, I thought *notdeadnotdeadnotdead. He never said she was dead.*

"I took her to the emergency room at Memorial Hospital." His voice cracked when he told me she'd been admitted. "That's where I'm at now." When he stopped talking, I thought he'd ended the call, then he sobbed.

I wanted to give him time to pull himself together, but the waiting was like watching your house burn down and not knowing if your family was inside. I was ready to scream questions at him when finally he continued, his words spoken so softly I barely heard. "They gave her steroids, which helped, but her body is still partially paralyzed. The MRI identified an irregularity, a cerebral lesion, they called it."

My mind and body were numb. I felt nothing. But within seconds, my brain caught up to my heart that had been pumping madly, and it screamed at my memory. *Standing at the window all those years ago, feeling the cold glass on my hand while the snow filled in Tim and Ali's footprints. Until there were no footprints.*

I hadn't been a mother since the day they left. *Who am I kidding? I've never been a mother.* I'd always been too busy, too tied up with my work. I always thought there would be time later. I thought they'd wait for me.

And now Ali was dying. I knew those symptoms. I knew what Tim was telling me, even if he didn't quite get it.

I swallowed and fought to keep my voice calm. "I'll make arrangements to have Ali transported here. We're better equipped to see what's going on." I added, "Try not to worry," ridiculous words that I told every family when naturally they would do nothing but worry.

My voice sounded like it always did when I spoke to the parents of my patients. Confident. Unemotional.

I called Gail and told her I would be in the office at eight. She made the arrangements for Ali's transfer and marked Tim as the first consult of the day. The only consult. I was only back for Tim. And Ali.

I felt no guilt knocking others out of her way. I would still be unavailable to patients who had been waiting weeks to see me and had opted to wait rather than see David. *I'm no different than Ned when he rushed into the ER with Kate in his arms, confident no one would stop him from plowing through doors where help could be found.* Except Ned had been Kate's father. I didn't know who I was to Ali.

By early afternoon of the day I returned Tim's call, Ali had been admitted to Lancaster General.

WHEN I FINALLY WALKED into Ali's hospital room, only the light from the hallway lit the way to the bed. I wanted her to be asleep so I could study nearly three years of growth. I wanted to look at my daughter without her looking back.

Minutes passed before I reached out to touch one small hand that rested pale and still on top of the blanket. I meant to touch her for a second, just to feel her skin against mine, but I pulled back quickly when Tim stepped out from where he'd been standing by the window.

"Oh! I—I'm sorry. I didn't know you were here. I just wanted to—" What could I say? *I just wanted to look at your daughter and soak in her beauty?*

"I didn't mean to scare you. I'm glad you're here. I wanted to tell you how grateful I am for seeing us..."

We stood within feet of each other, close enough to touch, far enough apart that the distance between us seemed insurmountable.

Tim spoke as if I were no more than the doctor assigned to help his daughter. A stranger whose job it was to save lives. And truthfully, I deserved no more than that.

I held up my hand to stop him from expressing his gratitude, and I put the rest of his words away—the unintentional pain he'd just caused by thanking me for something I would willingly give. "There's nothing to thank me for, not yet. What the doctors told you at Memorial is true. Ali *could* have a brain tumor, but let me finish reviewing the tests. Let me get David on board so he can schedule some additional scans. I'll talk to you in the morning. You need to go. Try to get some sleep."

I didn't believe in lying to my patients or their families, but in that case, I did. I'd already studied Ali's chart.

Normally, when I ended a meeting with the family, I reached out and lightly touched a hand or maybe an arm, a shoulder. If it was the mother I'd been talking with, I'd more than likely hug her. It was my way of letting them know I would do everything I could for their child.

But Tim wasn't just any parent. And I couldn't bring myself to touch him. Not that I didn't want to. I was just afraid it would hurt too much if he didn't touch me back.

Chapter 45

My office was my haven. It sealed me off from the offending ruckus of normal hospital life: rubber-soled shoes scuttling down hallways, moans of pain curling under doorways, the more than occasional requests for transport of one of the many pieces of mobile medical equipment to this room or that hallway.

It sealed off the smells too. Most of them, anyway. Rotting flesh, bodily waste, wounds left uncleaned far too long before the patient sought medical attention.

The moonlight was shining in so brightly there was no need for lights; my office was where I went to hide after I left Ali's hospital room. The last place I wanted to be was in the house where Ali had spent the first six years of her life. Where she'd learned to walk and talk and ride a tricycle and go on adventures with her father.

I sat alone on the couch—that place of comfort where heartache could be absorbed—and thought about the families who had sat there and listened while I described their child's death sentence. Maybe they came back from their grief, as much as they could, but they were forever changed. Maybe they didn't even know who they were when their hearts started to beat again.

I shrugged as if that would clear my thoughts. *It should be so easy.* I needed to sit somewhere other than that mournful couch that held no hope.

The sound of my footsteps, so different than during the day when they were swallowed whole by the urgency of everyday hospital life, were hollow against the tile floor as I headed to the cafeteria for a cup of tea.

I grabbed a muffin along with my tea and noticed Tim sitting in the farthest corner of the room, his hands wrapped around a mug of coffee, his face open and empty. His head jerked back when he looked up and saw me walking toward him. "Is anything wrong?"

I reached out to reassure him but stopped just inches from his arm. "No. No. Everything's fine. Try to relax." Without waiting for an invitation, I pulled out a chair opposite him and sat.

"I thought you were going to get some sleep?"

He blew on his steaming coffee. "I can't. I can't leave her."

I nodded. I took a sip of tea, unwrapped my muffin, and started to separate it into quarters. "Tell me everything." I wanted to hear the entire story, more than the specifics that had led him to call me.

Tim swiped his hand over his face. "When Ali didn't answer my knock, I opened her door, expecting to find her wrapped up in her comforter, sound asleep. Her alarm clock was blaring, and I couldn't understand how she could sleep through all that racket. She was going to be late for school, and I had a class to teach in thirty minutes. And... and I was exasperated. This wasn't like her. She's a good kid. Insisted when she started school that she wanted her own alarm clock so she could get herself up in the morning. But—" Tim swallowed, the look on his face reflecting the memory of what he'd seen.

"Take your time. I know this is hard, but it's important I know everything."

"She wasn't asleep. I could see that from the doorway. I yelled her name, but she never answered me. She seemed... rigid? Her eyes were open. Staring. I ran back down to the kitchen for my phone. I dialed 911. Unlocked the front door and raced back up the stairs."

I could barely understand the pain he must have felt. The fear. I regretted that he'd had to experience that alone.

"I didn't know what to do. I didn't know if I should touch her or try to hold her. I knelt by the side of her bed and looked into her eyes. I just needed her to know I was there."

"Here." The muffin was quickly turning into crumbs, and I offered him a piece before it became unrecognizable. Illogically, I smiled.

"What?"

"Sorry. I was just thinking how Miss Maggie says food solves everything."

Tim nodded. A slight smile danced across his lips as if he remembered too. "The ambulance came then and took us to the hospital. The sirens wailed, and cars pulled over to let us pass. I knew she was in trouble. I knew they didn't use the sirens unless it was critical."

He stopped, out of words, then looked around the cafeteria as if he'd just realized where he was. "It looks different."

"It was remodeled last year." I looked around too. The walls were painted a pale yellow, which made the room seem filled with sunlight, even in the middle of the night, and flowers sat in little vases on all the tables. Silk—because of allergies—but still, they added energy to the room.

When Tim was ready, he started again. "When we reached the hospital, I ran along with the gurney while the orderlies sprinted to the emergency room. I tried to answer their questions, but there was so much I didn't know. I didn't know how long she'd been unresponsive." Tim took a deep breath and closed his eyes for just a second. "How long *had* she lain there, needing help, unable to call out to me while I'd enjoyed my second cup of coffee?"

The image Tim painted was enough to break any parent's heart.

"I heard them talking while they lifted her from the gurney. 'Might be a stroke.' And I'm thinking, she's nine fucking years old. How can she be having a stroke? But then they mentioned a brain tumor. They ordered an MRI." He drew in a deep, ragged breath. "That's when I knew I needed you."

After the last three years of wondering how they were, I'd finally heard it all. The most Ali had suffered was scraped knees, a cold or two, and a broken arm when she'd conned a neighbor's kid into removing her training wheels and gone trailblazing down McCormick Hill, a feat no kid her age had ever dared before.

And Tim had handled it all, illnesses and accidents. Downright stupidities. None of it had been too much for him.

Out of what probably was sheer exhaustion, Tim started talking about things he had no right to talk about. "The hardest thing I ever did was walk out on you the night I told you I'd filed for divorce. But I couldn't live with a woman who devoted her entire life to medicine."

His words hurt, and at first, I thought he was attacking me. "Don't you think I know that?" I countered, knowing I deserved his words but somehow surprised that he'd brought them up. There. "Don't you think I'm sorry?" I started to rise, but his next words pulled me back into my chair.

"You wanted to tell me something that night, and I wouldn't listen. What was it?"

I bit my lip. I remembered all the words I'd had no chance to say. "It doesn't matter. That was a long time ago." I meant that, yet somewhere deep inside, the memory of where we'd started began to surface: that moment so long ago when he'd walked up behind me and wrapped his arms around me and promised he'd never let me go. And then he'd let me go, and I'd been helpless to stop him because of all my misguided beliefs and Ned's manipulations and deceits.

Tim nodded. We both knew it was too late to go back to that night and make things different.

"It's ironic, isn't it?"

"What?"

"I left you because you devoted your life to medicine, and now here I am, begging you to cure our daughter. Because you've devoted your life to this disease."

I would have smiled, but it hurt too much. "I guess it is." I couldn't talk about irony right then. I needed to concentrate on doing what I could, not dream about what might have been. "I've already called my office. You have the first appointment tomorrow morning. I'll see you then."

My final words to the man I'd once thought I would spend the rest of my life with were meant to offer hope even when I knew there was little hope.

Chapter 46

"Oh!" Gail looked as if she didn't know whether to move forward or turn around, go back the way she came, and slam the door behind her.

She chose to meet me head-on. "What are you doing here? Didn't you go home last night?"

I lifted my head from my desk and, for one quick second, wondered why Gail was in my bedroom. But then I remembered working late into the night. I must have fallen asleep. I vaguely remembered closing my eyes, promising myself I'd rest only for a minute.

"Sorry." Every muscle ached when I stood to stretch, and my mouth, oh God, my mouth felt like a cat had taken up residence between my lips. "Do me a favor?" I mumbled, trying to get my bearings. "Bring me a cup of tea? And maybe some aspirin? I need to splash water on my face and brush my teeth."

Gail gave me one long look, the one she reserved for people who felt the need to push their level of endurance into the land of stupidity. I'd seen it before, that look. It wasn't the first time I'd fallen asleep in my office, it wouldn't be the last, and my taking up residence there had never met with her approval. But I got the last word in before she turned back to her desk.

"And stop looking like you want to throttle me."

By the time Gail showed up with hot tea and aspirin, I had my desk in some semblance of order from where my head and arms had rearranged all the neatly stacked folders and files I'd placed there last night.

I swallowed two pills with the hot tea and told Gail to let me know as soon as Tim arrived. Until then, I planned on reviewing Ali's records again, even though every written word, every scan, was embedded in my brain. In my heart.

We've come full circle, this disease and me. It wasn't enough that I worked every day to save lives that the disease so thoroughly destroyed; it wanted my daughter too.

Last night haunted me: Ali, with her dark-brown hair spread across the hospital-issued pillow like the branches of a tree spreading out in search of sunshine, her face nearly as pale as the sheets on the bed. She'd looked so small and defenseless. Nowhere near strong enough to battle the tumor that, even as I'd looked down on her sleeping body, had continued to ravage her brain.

I'd watched the slow rise and fall of her chest, needing to know she still breathed, no different than when she was an infant and I'd sneaked into the nursery at night. Looking at her, I'd wanted to rub away the dark shadows that nestled under her eyes like bruises, but I was afraid that if I touched her, she'd wake and not know who I was. Or worse, recognize me and turn away.

Closing my eyes, I mentally shook myself. I'd never forgotten her, but I had to distance myself from those lost years. There wasn't time to dwell on tooth fairies and Christmas mornings with presents piled under the tree.

I picked up Ali's file again and held it in my hands. I wanted to toss the damn file into the depths of hell and watch it smolder and flare and turn to ash. My heart ached with all I'd missed: three years of my child's life. Every time I'd closed my eyes last night, all I could see was how silent and still she lay in her narrow hospital bed. She was so...

The sounds coming from the waiting room startled me. It was too early for Tim, but before I could question what was going on, my office door flung open, and Tim strode in with Gail following closely.

Ali's folder crashed to the floor when I stood, and all the notes and reports within it scattered.

"I'm sorry, Emma. I asked him to wait until I'd had the chance to let you know." Gail knew I would need a minute, maybe two, before we came face-to-face again, but Tim was in no mood to wait.

We had talked last night, but that morning, I took him in entirely. The full beard, the hollows in his face, the way his hair, damp from his shower, fell into his eyes. "Have a seat." I motioned, indicating the couch instead of the chair positioned in front of my desk. He looked like hell. I assumed he hadn't slept, and his face was scruffy from not shaving. I bet his stomach was already sour from too many cups of bitter black coffee.

Gail uttered one more apology, picked up my folder and all of its scattered contents, and backed out the door.

My office hadn't changed since the last time Tim was there, yet I felt we were both standing in foreign territory. The walls were still painted in shades of pearl gray and muted blues with a smattering of dusty rose; the furnishings, the fabrics, even the artwork geared toward placating the soul. So it wasn't the office that had changed. It was us.

Tim wasn't easily soothed, though, by furniture placement or paint hues. Instead, he turned toward me as if I might save his life. The catch in his voice was heavy, like a stone tossed down an old mine shaft that built momentum as it fell. "Just tell me, please!" he begged, his voice tight and laced with pain.

He sat then—or rather threw himself onto the couch—before I could open my mouth. He sat, I thought, not because sitting would change the outcome of what I said and not because I asked him to but maybe because he was too exhausted to stand any longer. What difference would it make when I told him the words he feared most?

I didn't make the mistake of offering him coffee. By the looks of him, he'd already had too much. And I put my thoughts of Ali away. Not for always, just for the moment. I had to. If I was going to help him, I couldn't hold on to my sorrow. I moved to the couch and sat far enough away that we wouldn't accidentally touch but close enough to catch the scent of the Kiehl's soap he used.

"I don't know how much they explained to you at Memorial, so I'll start from the beginning." The muscles in my face were frozen in place to ward off the pain in my heart. "The hemiparesis, the partial paralysis that you witnessed, could have been caused by a stroke or cerebral palsy, even multiple sclerosis. However..."

How do you tell the man you loved that his child is dying?

Chapter 47

I sucked in my breath and blew it out. "The biopsy confirms GBM." Knowing I shouldn't yet unable to stop myself, I moved to the chair adjacent to the couch so he would look at me. But he stared straight ahead, and I knew he didn't see me. I wasn't sure he saw anything.

I kept going. "The tumor appears to be in the early stages, which is good because that gives us some time." I stopped to let my words sink in. It was important for Tim to believe there was hope. "Research is moving forward." *Just not nearly fast enough.*

Speaking slowly so Tim could concentrate on each word, I continued, "I want to place Ali in a clinical trial to buy us even more time."

Those were words I'd used before. They were words that sometimes haunted me in the middle of the night after I'd used them to give hope when there was no hope. I remembered Ned saying close to the same thing when Kate was diagnosed. I remembered how little difference his words had made.

My finger itched to dig at the thumb on my left hand, but I didn't dare. I might just as well have screamed, "Ali is dying, and I don't know if I can save her."

Finally, Tim turned toward me and whispered, "GBM?" His face turned white. "Ali's going to die like Kate?"

Tim had heard nothing past GBM. "No. Ali's not going to die like Kate. We've come much further than when Kate died." What I didn't tell him was that the median survival rate for GBM was a little over fourteen months, and the sad truth of that time frame was that fourteen months was barely a chapter in a child's life.

I was wrong to promise that Ali wouldn't die, but if she had any chance of surviving, Tim had to believe she would.

The thing to remember when handing out news of that magnitude was the importance of time. Not *how much* time might be left in a child's life. I was talking about the time a family needed to swallow whole what took me no more than thirty seconds to spit out.

Tim sat hunched over his knees with his head in his hands, clearly crushed by my words, and I wanted to touch his shoulder, let him know I'd do everything I could, but my job right then was to let him feel his pain. I had to give him the time he needed to process what I'd spent all night processing.

"There must be some mistake. Two days ago, she was badgering me to take her to the mall. How could this happen so fast?"

Thinking back to Christopher, who'd displayed no symptoms, I believed that was unlikely to be the case with Ali. "It didn't happen fast. Most likely, Ali kept her symptoms hidden. Possibly for months."

His face screwed up in pain. "She *hid* this from me?" The very thought of Ali hiding her symptoms turned his eyes dark, as if they were drowning in pain.

"Oh, Tim, it's not like that." I tried to find the right words to comfort him, but what I really wanted to do was wrap him in my arms and hold him. "Kids don't like to rock the boat." I thought of Kate. *"Please tell my mom you think I need glasses..."* "Especially when they're scared."

I knew Tim blamed himself, but it wasn't him. It was me. Ali's disease was my punishment for thinking—even for one second—that I wanted her gone all those years ago.

"Can you remove the tumor?"

So he was aware of the procedure I'd created.

"It's not as simple as that. There are risks..."

I could see the moment he'd stopped listening. He stood and pulled me up with him. We stood inches apart, the closest we'd been in years. "David told me about the surgery. The procedure you created. Can the tumor be removed?"

David. David had spoken to Tim when he should have stayed silent.

"David's premature in discussing this with you. The surgery is still very much experimental. It's a last-ditch effort."

Tim stepped away, needing, maybe, to distance himself from me. Or my words. When he started to pace from one end of my office to the other, he was obviously trying to get his thoughts lined up just right. Some things were never forgotten.

I could tell from the way he held himself that he'd already been won over by David. Tim saw hope where little existed, and he dug in. I'd forgotten that about him: when he thought he was right, he never gave in.

"But Ned says the same thing. It's a phenomenal technique!"

"You talked to Ned?" I opened and closed my hands several times, slowly, giving myself time before I spoke. I took a deep breath before I said something I would regret. "This surgery could cost you your daughter's life."

Tim stiffened and spun toward me. "She's your daughter too." He bit off each word and threw it at me. "Yes. I talked to Ned. He called me when he heard about Ali. He told me about the cases where you've successfully removed the whole tumor. You need to do this."

"No." The word shot out of my mouth. I tried again, calmer. "No, I can't." I needed to slow down the conversation. "The procedure is experimental. It's meant for patients with less than three months to live. Ali is nowhere near that stage. There's still time before we need to discuss this."

I'd sidestepped his reminder of my connection to Ali. More importantly, at least at the moment, I'd sidestepped the patients who'd survived the surgery and currently led healthy, normal lives. "You need to trust me."

"I understand what you're saying, but I know what this disease does. How could I forget the nights you'd come home from the hospital devastated when you lost a patient? Devastated by their pain. Why would you want to put Ali through so much just to wait until she's near death to save her? Save her *now*." The energy between us was powerful. His will against mine. "Please."

It was hard to turn away from the plea in his voice. "I'm not going to throw the first shovel of dirt on Ali's grave." I pulled away from his hands that had grabbed onto mine when he begged for my help. I moved toward my desk, needing to put it between us as if it would protect me. "I can't! I can't take that chance. Not again. I can't be responsible for killing her. Ned and David both told you about the patients I've saved. Did either of them mention the children I've lost? The child who just died on my table from a brain hemorrhage? The child who..." I could barely continue, but I did. "Would you like to speak with their families? See how they're holding up?"

Confusion distorted Tim's face. I'd seen the very moment he'd flinched.

"Tim, I..."

He followed me to my desk and picked up the vintage glass paperweight I kept there. He rolled it from hand to hand as if he meant to heave it. I watched as he worked over my words. "What do you mean, *not again*? What are you talking about?"

After all those years, I still couldn't tell him. My doubts. My confusion about motherhood. Ned. I couldn't tell him how close I'd come to destroying our daughter. "Nothing." I hoped that with all we'd said, those words would be forgotten.

We each struggled for composure, and finally, I picked up where I'd left off. "There have been some positive results from injecting various viruses directly into the tumor. Polio, smallpox, even the cold virus has slowed, even stopped, in some cases, the progression of the tumor. I've made arrangements for Ali to enter that trial. We've had a few cases where the tumor disappeared completely."

Tim seemed to think about what I'd just said while he continued to roll the paperweight from hand to hand. He'd been married to me long enough to know that in some cases, clinical trials were no different from ten-car pileups. "How many?"

For one quick second, I again considered wrapping my arms around him. What stopped me was not knowing who I was looking to comfort, him or me.

"How many survived? How many patients are in the trial?"

There was no point in sugarcoating what I couldn't hide; those statistics were readily available for anyone who thought he needed to know. It wasn't like I was divulging some high-security secret, but when Tim heard my words, he closed his eyes.

"We started with twenty-one patients. Eight died. Three are in long-term remission. We are monitoring the remaining patients." The statistics rolled off my tongue. I only wished they were better.

Giving in to my initial urge, I walked around my desk and took his hands in mine. For a moment, we were both perfectly still, then his body began to shake. Slowly at first and then with a frenzy from all that had occurred in the last twenty-four hours. I could almost feel his muscles shred in an effort to get at his heart and rip it from his chest. His face was a river of grief, but he said nothing.

In that moment, I made my decision, yet I wasn't ready to share it. "Give me twenty-four hours," I told him, then I walked out of my office, forgetting that I was the one who belonged there.

Chapter 48

Some people feared silence and would do anything to avoid it, but I had built my life around it. It was as necessary to me as breathing.

My office was silent while I reviewed what I hoped would be the hardest decision I'd ever be called upon to make. David would perform the surgery to remove Ali's tumor.

While I waited for the review board to give me their decision, I pulled another folder from the files stacked high on my desk. I wasn't searching for answers; I was just looking. Remembering each case and each outcome, good or bad.

I thought I'd known what they'd felt, the families who'd sat in my office and listened to my prognosis when I'd advised them that their child had, at the most, only months to live, but I'd had no idea.

I shook my head at my own insensitivity. *You can't feel someone else's pain. Nor would you want to.*

I STRODE PAST GAIL'S office as if I were on a mission, but I really had no idea where I was going. I just knew I had to go.

When she heard me open the closet door, Gail looked up from her desk. "Wait! Where are you going?"

"Out. I'm going out."

"But isn't Tim due back here?"

"No. I told him I'd call. But before I do, I need to clear my head."

I skipped the elevator and took the stairs. I went through the lobby—and the visitors waiting their turn to sign in with their balloons and baskets of flowers in hand—and out the front door into air that wasn't recycled and purified. I stopped and took a deep breath. The sky was cloudy, and the air smelled like rain. But once I climbed into my car and put my hands on the steering wheel, I wasn't sure where I wanted to go. Yet I wasn't altogether surprised when I ended up parked in front of Miss Maggie's house.

"Why did you ring the bell, for heaven's sake? You know you don't need to do that."

"I know." I looked around the porch at the rocking chairs and the boot scraper and couldn't even remember walking up the porch steps. "I don't know why I rang the bell." I shook my head, amazed I'd managed to get there at all. "I need to talk."

"Well. It's about time. Don't look so surprised. The whole village is talking. Everyone knows Tim brought Ali home because she's sick."

"She's not just sick..."

"I know. I know. I'm going over tonight. Come in. I'll fix tea."

Tea was always Miss Maggie's answer. Tea or a story. A glass of wine. "Miss Maggie, tea's not going to fix this."

"I know it won't. But it'll give us something to do with our hands while we talk."

I nodded, walked into the kitchen, and sat in Anne's chair. I'd been sitting in that chair since I was a little girl, since Anne died, but I always thought of it as Anne's. "Tim wants me to operate. Well, not me. David. I haven't told him my decision yet."

Miss Maggie went about her tea preparation as if Anne were standing right there in the kitchen instructing her. Without asking, she looked up from Anne's teapot and turned toward me, her eyes filled with questions. I realized then that even though Tim had spoken with her briefly, I'd left her hanging. That was one more gray area when it came to who I was in relation to Ali: the mother who was devastated that her child was dying or the doctor who had to worry about HIPAA compliance issues.

"I'm sorry I didn't call you. I've been..."

"Busy, I know. You're here now. Talk."

Carefully placing the mugs of tea before us, Miss Maggie claimed her chair at the table.

"I requested the review board approve the surgery, even though Ali doesn't meet all the criteria."

"That must have been a hard decision."

"It was." The muscles in my stomach tightened. "It is."

When Miss Maggie commented on my actions, I realized I'd straightened the napkin beside my mug and positioned my spoon dead center on it. "You haven't changed all that much since you were a kid. Always needing to line things up. Make things right."

I was too tired to even nod.

"But you have doubts?"

"Do you think Ali's brave?"

I'd often thought that God—if there was one—only gave cancer to the brave. Because only the brave put up a fight. Only the brave soldiered on as though their burden were no greater than a beesting. Or a broken bone. I'd often thought that God saw cancer as a game, and the game was only over when he said it was. So I needed Ali to be brave.

"Of course she's brave. How could she not be? What's going on in that head of yours?"

I shrugged. "Just this theory I have. About God. Bravery. Sometimes, I wish I could talk to Ned." Just the thought of Ned and what he'd gone through and what he'd done made me close my eyes.

"No reason you can't."

My eyes popped open.

"Don't look at me like that. He's not the devil. He did what he did. He did what he had to do. He did what most of us, if we were honest with ourselves, wish we'd have the guts to do if we were in the same situation."

I knew she was talking about the night Kate died. But that wasn't why I'd just shot her that look. I'd almost come to terms with that night. I would never forgive Ned for his part in the night I stood at the top of the basement stairs with Ali in my arms, hearing in my head his voice asking me why I would waste my time on one child when I could save hundreds. Thousands. I would never forgive either of us. But I wouldn't tell her that. I'd keep Ned's secret. And my own.

Instead, I changed the subject. "What if I'm wrong?" I hesitated before completing my thought. "What if Ali dies?"

Miss Maggie sipped her tea. "What's going to happen if Ali doesn't have the surgery?"

"She's going to die."

"It seems to me you don't have much choice. I'm no doctor, but if the sure thing is death, I'd go for the not-sure thing. Seems like taking a chance is better than just watching it happen."

I couldn't argue with her logic.

"What do you think Ned would say if you did talk to him?"

"I'm not—"

"I know. But what if you did? What would he say?"

I sighed. "He'd tell me not to give up."

Chapter 49

What was it like to wake up and find that the only things that moved were your eyelids? What was it like to find your father kneeling by your bedside with a look of sheer terror stretched across his face?

I shook my head. It must have been agonizing for Ali when she realized she couldn't move.

Kate had said paralysis was like looking at staged mannequins artfully arranged into some holiday tableau in a giant department store window. "Only you weren't staring *into* the window," Kate had said. "*You* were part of the tableau. *You* stared out of the window. *You* searched for release while others stared in at you. It was fucking terrifying."

I'd have given just about anything to talk with Ali myself. Instead, I sent David in to find the answers to what I needed to know.

Ali didn't remember the ambulance ride to Memorial. She barely remembered the flight to Lancaster General. She did remember Tim telling her they were going home, and that had confused her. Wasn't Providence home?

"She's one scared kid. But she's tough too." David handed me his notes so I could see for myself.

The headaches had started about four months ago. At first, they weren't so bad. When they got bad, she swiped Tylenol from Tim's medicine cabinet, but when he caught her, she told him she'd used the pills for a science experiment at her friend Joanne's house.

When she fell or slipped, she'd make a joke over her clumsiness. And somehow, Tim never noticed. She knew she'd have to tell him, but she kept putting it off and hoping the symptoms would go away.

"If she hadn't experienced the paralysis, it wouldn't have been much longer until Tim noticed."

"Agreed."

"Was she very forthcoming?"

"She told me the pain was like someone had clamped a vise to her head—and just kept rotating the handle tighter and tighter. Apparently, Tim has a workshop?"

I nodded. At least he'd had one at our home. My guess was he probably had one in Rhode Island.

"Did she mention why she didn't tell Tim?"

"Pretty much like you thought. She knew he was happy, and she didn't want to do anything to make him sad. She said if something big was wrong with her and she died, her dad would be all alone, and their house would be too big with just him living in it. So she just kept hoping it would go away. You know what kids are like."

ALI HAD BEEN IN THE hospital twenty-four hours by the time I saw Tim again.

It was the middle of the night. Ali was asleep in her bed, and Tim was passed out in a reclining chair next to her. I leaned against the doorway and watched them. Ali slept soundly, barely twitching an eyebrow while Tim turned back and forth as if the devil himself were chasing him. *My whole life is in this room, and no one knows it but me.*

I yawned. I felt like I'd spent the night studying a problem from so many angles the edges were worn smooth.

Hoping not to wake them, I laid all the folders I'd brought on the table by the window. The oldest files were on the bottom, beat-up and raggedy, and the ones on top were crisp and clean. The very first one had Ali's name typed on it.

Tim woke just as I turned to leave the room. "Emma?" He looked around for a minute, unsure, maybe, of where he was, but I caught the look on his face when it all came rushing back. "What time is it?" His voice was husky with sleep, but he forced himself awake. He knew if I was there, I had something to say.

Looking at my watch, I was shocked to see the time. "It's a little after two. Sorry. I didn't realize how late it was."

Tim smirked. "Or you wanted to make sure we were asleep?"

I ignored his question and handed him the folders. "Here are the records of every patient who has undergone this procedure. The names are blacked out for privacy reasons, but all the information is here. As you can see"—I opened Christopher's file—"there are more ways to die than just from the scalpel. There's the unexpected, the..."

My words stuck in my throat, as I was unable to accept the loss of a boy who'd had such hopes for his future.

I swallowed and started again. "Tim, you need to understand the risks involved with this surgery. If you wait even three months, I can almost promise you that the risks of performing this surgery will be less. If you want this surgery now, I can't promise you that once she's wheeled into the OR, you'll ever see her alive again."

My words were harsh, and I meant them to be. Even though I'd agreed to the surgery, I wanted him to change his mind. At least for the time being. "I know you don't want to think about risks, especially where Ali is concerned, but you must."

Tim stayed silent. He placed Christopher's file on the table. He looked like he needed to lie down, no different from all the times he'd taken Ali for immunizations when she was a baby and he'd had to leave the room so he wouldn't get dizzy.

But he didn't leave the room. He listened to every word I said. He looked through more folders. Once in a while, he even nodded to let me know he was paying attention.

I didn't talk just about the kids I'd lost. I showed him the wins too—the kids who were back in school, the notes from families who couldn't stop thanking me.

"David... David's prepared to perform the surgery the day after tomorrow if that's what you want."

I knew Tim. He still hadn't wrapped his head around all that had happened. If he had a choice, he would go back to when life had been normal, when his biggest worry was Ali remembering her lunch money or some such thing. And now he had to make the biggest decision of his life. The biggest decision of Ali's life.

"Emma, I..."

I saw the pain and confusion on his face, but I couldn't make the decision for him.

LATER THAT MORNING, Tim showed up in my office with the consent forms for the surgery.

"The hardest thing I've had to do is sign these papers."

I nodded. I knew it was hard. Signing a paper that spelled out every possible scenario that could go wrong had to be one of the most difficult things any parent had to do.

"It is hard. I can tell you not to worry, but it's not going to stop you. I hope it helps to know that Ali's in good hands with David."

"I know. I wanted to know if..."

I looked up from verifying that everything was in order with the consent forms. Tim was struggling with something. "You wanted to know?"

"Ali. She says the scariest thing about this surgery is that she has to do it herself. She wishes I could be in there with her." Tim caught my eye. "I guess there's no chance...?"

I allowed myself to smile. "No, you can't be in there. What Ali's feeling is natural. You never feel more alone than when you know you've lost complete control over your body. Most adults hope to hell the doctor knows what he's doing. Kids worry that they'll never wake up. Especially when they have surgery for the first time. It's normal for her to be nervous, but the nurse will give her a pill to help her relax before she's taken to the OR."

When Tim's mouth tightened, I realized I'd said the wrong thing.

"There's nothing normal about this."

"No. There isn't."

Chapter 50

"I got there right as the prep nurse was covering Ali's shoulders with a towel." David leaned against the side of my desk to fill me in on what was happening in Ali's room, something I'd asked him to do for me. "She is some kid."

I smiled, even though I had no reason to feel proud. She was Tim's daughter. "How did she handle having her head shaved?"

David laughed. "She was fine. Tim winced every time the nurse cut a big swatch of hair and stuffed it into the bag. But I give him credit. He never took his eyes off her until the nurse picked up the electric razor. That was just too much for him."

I tried to picture it in my head, imagining Ali's dark-brown curls landing in a heap at the bottom of a bag. "Did either of them say anything?" I had put David in a difficult position, asking him to linger when he stopped in prior to the surgery, but I had to know how they were, and I had no reason to be there myself.

"He told her she'd had more hair on her head the day she was born."

My eyes blurred for a moment. That memory came fast. Holding her to me. Working up the courage to remove the blanket she'd been swaddled in. The little pink cap. Kissing the top of her head where little tufts of curls sprouted like baby endive.

I was so lost in my memories, I almost jumped when David spoke again. "Ali said her head felt like a bowling ball."

"Was she upset?" Some girls, even as young as Ali, were devastated when their heads were shaved.

"Didn't seem to be. She laughed."

"I bet she looked beautiful."

"That's what Tim said."

I nodded and pictured him telling her that. "Did Ali say anything?"

David shook his head as if even he was in awe of that child. "She told him everything would be okay."

MY PLAN HAD BEEN TO stay in my office until the surgery was over, but as soon as David left, I realized that if I didn't see her then, I might lose any chance of seeing her later.

I must have looked like I'd just seen my dog run over when Helen bulldozed her way into Ali's room, but she didn't bat an eye as she passed me while I was drawing in deep breaths and trying to gather the courage I would need to enter that same room.

Helen was there to give Ali the pill that would help her relax before heading into surgery. She was in a hurry; no matter how many nurses we hired, there was always a shortage, but as soon as she stepped over the threshold into Ali's room, she turned from a woman with her eye on the clock to the professional caregiver she was. I watched from right outside the door while Helen calmly introduced herself and explained how the pill in the little white paper cup would help Ali relax and maybe make her a little drowsy.

A look of disappointment flashed across Ali's face so fast that even someone who'd been watching for it would most likely have missed it. "It won't put me to sleep?" The tremor in her voice told me she'd been hoping for the kind of pill that would knock her out cold, but she swallowed it without complaint and handed Helen the empty cup.

"Don't you worry. You'll soon be sound asleep," Helen reassured her, watching to make sure Ali swallowed the sedative, because watching and reassuring was all part of her job. I knew Helen. She was a good nurse to see Ali through that part. Like most nurses, she had no time for dramatics, but she had a good heart.

I waited until Helen left and the pills meant to relax Ali kicked in, and even then, I hovered inside the doorway. "Good morning!"

Silently, I told myself I had every right to be there. But I was nervous, and my eyes darted around the room, at the closet and the door to the bathroom, the other bed that was unoccupied, the little gray metal table that held a jar of miniature sunflowers.

I took in everything before my eyes finally lit on the reason I was there, and then I realized that one quick look wasn't going to satisfy my need to soak in the last three years of Ali's life. And even though I was aware he was in the room, I never once looked in Tim's direction. Instead, I let my eyes rest on Ali and said words that had nothing to do with what I was feeling.

"I wanted to stop in and say hello and let you know you're in excellent hands with Dr. David. He's one of our best doctors, and he'll take good care of you."

I filled my eyes with her. Her pale face, her eyes, big and round. She was scared, and I wanted to tell her not to be; I wanted to tell her that everything would be all right. No matter what. It was what I'd always believed. But then I remembered I'd said close to those same words to Christopher, and I'd been wrong—it hadn't been all right. I knew then that only if Ali survived would everything be all right.

"When the surgery is over, your dad will be right here, waiting for you, so I don't want you to worry about anything."

My heart flooded with meager memories: the day I discovered I was pregnant. The first time I held her in my arms. The day I went home from the hospital after the Amish school shooting and nearly crushed her little body to me, forever grateful that she was whole and safe.

One more smile and I was out of there, never having said the things that needed saying: *I'm your mother. I love you. I'm sorry.*

Chapter 51

I never even gave them a chance to speak.

Ali's eyes had been clouded with medication when I edged back through the doorway, but Tim seemed to realize I was leaving and had maybe wanted to stop me then seemed to think better of it.

I walked out of Ali's room, but I couldn't walk away. Instead, I leaned against the far wall where I could watch but they could no longer see me.

"Will she come back?" Ali never took her eyes off the doorway, and her voice sounded hopeful, but maybe that was only my imagination. I'd hoped, foolishly, that she would be too drowsy to pay much attention to yet another doctor showing up in her room, but I'd seen the way her eyes had grown big and round as soon as she saw me.

Their voices were low, but I picked up most of what they said. Tim answered her in the only way he could. "I don't know, sweetheart. I don't..."

Then I left. I was headed to my office when I passed the OR nurses heading toward Ali's room; their job was to move Ali to the holding area outside the OR, a journey I'd seen so often I could easily imagine the trip.

One nurse at the head of her bed, the other at the foot, they would maneuver Ali out of her room while Tim walked beside the bed so Ali could keep her eyes on him. I knew he'd smile down at her. It might not be the smile I'd once known, the one that started with

247

his lips and didn't stop until it filled his eyes with joy, but it would be there. He'd do the best he could.

The sun was barely up, which meant only nurses and aides scurried down the hallways, entering and leaving rooms, switching lights on and off as they went. They would be the only witnesses to Ali's little procession, barely worth a nod from the staff who serviced the floor.

Tim wouldn't be prepared—no one was—for the shock of reaching the set of big double doors leading to the holding area outside the OR and being told he'd have to let her go the rest of the way without him. For him, that would be unfathomable. He was the kind of dad who would always have a hard time letting go.

But he would head to the surgical waiting room because that was what they'd tell him to do, and he'd want to show Ali that he was strong. That there was nothing to be afraid of, no matter what his furrowed brow suggested. I could only hope one of the nurses would assure him that someone would come for him when it was over.

They'd point him toward the bank of elevators—"Second floor, turn left once you get off"—and he'd repeat their words to himself because that was what he always did when faced with a set of directions that involved more than one turn. Then he would walk away.

I DIDN'T FOOL MYSELF into thinking I could sit behind my desk and sift through my current load of patient files while Ali lay prone on an operating table in a theatre alive with the energy of a surgical team waiting to save her life. I could barely sit still.

Instead, while gallery spectators leaned forward, eager to watch and learn, all wanting to see the miracle taking place before them, I performed each step of the surgery in my head. Because I had to. Because I couldn't do anything else. From the initial incision to the preservation of the vessels to the removal of the tumor, I mirrored the actions David would perform in the OR. All the while, I searched for any weakness in the procedure I'd built my life around.

The biggest issue, I reminded myself, was the tentacles attached to the tumor; they needed to be lifted away completely along with the main body of the tumor. For the surgery to be successful, for the tumor not to grow back, nothing could remain except healthy brain tissue.

And if the surgery did what it was meant to do, save Ali's life, it would be worth every day of the last three years I'd lived without her. It would be worth every childhood event I'd missed. Every promise I'd broken.

Every eye would be on David; the majority of the surgical team would barely give a thought to the child on the table. I understood that. It wasn't that they didn't care; at that moment, they needed to distance themselves.

"Do the best you can, and then move on. Learn from your mistakes. Because otherwise, you die a little every time you lose a patient." I'd learned that as a student, and that was what I taught my students.

The surgeon *had* to move on, but I wasn't the surgeon. I was the mother. And my only job was to wait. I'd forgotten how hard that was. The hours I'd racked up waiting for admission into Kate's hospital room after a middle-of-the-night ER run alone should have left me with some memory of what not knowing was like.

But I *knew* Kate was dying, and nothing allowed me to accept that Ali might.

Not knowing. Not knowing took my imagination to places I didn't want to go. Places where a nine-year-old little girl no longer existed. Places where her father could no longer stand the sight of me because once again, I'd failed him.

I swore I wouldn't forget that fear of the unknown when I directed the parents of my patients to rooms where they were meant to wait and hope.

WHEN GAIL KNOCKED AND came in with a cup of tea, I'd almost forgotten that she'd refused to go home. There was no reason for her to be there, but she'd refused to leave. Everyone I loved was with Tim, and if Gail hadn't been there, I'd have had no one. That was what she'd told me, and she was right.

"Thanks." I brought the cup up to my mouth, but when I realized I couldn't swallow, I placed it on my desk. Maybe later. Maybe when the surgery was over.

Instead of turning back to her desk, Gail moved to the couch and sat, patting the spot next to her. "Come, sit." And when I did, she got down to why she was there, with a cup of tea and words to say. "Now, don't get mad..."

Gail couldn't possibly think it was the right time to tell me that she'd done something I wouldn't be happy about, not that I could even think of anything she might have done that would upset me.

"What?"

"I know you don't believe in God..."

I felt my eyebrows squish together, and maybe when I asked again my voice was a little sharp. "*What?*"

Pushing her glasses up on the top of her head, she took my hands in hers. "I just thought that if you had something more to hold on to, more than just yourself, it might help."

"This isn't the time—"

"Emma, it really is the time. Being strong isn't always enough. Sometimes, even strong people need help."

And even though I was experiencing the most important day of my surgical career without being in the OR, I laughed. I almost laughed. "You remind me of Kate."

The look on Gail's face was one of relief, perhaps that I hadn't kicked her out of the office.

"Tell me."

"Kate was big on God. She swore God would save me if only I asked. She was hell-bent on making me see it her way. Even dragged me to church once. The closest she got to turning me into a believer was when she loaned me a book."

"The Bible?"

That really made me laugh. "No, Kate would never be so obvious. I don't remember the name of the book, but it was a story about a little girl who talked to God as if they were on a first-name basis. As if they were friends. I'd found the book lying facedown on her pillow and made the mistake of picking it up. I'd turned it over and quickly flipped through the pages and started to put it back where I found it when Kate stopped me."

I realized what Gail was doing. She was keeping my mind off the surgery, and for maybe a few minutes, it was working.

"'Borrow it,' she'd said. Kate never loaned me her books. To Kate, books were sacred, and to me, they were just a source of information. Plus, I had a terrible habit of folding a corner of the page over as a place to mark where I'd stopped reading. The truth of it was, once I'd retained what was inside, I had no further use for books. It had taken until I met Tim to understand the beauty of fiction." I thought about his books lined up on the shelves in my library. It still amazed me that I'd married a writer.

"Kate's offering me that book should have been my clue to back away from it, but instead, I took it home."

"I don't think I know that book. Maybe it's because I had boys instead of girls?"

I nodded. "Maybe. The thing is, Kate only got part of her way. That book didn't make me believe, but it made me wish I did."

Chapter 52

Once Gail left, sitting was no longer an option. Ten steps took me the width of my office. Twelve covered the length. My shoes lay in a heap where I'd kicked them off, and even though I promised myself I wouldn't check, time seemed to have stopped.

Will Ali survive if I remember the name of that damn book Kate wanted me to read? If I go to church and beg for forgiveness? Would that help? What would assure me of Ali's life? Anything?

Startled by the knock on the door, I plowed into the chair set to the right of my desk. "Damn!" When I leaned down to rub my shin, I heard the knock again. *Where the hell is Gail? Why doesn't she send whoever it is away?*

"Emma?"

David. My chest filled with pain. The surgery was over? I looked at my watch. Ali had been wheeled into surgery six hours ago. So it *was* over. But it was too soon. I didn't want to know. Not knowing was better. If I didn't know, I could hope.

The only reason for him to get here this fast is to make sure he reaches me first.

"Emma? Can I come in?" David's voice was weary, like he'd been doing his job so damn long he just wanted to be done with it. When he walked into my office, his face was the color of ashes, shades of gray with no sign of light. No sign of life. His surgical mask hung loosely around his neck, and his good-luck surgical cap still covered his thick blond hair.

253

Specks of red spotted the shirt of his scrubs. I blinked, but those dots didn't disappear.

We looked at each other for what seemed like a lifetime.

"Emma, she made it."

But I didn't understand. *Just stop where you are, and I can pretend you're not here. Just stop. Don't come any closer.*

Then he moved, and my chance not to know disappeared. In two quick strides, David covered the space between us and pulled me into his arms. I stiffened and stepped back, but he followed and pulled me against him more tightly. He wrapped his arms around me as if they would keep me from drowning. "Did you hear what I said? She made it!"

It was the kind of hug someone gave to a total stranger on the street while they both stood helpless, unable to do more than stare at flames shooting out of a bus filled with children. It was the kind of hug someone gave when there were no words to say what needed to be said.

Slowly, David moved me from where we both stood in the center of my office and inched me back with him until we reached the couch, where he urged me to bend, to sit.

"Emma!"

I heard the clock on the wall, ticking, ticking. I heard the beating of my heart. I heard every breath I took, shallow and quick. Somewhere outside my office door, I heard a page for Dr. Mendez in Pediatrics. *Pediatrics.* And my heart howled.

I couldn't look into David's eyes; I didn't want to see his pain. Just like I had avoided my father's eyes so many years ago when he talked about the puppies he couldn't save, I watched David's mouth. The words would come from there and strike me down.

I thought about how I'd said the same words. Slowly, calmly, leaving no room for misunderstanding. I thought about the way I looked straight into the family's eyes when I spoke, how I grasped their hands, how my heart broke when I said the words that needed to be said. Words that David clearly struggled with right then. Then I stopped thinking and pulled myself into my silence, hiding as best I could.

When David reached for my hand, I flinched; I wanted no part of his sympathy. I pushed away from him until I was back where we had started, in the middle of my office. Away from those specks of red.

"Don't you see? If I can't give Ali back to Tim the way she was born, perfect and whole and healthy, then I've ruined all of our lives."

"Emma—"

"No!" I struggled with the words I needed to say, but I forced them out. "Don't tell me she's dead." Stepping back even closer to my desk, I fought to say all of it. "You don't get to say those words. She can't be dead." *She can't be dead. I will not allow her to be dead.*

"I don't have any more to give, David. Please."

"Emma!" David's voice grabbed hold of me but for only the briefest of seconds. "Emma. *Listen* to me. Calm down."

But I couldn't calm down. I couldn't. I saw Ali on that table, alone, and still, bright lights shining into the gaping hole in her head. I didn't need to be there to see everyone step back from the table in a well-executed move, looking to David for guidance. Waiting for him to say the words that must be said before they took another step, either toward Ali to make one final, last-ditch effort, or away from her, removing their masks and gloves as they walked off slowly.

David lifted me from where I'd sunk to the floor and once more forced me to sit on the couch, the same couch where I told other parents their child was soon to be dead. Or was already dead. And that time, I yielded. I knew what he was going to say; I just wanted it said.

"Emma, *look* at me. Will you look at me?" David gently turned my face toward his. The only way to avoid his eyes was to close mine, but I couldn't close my eyes because every time I did, I saw Ali on the OR table, all the tubes and IVs removed. She looked like she was sleeping. But she wasn't breathing.

"Ali's alive." He spoke slowly, his hands on either side of my face so I was forced to look at his mouth. There was no chance I would misunderstand. "The tumor is gone. She's in recovery. She's stable."

I thought he was saying *other* words, words of grief, of condolence, but instead, he spoke of survival. Of life. I closed my eyes then. When I opened them again and looked up into his face and saw his smile, I knew he was telling the truth.

"*Alive?*" I whispered as if I'd never heard that word before. As if that word alone brought miracles right into the room. "Alive?" I whispered again. And again. And *again*. I couldn't get my fill of saying it.

"Has Tim seen her?" I couldn't help myself. I thought of him first.

"Just for a second," David said, gently wiping away one lone tear of gratitude that had worked its way down my cheek. "Come on, and I'll take you to her." David stood and pulled me up with him, intent on getting me out the door and into the recovery room.

"No! I can't." I struggled to break his hold on me.

"Yes. Yes, you can!" Again, he urged me out of my office, but I couldn't go. Just the thought of intruding on Tim terrified me.

"No!" I pushed free.

David's eyebrows squished together until they were one. "Why?"

Again David pulled me into his arms, but instead of crushing me to him, he held me gently away. He searched my face for my truth. "Why can't you go?"

His eyes were so blue and honest, and he would never understand that what I'd done was intentional, and I'd do it all again if I had to. "I gave her up, don't you see? I gave her up. I've no right to see her."

"Look what you've done! If anyone has a right to see her, it's you."

"No!" I pulled away and stepped back, my voice finally filled with determination. "Tell Tim I'm happy for him. Tell him you'll monitor her progress and let him know when he can take Ali home. Tell him... I'm glad I could help. Tell him he's raised a beautiful little girl. Tell him..."

"Tell him what, Emma?" David's voice was tight with frustration. "What else do you want me to tell him?"

"Nothing. Nothing else."

Chapter 53

A li remained in the hospital for five days.

Sometimes, patients were released in less time, but because of the nature of her surgery and her age, David and I agreed to keep her as long as we could. We were so lucky that her speech and her small and large motor skills were unaffected. Within days of the surgery, she was, according to Tim, close to the same little girl she was before the tumor invaded her brain. There was every reason to believe she would recover fully.

We were so lucky.

I wanted to see Ali one last time before she left the hospital and went back to her life with Tim. I knew I should visit during the day; I knew I should have the guts to face my child and answer her questions truthfully, but again, I chose darkness. I wanted one last look at her, but I was afraid that she wouldn't want to see me, or worse, that the sight of me would be meaningless.

Head bandaged, sheet pulled up to her neck, Ali looked small and pale in her hospital bed. And beautiful. And alive. Watching her sleep reminded me of the first time I saw her after she was born, those beautiful first few hours when she was mine. When I was so sure I would be able to keep her safe.

Tim watched with a smile on his face as I pulled up the blanket folded at the end of the bed and tucked it around her. "It's important to keep her warm after surgery," I whispered, not wanting to wake Ali. I wasn't surprised to see him; I'd just hoped he'd be asleep.

"I don't know how to thank you." His voice was thick with exhaustion, and when I looked into his eyes, they told the story of the last two weeks. No doubt the hardest of his life.

"You don't need to thank me. Just... be happy." I reached out and took his hand, entwined his fingers through my own, and held it for the briefest second. I gave it one quick squeeze before I let go. I wanted so much more. I wanted to put my arms around him and hold him to me. I wanted to never let him go. But it was too late, and I'd already let him go. I'd let them both go.

Chapter 54

Taking a few weeks off was the biggest decision I could make after Ali was discharged from the hospital, and by week two, when my mind and body searched for something to motivate me, I remembered there were windows that needed washing.

The bucket and rags and cleaning solution were where I'd dumped them on the day Tim had called and begged me for help. It was hard to believe that was only a few weeks ago when so much had changed in that short time.

Maybe I'll get a dog. I ran hot water into the bucket, pouring in the cleaning solution and a dollop of vinegar that was the secret to sparkling windows. At least according to Miss Maggie. *Maybe I'll teach and hold regular hours. Come home at dinnertime and cook a proper meal. Maybe I'll travel.*

I laughed at all my crazy thoughts. *Maybe I'll just finish these windows and take one day at a time. But a dog? A dog might be nice.*

I laughed again when I remembered the looks on the faces of both Gail and David when I announced my leave of absence. "You both look like you're trying to catch the same fly," I'd joked. But neither of them had tried to talk me out of it.

When the doorbell rang, I had just started the upstairs hallway window that looked out onto the front porch. After days of silence, the ring echoed in my ears. I peered over the windowsill carefully, not wanting to be seen, then slowly leaned back on my heels. *What the...*

The wet sponge still in my hand, I peeked out again to make sure I was seeing what I thought I'd seen, only that time, I wasn't as careful and met Tim's eyes as he rang the doorbell of the house that had once been just as much his as mine. And Ali was standing next to him.

"Emma?"

The doorbell rang again, and Tim's voice floated up to me from the open window. I looked at myself: ripped jeans, and not the kind designed that way, and a T-shirt stained with I didn't even know what. *Answer the door? Hide?*

I threw the wet sponge into the bucket, stopped long enough to pull a clean sweatshirt over my head, and raced down the stairs. *What do they want? Why are they here? What will I say? Just open the damn door.*

Wiping my hands on the sides of my jeans, I took one deep breath and opened the door.

Tim was smiling, close to laughing. So was Ali.

I took a step back. "What? What's so funny?" If it was a joke, I didn't get it.

Tim took one step toward me, and I stiffened, but he only smiled. Maybe it was more of a smirk. He reached out and pulled a pencil out of my hair.

"You are the only woman I know who washes windows with a pencil standing straight up in her hair." His laughter made his eyes crinkle in a way I barely remembered.

Grabbing the pencil out of his hands, I tried to explain that it must have dislodged from behind my ear when I'd pulled my sweatshirt on over my head, then I stopped. "How did you know I was washing windows?"

Leaning even closer, Tim plucked several drying cloths hanging from my pocket and handed them to me.

"Oh!" Feeling foolish, I imagined the sight I made from his side of the doorway. I had no idea what to say. I looked from Tim to Ali and back at Tim again. "What are you doing here? The both of you?"

"Can we come in?" Even as he spoke, he moved forward, bringing Ali with him until I had no choice but to step back and allow them in.

Once we were all in the front entryway, I watched as they looked around. I folded my arms across my chest and hugged myself warm, even though sweat trickled down my back. "Nothing's changed."

I felt the need to justify never having made one decorating change in the last three years, so I reiterated, "I've left it all the same."

"I see that. Can we sit down?"

I only noticed the small satchel Ali carried when she placed it on the floor and nudged it to the side, almost as if she wanted to keep it out of sight.

Dragging my eyes from the satchel, I turned to Tim, but he was already moving toward the library. "What are you doing here?" I asked again, at a loss for words in my own house. I tried to catch up, but clearly, I was at a disadvantage. "How did you know I'd be home?"

Tim smiled again. I was beginning to remember how he did that, smiled when he thought he'd pulled something over on me. "David told me."

It felt like years since I'd seen them. Tim's face was freshly shaven, the beard he'd worn while Ali was in the hospital gone, but he still needed a haircut. Ali looked, well, Ali looked like a healthy little girl who was near bursting with a secret. Which reminded me of her satchel.

"Ali wanted to thank you for everything. She wanted to thank you in person," Tim explained, moving toward the leather wing chair that had always been his favorite, but I stopped him before he reached it and pointed at the satchel. "What is this for?"

Again, that smile reached his lips. His eyes grew bright, and his eyebrows wiggled. "That's for later. You'll see."

Ali was tall enough that her feet touched the floor when she sat on the settee, but when I looked at her, what I saw was the six-year-old whose little legs dangled toward the floor, not the almost young lady who sat before me.

I started to deny the need for thanks, but the look on Ali's face stopped me, and I let her talk.

"Dad says you both made a mistake." Ali took a deep breath before she continued. "He says when people make mistakes, it's important to forgive them if they're sorry for what they did. Dad says you did what you had to do, and he did what he had to do. And maybe not all of what you both did was the wrong thing to do."

She stopped then and looked from Tim to me, and when she continued, I got the feeling she'd suddenly gone off script. "I wish..."

The grandfather clock in the parlor struck eleven while I waited for her to continue, but the one in the entryway stayed silent—it had stopped announcing the time about six months ago, and I'd never bothered getting it fixed. Tim's head was cocked in anticipation, and when he didn't hear his second chime, he looked at me, and I shrugged. Running an efficient household was overrated.

While I waited for Ali to continue with her wish, I looked at her fully. Her hair was slowly growing back, curlier than ever. She would be tall, like Tim. Her eyes glowed with intelligence and curiosity. She was beautiful.

When she didn't continue her thought, I nudged. "What do you wish?"

"I wish I knew you better."

I sucked in my breath: That was how children were. They gave you their hearts because they thought you would give them yours in return.

Keeping my eyes on Tim, whose own eyes had grown large at hearing Ali's wish, I offered the only apology I could. "Sometimes, a person makes a decision and doesn't see the repercussions right away. Sometimes, she never sees them. Do you know what I mean?"

Before Ali could answer, Tim turned to her and asked her to check on her bedroom upstairs. He asked her to see if I'd changed it into a sewing room.

After Ali left the room, Tim moved from the chair he'd been sitting on and reached out to pull me up from the old ottoman I could never get rid of. It had been in Kate's bedroom, and after she died, I took it as mine. His face grew quiet. His face always grew quiet when he had something important to say, but I stopped him before he could say anything.

"You know I don't sew."

Tim smiled. "I know you don't sew."

"And what's with the satchel?"

Again, Tim got that look on his face. "You'll just have to wait and see. Now let me say what I came here to say. I am so grateful..."

I'd never been comfortable with praise or thank-yous or anything that drew attention to me. "I didn't do anything. David—"

"I know David performed the surgery, but it was your procedure. Yours. You never gave up."

I'd spent my entire life pondering just that. *Was it a good thing?*

"Look what it cost me."

"Look what it saved."

My thoughts were all over the place, but they kept going back to Kate. "Do you remember when I told you I thought I needed to save Kate, even though I knew she was dead?"

As soon as I mentioned Kate's name, a look of pain crossed Tim's face. I continued quickly so he would understand I wasn't placing blame. "Do you think everything had to happen this way? I don't know, not for sure, anyway, but maybe Ali's the reason GBM struck

Kate's brain and not mine. Maybe Ned and Laura and everyone who loved Kate can finally accept Kate's death because something good came from saying goodbye when we should have been nowhere near goodbye."

Epilogue
Kate

I couldn't grow up fast enough. Emma was thoughtful and kind, careful. Everyone thought she was the one who needed me, that she would always follow in my footsteps, but really? That was not the way it was. I was a flare; I burned bright, and I burned out fast. Emma was a candle; her flame glowed soft and sure.

I liked to think I was brave, but the truth was that Emma was the brave one. I was just along for the ride.

Oh, and the satchel? It was filled with three years' worth of pictures and memorabilia. Ali and Tim at the beach and hiking in the mountains. Skiing at Seven Springs. Standing in line at Disney World while they waited to get on Space Mountain. Playbills from when Ali played Dorothy in her school's performance of *The Wizard of Oz*. Coming in second at the spelling bee. It was all there. Every minute of the last three years.

Acknowledgments Page

B ooks are like small children—it takes a village to raise them from that very first spark of an idea until they reach the hands of a reader.

Welcome to my village:

Lynn McNamee – Owner of Red Adept Publishing. Thank you for taking a chance on me. I will be forever grateful.

Angie Gallion – Content Editor with Red Adept Publishing. Thank you for making sense of my story.

Angela McRae – Line Editor with Red Adept Publishing. You went above and beyond, from insisting I keep my actions in chronological order to placing my modifiers where they belong to helping me make sense of it all. From the bottom of my heart, I thank you.

My mentors – Suzanne Warr and Erica Lucke Dean for answering my questions and keeping me sane.

Leah Ferguson – Leah directed me to the Women's Fiction Writers Association (WFWA). If you write, you want to belong to this group. You can find them here: https://www.womensfictionwriters.org/

Rachel Lipetz MacAulay and Wendy Gold Rossi – There is a special place in Heaven for first readers.

Lisa Roe – Lisa taught me everything I needed to know about nursing mothers and how much drama is too much drama.

Jennifer Klepper – We became critique partners and promised not to muddy the waters by correcting each other's grammar or punctuation errors. Thank you for loving my Kate and for always offering encouragement.

Kathryn Barrett – My everything partner. Kathryn read this story numerous times and tried desperately to teach me about dangling participles.

Dr. Bradeigh Godfrey – Bradeigh clarified medical scenarios other than those specific to GBM. Any errors relating to GBM are mine alone.

Kimberly Lynne – Kimberly provided a beautiful and honest answer to my question: Can you learn to live with guilt? And then she graciously allowed me to include her response in this book.

My family – For your excitement and encouragement. I love you always!

Renee Anderson – You never seemed to doubt that I'd finish this damn book.

The Beagle Freedom Project is real. If you have it in your heart to donate or adopt a rescued beagle, you can find them here: https://bfp.org/

GBM is real. Many reputable research facilities would love your donation.

About the Author

Barbara Conrey worked in the health care industry for many years before opting for an early retirement, which lasted all of three months. She then accepted a position in finance, for which she had absolutely no background, with a national company, and four years later, she decided to write a book. But not about finance.

In the early morning hours, people can find Barbara walking her neighborhood streets, head down and deep in thought.

Travel is her passion, along with reading, writing, hiking, and exploring antique shops. Her greatest love is Miss Molly, her rescue beagle. There are stories to be told about beagles, and Barbara hopes to incorporate some of them into her books.

Barbara lives in Pennsylvania, close to family and friends.

Read more at https://www.barbaraconreyauthor.com/blog.

About the Publisher

Dear Reader,

We hope you enjoyed this book. Please consider leaving a review on your favorite book site.

Visit https://RedAdeptPublishing.com to see our entire catalogue.

Don't forget to subscribe to our monthly newsletter to be notified of future releases and special sales.

Made in the USA
Monee, IL
21 May 2022

96829451R00163